SHATTER DARK

By R. Graeme Cameron

Shatter Dark

By R. Graeme Cameron

Cover art by M.D. Jackson

ISBN: 978-1-998703-10-4

Category - Adult

Genre - Science Fiction Satire

© R. Graeme Cameron 2025

All rights reserved, no duplication by any means, or training with AI or other similar program except by explicit permission of the publisher.

Celticfrog Publishing

Clearwater, BC

DEDICATION PAGE

My mother wanted me to be a Rhodes Scholar.

My father wanted me to memorize the times tables.

I disappointed both of them.

Nevertheless, their lifelong support for my writing goals never wavered.

Had they lived long enough to read my novel, I'm sure they would have been pleased.

I dedicate Shatter Dark to Mom and Dad.

AUTHOR'S BIOGRAPHY

R. Graeme Cameron has been a science fiction enthusiast since seeing live television broadcasts of "Tom Corbett Space Cadet" in 1955.

To date, he has received seven Aurora awards and was inducted into the Canadian SF&F Hall of Fame in 2019.

He is noted for his numerous fannish publications, his years presenting the ELRON Awards, two decades moderating writer workshops at VCON, his stand-up comic performances as "Moog, the Magnificent Martian," and his co-presentation of the "Godzilla Sex Life" lecture two-dozen times at various SF conventions.

Currently, he writes reviews of Canadian Speculative fiction for "Amazing Stories Magazine" (since 2014), publishes and edits "Polar Borealis Magazine" (since 2016), and publishes "Polar Starlight Magazine" (since 2021) which is edited by Rhea E. Rose. Both magazines are devoted to promoting Canadian authors and artists. They are read in 126 countries.

He is a member of SF Canada, Wordstorm, FBCW, SFPA and SFWA.

Shatter Dark is his first published novel.

CHAPTER ONE

"You're too easy to kill. That's why you are still alive."

I shifted uncomfortably in my chair.

I know, my dear Buddy-bod. To state the obvious is to state the obvious.

"Seneferu is in the outer office. He believes you are a pure biologic. He has no fear of you. What if he is an assassin?"

I glanced out the window beside my desk. From my office just below the crest of Grouse Mountain I could see the dull, leaden sea pressed against the base of the slope. Always bugged me that ignorant people claim there used to be a city down there. Obviously not. Nothing but water.

Don't ask me. Ask Myriad.

Silence. More musings.

"Her mate says his Mate is sweeping. Detects everything. Knows how powerful she is."

I snorted, almost a laugh. *Then he knows he can't flee past her once he's slain me. No chance. Dead man. Any indication he wants to be a martyr?*

"None. A cautious man craves sanity."

I think we can handle him… unless… does he know I'm fake?

"No. He thinks you're legit."

Good. It's more fun conning someone when they don't realize they're being conned.

A tentative knock on the door. It swung open. My secretary Myriad leaned into the room, her golden eyes gleaming bright above her golden breasts. Evidently the colour of the hour was gold. She'd been quite scarlet when I first saw her this morning. I had to admit, her Minoan style dress was most fetching. Showed off her chameleon-algae to best advantage. *Seneferu must be impressed.*

"Actually, I doubt it. He's... different."

"What is it?" I inquired, with a decisive irritation in my voice. Have to set the tone after all. I knew the client was listening.

"A Mr. Wolfgang Seneferu to see you. He's on schedule."

My schedule. "Direct him to enter."

Myriad withdrew, to be replaced by the waddling Seneferu, a man hard to respect on first sight. For one thing, he sidled through the doorway as if afraid he wouldn't fit. Yet he was young and slender, devoid of excess fat. I pointed to the seat before my desk. Seneferu obediently sat, or rather, settled down, patting nonexistent folds of flesh beneath his absurdly large cotton tunic. It hung on his frame like a collapsed tent. *Expensive stuff, cotton.*

"His implant cost a billion."

Then his country doesn't value him. Neither should I.

"The techgrid values YOU. I cost an icy trillion."

You only say that because you love me.

"Rudwulf, sir, pardon me while I catch my breath," Seneferu pleaded. "My excessive bulk handicaps me. Makes life difficult."

Has he always been like this?

"Eunuchs are generally obese."

This one isn't.

"Why in Shamash don't you have a sane office?" Seneferu asked, pretending to be annoyed. "My Mate detects no technologic whatever." He glanced at the bookshelves lining the walls. "Is that genuine wood?"

"Vat grown, not extruded. I like natural things. Nothing but the best biologic for me."

"My Mate tells me you are Mateless. How is that even possible?"

"I abhor the unnatural. The very idea of an implant upsets my gonads. Besides, I'm *very* rich. The law doesn't apply to me."

"But you're all by yourself inside your skull. Who do you talk to when you're alone?"

"No one. No one at all."

Seneferu sat back with an exasperated expression on his face. "You are abnormal beyond all measure."

"Thank you."

"*He really does believe you are odd. Maybe even insane.*"

Is he mentally discomforted? His concern is only useful if I disconcert him.

"*No. He has too much contempt for you to be afraid. But he is curious, very curious, and eager to hear what you have to say.*"

Then I'll keep quiet on the important stuff. "My dear Wolfgang, I perceive you love nature as much as I do."

A brief but brilliant flash of shock distorted Seneferu's composure. "Really? How disgusting. Whatever do you mean?"

"I may lack a Mate, but even my internal solitude can see you are perspiring enough to drown the Nile. I have rubbing alcohol in my desk if you need it."

Seneferu laughed lightly, a tinkling sound, almost charming. "Shows how much you know. I sweat on demand. Dark stains a useful distraction in debate. I'll switch off now."

Leaning forward, I sniffed loudly. "I have a very good sense of smell. Why is your sweat odourless?"

More laughter. "I'm good at contact tactics. I'm never rude."

"*He thinks he is running laps around you. Getting quite smug.*"

Good. I like it when enemies underestimate me.

"How do you know he is your enemy?"

Isn't everybody?

Seneferu leaned back, his black eyes suddenly intense. It would be intimidating, except it wasn't. Not to me.

"If I may say so," Seneferu stated, knowing full well he was being presumptuous, "your lack of a Mate is a preposterous handicap. It renders you artificially autistic compared to us technologic augments. No context. No environment. No clues."

"*Told you he's getting smug, damn near giddy with complacency.*"

It was my turn to smile. "I find my absence of awareness refreshing and invigorating. Focusing on the superficial requires surprisingly little effort. Consequently, I find reality rather pleasant."

"But Implants shift the burden, freeing everyone to be equally unaware. We're *all* happy."

"I find that hard to believe," I replied. "So much suffering in the world."

Expression of distaste. "You're talking about the poor? They *enjoy* suffering. Everyone knows that."

"The hunted enjoy the hunt? Interesting idea. I must mention that to my PR hacks."

Seneferu actually had the gall to point at me. "But you… your reality offends me. No implant. Like a man deliberately cutting his own balls off. Not natural. Against the will of the Gods."

"*He's getting flustered. His mate adjusting hormones to calm him.*"

Let's hope it sedates him insensible.
"That would be amusing."
I adopt a serious tone. "Don't let me keep you, Wolfgang, if you find my presence uncomfortable. But if you find you can tolerate me, stay, and let's get down to business."

Regaining his equilibrium, Seneferu pressed his fingers together beneath his chin in a futile effort to appear competent and confident. I had the impression he thought he had multiple chins.

"I expect you've read the contract?" he asked.

"Of course not. I refuse to focus my eyes on technologic displays if I can avoid it. I've been *told* what the contract says. But I suppose I should read it nonetheless."

By the way, is his copy correct?

"His Mate is under the impression it is identical to what was negotiated."

That'll do.

Seneferu grunted as he reached within his tunic to pull out a scroll that he'd tucked under his belt. "Please excuse the fact I kept it pressed between folds of my belly fat. Gross, I know, but as secure as a safe."

"The only gross thing about this idiot is his obsession. He weighs less than you do."

Why is he like this?

"Something to do with his father, maybe. Said to be quite the authority figure."

The whitish-yellow scroll, only six inches long, and a mere inch in diameter were it uncompressed, lay on the desk like something dead.

"Cost a fortune, stupid thing," Seneferu muttered. "First one manufactured in centuries."

I felt my lips curling. "Manufactured?"

"Handmade. Handmade of course!"

"Paper?'
"No. Papyrus."
"Thought that was extinct."
"Of course it is. Till they brought it back in our labs. Hence the expense."

My hand hovered over the scroll. Continued to hover. "Lab grown?"

Seneferu shrugged. "Don't know details. First one maybe. This from a second-generation plant grown in the vats on my father's delta estate." He smiled.

"I'm perfectly aware your father is enormously wealthy. No need to boast. The whole delta his private estate?"

"The whole country. Anything and everything he owns, he owns entirely. Habit of his."

I popped the scroll back into cylindrical form, then slowly drew it past my nose, my nostrils lightly scraping the fabric. "Divine."

"I told you my sweat doesn't smell. What are you talking about?"

"The Papyrus. Subtle, yet noticeable. I like it."

"I expect it's the ink you detect. Made from cuttlefish and ash, or the ash of a cuttlefish, or something. Also expensive."

"He's very impatient."

I don't care.

Unrolled, the scroll displayed tiny script composed in an unsteady, shaky hand by a scribe who hadn't known what he was doing. "Not very professional."

"There are *no* professionals, not for something as archaic as this. My Mate told me how to form the letters, guided my hand. I did good. My father was pleased. That squiggly line at the bottom is his signature, by the way."

I glanced down the length of the scroll, a mere 16 inches or so, in less than two seconds, my eyes taking in nothing. "Done. Acceptable."

"Nobody reads that fast," Seneferu protested.

"It's called speed reading. An ancient tradition I've mastered."

"Nobody reads that fast."

"His mate advised him to insult you."

Testing me? Pathetic. Can't come up with something more virulent?

"His Mate doesn't think so, but it is tired of feeding him lines."

Oh really? Heading for a divorce, are they? Delightful.

"Unlike us. I never know what you're going to say next. Saves me a lot of bother."

Yes, made for each other. Both of us crazy. I love it.

"Communing with your imaginary Mate?" Seneferu inquired.

I laid the open scroll before the Egyptian. "You can sign this without any further insults. I'm too proud of my celibacy to care what you say."

Seneferu reached back into the folds of his tunic as if thrusting his hand deep into his flesh. The man genuinely thought he was immensely obese. And now he looked puzzled. Withdrawing his hand, he stared at a black smear darkening his fingers. "Ugh. Must have broken."

"Your hand?"

"No. The stick of charcoal he was carrying."

"Just let me sign the damn thing." Seneferu muttered, pushing the nub of the charcoal twice across the paper. "There's my X." He swung the scroll about and shoved it toward me. "What are you going to utilise, some pen out of a museum?"

"Don't be silly. Just because I don't normally use technologic doesn't mean I never take advantage of it." I stuck the index finger of my right hand in my mouth and swirled my tongue around it. This made Seneferu blink and lean away from the desk, pressing hard against the back of his chair.

"His mate is assuring him you're not being homoerotic, that you're not coming on to him. That you are most likely simply trying to intimidate him. He will respond accordingly."

I drew out my wet finger and rubbed its moisture-gleamed tip across the surface of the scroll next to the charcoal mark. "Now my DNA is on record."

"Not yet it isn't. On record I mean."

"Nor yet *your* DNA."

Seneferu smiled, rather enthusiastically. "How's this?" He grabbed the scroll back, spat a glob of thick saliva on top of his charcoal X, then pressed the oddly green-tinted goop into the papyrus with the palm of his hand. "Good enough?"

"Excellent. You may transmit."

Seneferu glanced at the scroll, his eyes intent and focused. He blinked. "My Mate copied it to the Alexandria library, DNA and all."

"So you say. I'll have my secretary check on that." I swept the scroll into an open drawer. A slight hum from the chem lab inside. Really superb shielding, as there was no reaction from my visitor. My technologic top notch, completely undetectable. "I'll keep the scroll. A souvenir."

"Fine," Seneferu said. "I don't care. Nobody cares."

"Now that we are on a friendly basis, may I ask you a personal question?"

"Ask my Mate... oh right, you can't. Okay. Ask me."

"You mentioned Shamash. Your personal God?"

"No. Nergal," Seneferu declared, looking bored. "But I accept the whole Neo-Babylonian pantheon. The Great King of Assyria converted me. Ashurbanipal and I, we're pals."

"Yet your father is Pharaoh? Shouldn't you worship Ra or somebody?"

"He's getting irritated."

"My father forgives his children one vice apiece. Makes for an interesting family."

"Remind him what his father did to him."

"According to the endlessly repeated revelations in the tabvids, your father made you a eunuch," I commented, trying not to smirk.

"You think you can make me sweat again? I remain switched off."

"No such intent. Just curious."

"But it's common knowledge. The good Pharaoh Hermann Horemheb caught me wallowing in my preferred vice."

"And that was?"

"A torrid love affair with my sister, my one true love, the mother of my son."

I laughed. "Seems in keeping with the hoary traditions of the Royal House. Perfectly patriotic. Why should he mind?"

"He was married to her at the time."

"Oh." Why didn't you tell me this in the briefing?

"I didn't think it was important."

Seneferu sighed. "You know how it is. Our bloodline being German, the security of the throne in Thebes is fragile, subject to the volatile whims of the fellaheen. The Securitas claims the peasants would prefer a Brazilian Emperor to a German Pharaoh. Damned if I know why. Something they saw in the soapvids, I suspect."

"Plausible."

"At any rate, Pharaoh cannot be seen to be disrespected by his own son and brother-in-law. Hence my punishment."

"I'm sorry for you. Genuinely sorry, all business aside."

"Me too."

Stop showing off your false empathy.

"You do the same."

Shut up.

"Rudwulf, sir, it was kind of you to step out of business for a moment," Seneferu said, bracing to rest his imaginary multiple chins on his chest. He looked almost benign. "Allow me to return the favour. They intend to kill you."

"Who does?"

"The Mayan Druids, or so my father informs me."

Buddy-bod, why didn't you inform me?

"I can only scan what his Mate is thinking. Not what he has buried in the recesses of his shallow mind. Comes as a revelation to me too."

"Mayan *Druids*?" I spluttered. "Not the Mayan Mormons?"

"It's a new sect, Quetzalcoatl Reform Druid. Beedlewood is their prophet. He's English."

"What am I to him? What has he got against me?"

"Nothing personal," Seneferu said, smiling, patting his hands together as if he wanted to rub them gleefully. "You're the last living Smiter on Earth. The perfect sacrifice."

"Then I should avoid visiting Quintana Roo. That Kingdom is lousy with English Mayans."

"That would be my recommendation."

"What's his game, I wonder? His Mate doesn't know. Seems astonished."

"And Wolfgang," I went on, "you are generously warning me because?"

Seneferu grimaced. "I may have deserved to have my balls cut off, but my father knows I am no traitor. He and I both want you to live long enough to crush the armies of Assyria. I hope to be installed as Governor in the palace at Nineveh. My future depends on you."

"And you already worshipping the Gods of the people you hope to rule. That's handy."

"Yes, ensures I will be welcome. And now, may I ask you the name of *your* personal God? Allah? Yaweh? Yewah? Jehovah? Bert?"

"Loki."

"What?" Great shock. "My Mate told me you were Christian!"

I chuckled. "I may be old-fashioned, but I'm not *that* obscurantist. Besides, Christianity is too fixated on divine punishment for my taste."

"But the Norse Gods? Why them?"

"Let me put it this way… Christian attitude: 'Damned to Hell.' Norse attitude: 'Oh, what the Hell.' See the difference?"

Seneferu pursed his lips. "Not really. I prefer the Chaldean setup. It's very contractual. Once you've performed the appropriate rituals, the Gods do what you command."

Again, I laughed. Getting to be a habit. Creating a bad impression? "A good religion for accountants. Mine is suitable for berserkers."

"Hmm?" A respondent chuckle, a nervous chuckle. "That makes sense. You do like to kill. You are well-suited to your profession."

"Good! He's fallen for our publicity hype."

"But, Wolfgang, my friend," I said, "I have need of your opinion. Speaking of Pharaohs and Assyrian Great Kings and such, don't you think the modern fad of reviving ancient cultures is utterly absurd? It complicates planning for the future. You'll note we have none of that here in Vancouver. We're far too progressive."

"The Reality-Revisionists insist on it. After all, the techgrid is on the verge of collapse and the only way we can survive is to embrace the stone age."

"And you believe this pseudo-scientific, pseudo-religious crap? This folly? This proof that the average person is a moron? When the vats produce wonderful things like Watermelon Bourbon? You want to give that up?"

Seneferu managed to look both uncomfortable and sheepish at the same time. "My father embraces it... reluctantly. He relishes being Pharaoh, but also modern weapons. Me? I do like wonderful vat stuff. Especially food. But I tell you, frankly and sincerely, it is even more wonderful to be the son of a Pharaoh and a friend of our enemy the Great King of Assyria. That's what the past offers in abundance: prestige and power. I'm all for it."

"Yeah? What if the techgrid *does* go down? How are you going to hang on to your prestige? By waving a stone dagger at people? Think that'll work?"

"He's worried. You've set him on edge."

Excellent. "You may go, Wolfgang. Good living."

Seneferu struggled to his feet, as if the oscillations of his pretend-flesh threatened his centre of gravity, causing him to wobble from side to side, in risk of toppling. Slowly, he steadied. He stuck out his hand.

I stared at the man's glistening palm. "Still wet."

"Oh." The offending palm was drawn across Seneferu's close-cropped scalp. "Dry now."

We shook hands. It felt like I was shaking hands with an oyster.

The Egyptian turned to leave, paused, then looked back coyly. "Now I know why you're so chatty. Just occurred to me."

"I'm not aware of any confession on my part."

"I've learned more about you than you suspect."

"Suspect? I don't care enough to suspect."

An oddly triumphant smile played about Seneferu's lips. "Because you're alone when you're alone," he said. "So, when you meet someone apart from yourself you blurt out the first thing that comes to mind. Bad character trait. No self-discipline. No business sense at all. It's almost embarrassing to joust with you. Like taking candy from a crèche."

"The generosity of your perception overwhelms me." *What an idiot.*

"His Mate is thinking the same thing about you."

Buddy-bod, are you positive his Mate doesn't detect you? Hasn't scanned you?

"It isn't capable of that. No technologic is."

Because you don't exist? Figment of my imagination?

"We've argued this too many times. Whatever I am, I'm useful, no? Leave it at that."

Seneferu looked smug. "Stunned you, have I? Should I be pleased with myself?"

"Sure. Why not? Good living. *Good Liv... ing.*"

Seneferu shrugged. He ponderously drifted to the door, fumbled at its unfamiliar opening device, finally figured out how to turn the glass knob, paused. "This contract... it's a good one, yes? The biggest yet? Profitable?"

"Like candy from a crèche."

The expression on Seneferu's face was wistful, haunted, even envious. "How *do* you plan to exterminate Ashurbanipal's armies?"

"I don't know… I'll think of something. I always do. Never let a client down yet."

"Normally, you just cull civilians."

"True. I may have to kill a few, to stay in practice."

"Won't include me, will it?"

I just smiled.

CHAPTER TWO

The chill wind whipping across the open expanse of the runway grafted atop the mountain had zero effect on the low-lying overcast toying with the peak of the hangar. The grey ceiling hung motionless. Too thick to be moved, perhaps.

I drew my cloak close about my body. Good old Vancouver, best place in the world to appreciate all the subtle shades of grey. Wonderful lack of annoying colour. Must have driven Seneferu nuts. Not seeing the sky.

"It did. Educated in England, he's used to occasional clear skies. Used to seeing the Moon with the naked eye. Not like here."

He didn't seem like much of a negotiator to me. More like a third-rate salesman.

"In truth, just a courier."

What did Lenin call the type? Useful idiots?

"Stalin, I think. Or maybe Disney."

Ah, right. Disney. I remember now.

"You shouldn't underestimate Wolfgang. His mate plans to make him Pharaoh next year."

And how does Big Daddy of the double crown feel about that?

"Doesn't know. Not yet. We could tell him."

Not till it becomes useful, or necessary, or profitable, or suitable as an act of revenge. Otherwise, none of our business.

"Suit yourself."

Always do. I pondered the tarmac. Cracks everywhere. In a curiously repetitive fashion. *Nature can be weird.*

"Man-made. Purposeful. Relieves stress in the concrete. Prevents cracks."

Cracks to prevent cracks? Brilliant.

"Your grasp of technologic humbles me."

Your grasp of the irrelevant humbles me. Technologic serves. Don't need to know anything about it.

"And you certainly don't, what with pretending to be a technophobe, to be a man who sticks to his ignorance. I call that highly principled."

Don't be sarcastic; I know a thing or two.

I pointed at the crack immediately in front of me. Deep enough to reveal the orange platform beneath the pavement. *Remember the orange?*

"Yes. I wish the Gogetters were still functioning."

It used to be so much fun. Make a wish and there'd we be. In Thebes faster than a blink.

"Or Mars."

That was before my time. Assuming it was ever true. Which I don't. And what is the damn hold up?

"Myriad checking out your fellow passengers. Pays to be careful."

I studied the squat, grey sausage of the transport, its slanted wings brooding like… brooding like a broken porch swing I remembered from my crèchehood.

"It's supposed to be like that. Generates lift."

I know. I've flown… what… a dozen times before?

"More. You've forgotten most of them."

Yeah, my memory sucks. Useless thing. Fortunately, I have you.

"And what does that get me?"

The thrill of being the fly on the shoulder of Rudwulf the Smiter.

"Oh, THAT thrill..."

The curved props stirred on one of the six engines, began to revolve. There was a faint whiff of kerosene in the air, growing stronger. *See? They're leaving without me.*

"It means it is time for you to board. Myriad says it's okay. Safe."

I strode rapidly toward the plastic boarding steps. Bank account the size of Switzerland and they won't let me take a sub-orbital.

"You can't handle the apogee spree. You'd throw up. Besides, you hate advanced technologic, remember?"

Yeah... but forty hours instead of forty minutes.

"At least we'll get to Thebes before Seneferu."

Why? Is he walking?

"He's leaving later today aboard 'The Wrath of Ra,' his father's personal yacht."

A little bitty yacht to cross the wide Pacific? How cute.

"Bloody big nuclear submarine. Quite the antique. Centuries old. World's largest rust bucket."

Your wit begins to bore me. Makes me tired.

"So, sleep. You like sleeping. Any particular dreams you want?"

I shook my head as I climbed the rickety, slightly swaying steps.

You know I hate to be separated from my favourite book. I'll read for a bit first.

"Show-off. The other passengers will hate you."

They need to understand I am richer than they are. Puts them in their place.

I popped through the hatch, surveyed the cavernous interior of the fuselage. About forty relaxation pods I estimated, half of them occupied by Myriad. "You brought your clones?"

The Myriad closest to the open cockpit door waved. "Duplicates. Not clones. Duplicates." She pointed to the empty pod beside hers.

I walked towards my waiting relaxitron. "I like how few pods there are, but I don't like the fact all the strangers are behind me, staring at my back."

"No, they're not. They're staring at my breasts. All of me are sitting facing the passengers, watching them."

I plopped down into my couch which promptly conformed to my body and began a tentative but welcome massage. "Why so many of you?"

"So it won't take me more than a few seconds to kill the passengers if I have to. Just thinking ahead is all."

I noted the pupils of her eyes were now a glittering steel grey. All business today it would seem. I studied her voluptuous form hidden beneath her clinging orange jumpsuit. Giving her nano-algae a break apparently. But at least her duplicates were completely naked.

"Don't even think about it."

"How about a quickie?" I asked, displaying my trademark boyish, quizzical smile.

Myriad smiled back, slightly tossing her neutrally grey hair as she gave a brief shake of her head. "You knows I luv my sweet, walking, talking, innocent dildo, but, my dear virgin honeykins, keeping you alive is more important. Besides, sex is bad for you, bad for everybody. You *are* my responsibility."

"How about I screw one of the duplicates? It would help infuriate the passengers."

It seemed to me her hair flushed steel into the grey. Her eyes had turned black. Focusing her energy. Not a good sign.

"I mean," I continued, no doubt digging myself a deeper grave, "it would be pure pleasure for you. Sprawled out doing nothing, yet peaking second-hand as it were."

"I keep telling you, I don't experience my duplicates except through our Mates. All of me are not a single being. Each of us are unique individuals, apart from looking the same and having identical implants."

"I know that."

"Then why do I keep having to remind you?"

"I'm not allowed to have sex. Fantasy is all I got. Why spoil it?"

"You're being childish."

"She's right. You ARE being childish."

Hey, I'm twenty years old, practically middle-aged. My inner child keeps me young.

"Tell your inner child not to throw up."

I jerked my head around to face the open cockpit door. I could see both pilots leaning back, their fingers interlaced behind their heads, no doubt grinning inanely as the end of the runway hurtled toward us.

Oh, bugger Odin. I hate this part. I hate it! I clutched the edges of my pod. Sensibly programmed, the pod clutched back, holding me firm, almost as firm as the tensed muscles of my face. Bugger it!

The view tilted sharply downward as the craft plunged off the end of the runway and raced frantically toward the sluggish waters below, fuselage shuddering, passengers screaming, pilots pumping the air with their fists. Make it stop! Make it stop!

Giant clumps of moss and lichen flashed underneath, like a green and yellow carpeted treadmill rolling insanely out of control. Touch and smash. Rocks underneath. Touch and smash. The slope of the mountain a deadly trap scant feet beneath us.

"*Lift effect building up.*"

The dimpled, bulbous nose of the airplane slowly rose. The ocean dropped out of sight. No more shuddering. We were at one with the sea, skittering along just above the immensely wide but slow-moving swells. The pilots settled down to a game of cards.

They really shouldn't do that. Proper pilots pilot nonstop, round the clock.

"*They ARE piloting, or at least their Mates are. They're in constant thinktalk with the ship's Mate. They'll give me plenty of advance warning of a fatal crash. I'll make sure you're unconscious when we hit. No worries.*"

Cigar and rosewood. With a hint of mint. Wonderful perfume. Ah yes, a stewardess. *Very pretty. Very natural looking.*

"*The crew was briefed. They know how much you love natural, you kinky old bastard.*"

The stewardess had a pert nose, wide grey eyes, and yellowish, uneven teeth with a touch of grey metal fillings. Hips far wider than her shoulders. One leg shorter than the other. Perfect!

"Care for a meal, dearie? Chef's heating up the vat."

Her grin was endearingly lopsided. I found myself experiencing a mild arousal. Perhaps the trip wouldn't be boring after all.

"What's available? Is it real?"

"Sure thing. Asparagus mixed with broccoli mixed with pumpkin and a separate block of roast beef thick enough to gnaw on."

"But is it *real*?"

Puzzled, the stewardess replied slowly as if speaking to a crèche squirt, "Of course it's real. Finest turnip flesh and the best coal tar derivatives on the planet. Other than raw moss that's as real as real can be."

"Fine. Sounds good."

"Be about an hour. The chef's having trouble mixing the ingredients. Lost his measuring spoons." She turned and sauntered away toward the galley at the rear of the plane, her broad hips swinging in an ungainly fashion. Rather seductive, that.

I suddenly noticed all the Myriads were staring at me. The passengers too. Vaguely unsettling. I turned my attention to *the* Myriad. Out of the corner of my eye I observed the other Myriads swiveling their heads back toward the increasingly self-conscious passengers.

I leaned toward the true Myriad. "Stewardess didn't ask if *you* were hungry," I commented.

"I talked to her via thinkMate," Myriad replied. "She only came forward because I told her you were a Mate-less gimp. You sure spoiled her curiosity quickly, though. Very quickly."

"Unhealthy thing, curiosity."

"Be quiet. I've got work to do." She stretched out full length, her pod adjusting into a comfortable recliner, and closed her eyes.

"She is concentrating fiercely on what her multiple Mates are observing."

Jolly for her. I'm going to indulge in my private pleasure. Did Myriad remember to bring it aboard?

"Of course. She knows you never go anywhere without it. The pod's extruding it now."

The hard-cover book emerged from the armrest and plopped into my lap. I picked it up and pressed it against my lips. A faint, musty, rather tangy smell assailed my nostrils. Parting my lips, I let the tip of my tongue feel the book's rough texture. Then I held the book out at arm's length. The title, in vivid black ink strident against the gilt cover, jumped at my eyes.

"Yargo," by Jacqueline Susann.

I opened the book at random. A sentence. "He was exactly as Sanau had described; half man, half bee."

Oh, they were giants in those days. Prophets. Masters of metaphor. Too bad none of her other work survived. Too bad hers was the only twentieth century masterpiece extant, the only one complete and unabridged. What a treasure it was. How kind of the World Emperor to present it to me. I could never thank the Duce enough. Which is no doubt why Mussolini gave it to me in the first place. Now I was forever in his debt.

"Something insipid this way comes."

I looked up with a start. A thin, hunched-over man with a withered, jaundiced visage was approaching holding an object hidden in his hands. *Should I be alarmed?*

"One of the Emperor's acolytes. Okayed by Myriad. And by me."

Gods, he looks disgustingly ancient. Decrepit as hell.

"He is old. Pushing forty."

The elder, dressed in red and black robe and tunic, had eyes only for the book. "'Yargo.' You have 'Yargo.' What a blessing from the Duce. I bask in your reflected debt."

"And you are? Wanting what?"

The man drew himself to his full height, nearly seven feet. Almost impressive were he not so weedy thin. "I am Titus. His majesty sent me. I got here just in time to learn you were going, so I got onboard to make sure I'd go with you. Not that I want to go to many-gated Thebes, you understand, but wherever you go I go because—"

"Get to the point."

"Another gift from the emperor," Titus stated, bowing and extending a scroll. I took it, then watched as Titus backed away, scrambling along as fast as his heavy robes allowed till he had returned safely to his pod.

"Another scroll? Is it papyrus too? That would imply an alliance with Seneferu."

I examined the scroll closely. Looks linen-like, but I think… just titanium foil that's been textured and coloured. I took a closer look, started reading.

Hah! It is the emperor's pet project. Listen to this. I began reading aloud.

"Dear Rudwulf, thought this would do you some good. Take it to heart, your loving friend, Mussolini the Invincible.

Martius 31st: reserved for worshipping the Moon Goddess from atop the Aventine Hill. Good excuse for a moon-lit picnic. You might get laid.

Mai 22nd: festival of 'Tubilustra' dedicated to cleaning the trumpets used in the worship of the God Vulcan. The one day of the year you don't have to listen to the damn things.

Junius 7th: festival of 'Vestalia' in honour of Vesta, Goddess of the hearth, when her temple is opened by the Vestal Virgins to admit Mothers of families—normally forbidden to enter—for non-stop partying or, as they tell their husbands, a dull affair pouring purified water into a clay vase incapable of standing up on its own—much like the women by the end of the day. What say you? Sound like fun?

Cheers! Your Pal Musso, World Emperor, King of Italy, etc., etc."

"Lost his mind, has he?"

No. Still trying to convert me. At odds with the Vatican, it's easier for him to rule if everyone jumps to his screwy version of Roman paganism. By reconstructing the ancient calendar of festivals, trying to make them seductively attractive, throwing in sex and alcohol wherever he can, he guarantees his followers will remain faithful. Nothing builds loyalty like drunken orgasms.

"If that's the definition of Roman, I'd say you Thor-thumpers are the most Roman of them all."

Which explains why I was able to suggest he do it. After all, what do war and sex have in common?

"Death, of course."

The perfect Smiter cull. No wonder Musso loves me. I did him proud.

"Yes, but... why insult me by reading aloud? I share your every thinktalk. What makes you believe I crave the sound of your voice?"

It's not about you. I just wanted to make the passengers jealous.

I pushed the scroll against the armrest, watched the two merge and become indistinguishable. Reluctantly, I gave the screed some thought. Musso probably believes his syncretic religion is going to catch on like a burning city. Probably not. Most people, like me, treasure our individual obsessions obsessively. *Musso is very naive, I'm afraid.*

"That's to our advantage, surely?"

Absolutely. I pressed "Yargo" into the plasticity of the armrest. The book was absorbed in less than two seconds.

Buddy-bod, I'm tired. Be a good Mate and sedate me, will you? Wake me up when the food comes.

I started to dream. Formless dreams at first, kaleidoscopes of raw images, flashes of impressions, nothing to latch onto, until—

I am an Italian soldier assigned to guard a crossroads in a wooded landscape. It's snowing, and very quiet, as only a snowscape can be. Even though it's very cold, my sentry box is a burnt-out tank, and I have no fire, I am reasonably content, busy sorting through a fistful of Christmas postcards looking for one suitable to send my family.

First postcard: beautiful full-length portrait of Jesus facing the viewer and throwing the Fascist salute. Inscription at the bottom states: "Jesus and Il Duce salute you!" Nope, not that one.

Second postcard: Manger scene. Baby Jesus is surrounded by his family, animals, shepherds, the Magi, and an adoring, beaming Mussolini. The inscription? You guessed it. "Jesus and Il Duce salute you!"

Damn! Aren't there any old fashioned, traditional cards? Don't want this modern crap.

I look up, a gaggle of teenagers approaching. Always get nervous when this happens. The usual thing, guys showing off for the girls, a bit of swaggering, a lot of sniggering, frequent "F" word, one or two illicit cigarettes being smoked, a lot of pushing and shoving... yeah the usual thing... wearing Fascist Cadet uniforms... weapons slung carelessly over their shoulders...

I'm unarmed. I smile weakly as they saunter by.

Dodged that bullet I think, prematurely as it turns out. A column of elite Bersaglieri comes jogging along. Crisp uniforms. All manner of weapons. Firm, purposeful air. One of Italy's best units.

Loki, they almost look German.

The column halts. The Commander, who is quite tall, stares down at me with contempt in his eyes. "We're looking for a figure of authority." Evidently, I'm not it.

I make up a story. "Bunch of German mountain troops just went down the side road."

"Great! Show us the way."

Damn! I start jogging through the snow, surrounded by my unwanted comrades—

"Wake up, Rudwulf! Wake up! Wake up!"

I opened my eyes. I could see the pilot pounding his head with his fists. His co-pilot was leaning over the throttles, vomiting. Something brilliant in the murk. A flashing streak of light heading straight toward the cockpit, swerving to one side… a tremendous noise! No, a hammer blow to my body! From my body! Everything inside bursting. Everything outside bursting. *What the Fensalir!*

"*Go back to sleep! Go back to sleep!*"

Make up your mind. Why are my arms flailing? I stared at my thrashing arms. Make them stop!

A heavy body, clutching my arms, crushing my arms. It was Titus! "Help me! Save me!" the old fool shouted.

Tumbling. Tumbling. More arms. Myriad! On top of Titus. "Prepare to crash," she yelled. Came a tumult of shrieking passengers and ripping metal.

Buddy-bod!

"*I'm busy. Go to sleep. Sweet dreams.*"

Fire racing along the ceiling. Fire everywhere. *Loki! Put it out!*

"Only atheists in foxholes," hissed Titus, his face obscenely close. "No Gods. We're going to die!"

The pod slid shut. Darkness enclosed us. No more flames. No more light. No more noise.

I'm too old to die. Not ready for afterlife. I exist. I exist! Oblivion.

CHAPTER THREE

Palm fronds waved overhead. Stupid weeds. Worse than the pine trees on Grouse. I felt a hot, sluggish breeze. Rather unpleasant. I looked down the length of my body. Naked. Lying on sand. My body covered in beads of sweat. Tiny, tiny bugs alighting in the sweat. Stupid bugs. This is why so many die in amber. Too dumb for their own good. Just like humans.

"Good. You woke up. For a while it seemed like you didn't want to."

I turned on my side, away from the trees, and stared out over a sullen sea lapping reluctantly against a sandy shore. Incredibly flat islands not far off, inches above sea level, each crowned by a straggling line of damned palm trees. *What the Eldhrimnir? Where are we?*

"Don't know. Somewhere off Mexico, maybe, or further south. Sure isn't the Emperor Norton's California."

Myriad was purposefully up to her waist in the lack of surf. Hunting for something. *What do you mean you don't know?*

"The techgrid is down. No GPS. All I can contact are the Myriad and Titus Mates. Everything else is gone."

Raising my head, I glanced up and down the beach, spotted Titus huddled against the trunk of a palm tree about a hundred yards off, head buried in his folded arms. He was naked too. *What's with him?*

"In a bit of a snit. Can't contact his beloved Mussolini. Feels lost. And jealous of you."

Why?

"That dream you had before the crash. It was Mussolini's dream via Titus. Musso wanted you to see it, wanted your opinion. I suppose he's still questioning his faith. Ever since the Naples super-volcano buried Rome in ash and the Vatican moved to Lake Garda. he's had doubts about everything. What a loser. Why do you keep in touch with him? Waste of time."

Once a client always a client. But don't change the subject. His dream was vivid enough to be mine. Perverse of you not to credit me with an imagination.

"That you possess in abundance. Quite the handicap."

More to the point, why are we naked? And where's the pod?

"Washed away. It had gone dormant not long after we crashed. A missile took us down. We spent ten days and nights floating about till the pod grounded on this island."

A missile? Who fired it?

"One of those boring people who want to kill you. Beedlewood, maybe."

I had a brief vision of a drunken Englishman in a loin cloth struggling to stand upright on a balsa-wood raft while firing a shoulder-mounted anti-aircraft missile. Seemed unlikely.

"Just after we hit the water the pod said something about sensing a periscope."

Seneferu? After I signed the contract with Horemheb? Why would he risk offending his father?

"Maybe he's a traitor to dear old dad."

Doesn't make sense.

I heaved myself to my feet, sweat mingling with the sand between my toes. The view was uninspiring. More islands in the distance. The rippling waves giving off an oily sheen. *Why didn't you summon a rescue? I'm rich enough.*

"Not anymore, not with the grid down. Meanwhile we Mates kept you three asleep, but we couldn't initiate hibernation without the grid. Fortunately, your escape pod complied with my demand that it release its emergency supplies. Moments later it would no longer respond. At least the air circulation kept going. We Mates made you eat and drink. Despite the three of you piled atop one another your bodies functioned. Pretty filthy by the time we drifted ashore and the pod popped open. We had you strip and wash your clothes in the sea. Then yourselves. All the while unconscious. A neat trick."

I shuddered. I was rather glad I couldn't remember arriving.

The explosion crashed your connection to the grid? How soon before the techgrid repairs itself?

"Never. I told you. It's dead. The Reality-Revisionists were right."

Get off! With all the techgrid's nanotech ability? Pull the other one.

"Not being funny. You biologics used to worry about A.I. Not only would it take over, but take over forever, because immortal and self-repairing and so on. But the quasi-nuclear war and rising of the oceans was a double whammy. Just like us, the techgrid was reduced to living off scraps and debris. Ten days ago, it decided it was time for it to die."

I find that hard to believe. We're shot down and the world comes to an end. Can't be a coincidence. Someone or something must be responsible.

"Save your conspiracy theories for your masturbation sessions. I was the only part of the grid that cared about you. Still do. You can rely on me to keep you informed."

If you know so much, answer me this. Why did Myriad and Titus climb into my pod? Crazy with fear?

"I told their Mates yours was the only pod equipped for escape. Good thing they reacted before the pod sealed over you."

And our clothes?

"A pair of biologics came along in a dugout canoe. I think they had been out spearfishing. They made off with everything before we emerged from the palm trees. My fault for insisting we explore the island. I didn't even know of their presence till we saw them shoving off."

I think I'm hungry. My stomach hurts. What about water. Any water?

"Nope. Not a drop. Just sand and palm trees. There are coconuts, lots of coconuts, but we've got nothing to smash them open. Myriad is out looking for rocks. Then, maybe, we can have coconuts and coconut water. Even better if the rocks have limpets. Good eating."

I stared at Myriad. She was splashing the water with her hands, not for fun, but apparently out of frustration.

What, no rocks? And no other Myriads?

"All dead. No loss. They were only duplicates."

Quite a waste if you ask me.

I shaded my eyes from the dull, diffuse glare of the clouds and made a fleshy, glassless telescope by touching the tip of my left thumb to curved fingers, then peered through it with my left eye. Somehow it helped me focus. *I see something. What are they? Do you sense them? Can you thinktalk with their Mates?*

"No. Strictly biologics, but I see what you see. Three... canoes? Two men in each."

Myriad saw them too. She came splashing out of the water and strode purposely and forcefully up to me. Not that that meant anything. She always walked like that. I noted her beautiful skin was devoid of anything other than her natural, blotchy, pinky-white colour, all traces of the chameleon nano-algae gone. Her finely toned muscles rippled to advantage. And those giant pink nipples. Damn she was beginning to look super-attractive. The natural look suited her. Too bad she was so perfect. Almost inhuman.

"Focus, Rudwulf, focus! Those natives have spears. We could be in trouble."

"I hate this place," Myriad muttered. "No water. No food. No privacy. But if I kill those guys, maybe we can eat them, or at least steal their boats. Go somewhere else."

No, not spears, I noted as the strangers approached. Standing upright, they were using lengths of bamboo to pole themselves along. Water must be shallow everywhere. At least, between the islands.

The dugouts, carved out of individual logs twelve feet long and two feet wide, quietly crunched ashore. The occupants leaped onto the sand, dropping the poles onto the beach beside the dugouts. Short men, about five feet tall, but muscular, wearing only thin pants and well-worn, shapeless derby hats with most of the felt worn off. Not exactly high-tech but an indication of trade relations of some sort. Contact with the greater world?

The men grinned as they approached, their fine, near-perfect teeth practically glowing amid the light brown of their faces. Strikingly black hair fanned out from beneath the brim of their hats. They seemed friendly.

You sure these are biologics? They seem too good-looking for that. Surely, they possess technologic augments?

"Not that I can tell. One thing for certain, they have no Mates. I'm useless in this situation."

The six locals stopped in front of us, still grinning, but glancing at our faces with a kind of gleeful curiosity. Myriad struck poses, thrusting her breasts in their general direction, seeking to overawe them, but her efforts had no visible effect. Odd.

31

Once they begin to speak, you'll be able to transition what I hear? Like you did with Seneferu? In my mind's ear he sounded like he knew English well.

"That's because he WAS speaking English, you idiot. Nothing to do with me. I doubt I know the local language."

You know every language, so what's the problem?

"Only when I was connected to the techgrid infinite-knowledge banks. Now I'm constrained by the limits of your memory, and you know bugger all."

Oh, damn. The implications of Buddy-bod's words began to burrow into my brain.

Myriad relaxed her body, stared quizzically at the natives. "These guys have no fantasy life. Or they're satiated. One or the other. I guess that means they're harmless."

Still attentive, still grinning, the men began pointing at us, at the dugouts, and back again. "Cayuca," they said, over and over. "Cayuca."

"They want us to go with them," Myriad said. "Might as well. Wherever we arrive we'll be more welcome than if we showed up by ourselves."

We started walking down to the dugouts. Four of the natives accompanied us. The other two trotted off toward Titus.

"I told the old git's Mate what's happening. Titus is near catatonic."

Frozen in fear?

"Frozen in disgust. He's pissed off at the world."

On reaching the nearest dugouts one of the natives patted its side, repeating "Cayuca" over and over. Then it became clear, courtesy of extravagant gestures, that I was to kneel in the centre of the cayuca, sandwiched between natives fore and aft. As I clambered over the gunwale I caught a quick impression of Titus, arms still folded, legs tightly drawn up beneath him, being manhandled like a disrespected idol towards the beach, the men carrying him laughing quietly. Such a jolly bunch.

That both locals remained standing as they poled my dugout off the beach was disquieting. Centre of gravity way too high. Nervously I leaned forward as low as possible. Kneeling as I was, the rough bottom irritated my bare lower legs. I couldn't help but notice the interior of the dugout seemed more burned than chiselled out. Low tech indeed. I thought I loved everything natural, but this precarious craft reminded me how natural death is, and that is one embrace I intend to avoid.

"Stop worrying. Enjoy the ride. Look at Myriad."

Yes. Myriad appeared *very* relaxed in her cayuca. Both arms dangling in the water to either side, her body bowed so far forward she looked like she was worshipping the ankles of the man standing in front of her. I glanced at the bare feet of the man before me. Bottom of the feet so thick and gnarled it looked like he was wearing sandals. Probably never worn shoes in his life. A true man of nature. Great.

Myriad's back, though. Was it beginning to tinge red? What about me? Suddenly felt itchy all over. *Oh gods, sunburn?*

"We are closer to the equator. Yet the cloud cover is as dense as ever. More so, maybe. Nobody gets sunburn nowadays. Except maybe in England. Not like the old days."

There was a faint bluish tint to the water amid its sluggish ripples. Or was it my imagination? No doubt under brilliant sunshine it used to be sparkling blue. But that was centuries ago. At least it wasn't glittery-orange like the algae-scummed waters off what's left of Vancouver Island.

The cayuca was a perpetual-motion machine, constantly rocking in multi-directions. It reminded me of certain annoying mechanisms in the playground of my crèche, only not as rusty. Still left me with a propensity to vomit, though.

"*Ignore your body. Be like me. Have no body. Just watch with your eyes.*"

Good advice? I glanced about. We were making good progress. Surrounded by islands now. The natives, poling their way through them like penetrating a maze. Bigger islands. Some of them a dozen feet or more above sea level. Some of them covering acres of sand, bearing hundreds of trees, associated brush, probably man-eating crocodiles. Or carnivorous plants. Long-extinct dinosaurs now hungry for flesh?

"*What are you going on about?*"

Just using my imagination. Like when I was a kid.

"*I told you. Bad habit. You know your imagination isn't good for you.*"

Keeps my wits sharp.

"*Rather the opposite, actually. Reality is better. Example dead ahead.*"

We seemed to be heading for a particularly large island. Dense growth of palm trees. Best of all, a long row of large huts with sharply slanted A-frame thatched roofs. As we got closer, I could see people lounging about in the shade of overhanging eves. Men. No women. Just men. All wearing derby hats, dirty white pants, and a few of them, faded white shirts hanging loose. None seemed in any rush to greet us as our cayucas pushed ashore.

Young children were scattered everywhere, naked, their skins varying in colour from light brown to mahogany. They, at least, were full of curiosity. They came running as a quietly chattering mob. Soon we were surrounded by them.

"So many," Myriad said with a broad smile. "I think they're adorable."

"Too many," I said. "It's not natural."

"No crèche. They're as natural as you can get. They run free."

I gazed into their smiling, friendly faces, astonished by their open curiosity. I noted even the youngest girls bore gold rings dangling from the septum of their noses. "How *can* there be so many? At least forty. Yet I count only twenty huts. Twenty families? Two per family? One man fathering them all?"

"Should be the case. But these young ones are so diverse there must be more than one father."

That's not statistically possible.

"Maybe *all* the men are virile," Myriad observed. She seemed excited by the concept.

I drew in my breath. I was shocked. "What are you saying? That the village is a nest of throwbacks? Mutants? That can't be."

The men who had brought us, having drawn the cayucas entirely free of the water, joined their companions at the lounging line along the huts. They didn't appear motivated to help us any further. Rather annoying. Piss-poor hosts.

I began to stroll toward the huts. Their walls were made of upright bamboo stalks thrust into the sand and tied together by sloppily applied vine ropes. The bamboo was as dry and grey as the thick palm-leaf thatch weighing down the steep roofs. Everything looked as if it would ignite like a flare if touched by flame. The huts were jammed so closely together there was hardly any room between them. The whole village could be destroyed in seconds. *Are these people insane?*

"Maybe just very careful, and lucky. Or maybe they don't use fire."

The huts were windowless. The single doorway of the hut opposite us suddenly disgorged a line of giggling women bearing food in wooden plates and drink in coconut husks. The liquid in the husks was a slimy whitish mess but it smelled like nectar. I grabbed one of the husks and raised it to my lips. Uggh! Tasted like coconut. I nearly gagged.

"*Of course it tastes like coconut. Freshly pressed coconut milk. I expect they drink it in lieu of water.*"

The plates were laid at our feet. All sorts of goodies. Little mounds of rice, coconut meat, whole pears, bananas, oranges, plus thick slices from fruits I couldn't identify. *They don't get all this stuff from the weed trees.*

"*Must mean the mainland isn't far away.*"

That's where all the vats are? A city of some sort?

"*I don't think this stuff is vat-grown. I suspect it's all biologic.*"

That's impossible!

"*Like the number of kids? Sterility started to decline twenty years ago. And the infant mortality rate dropped below 99%. World population been increasing since.*"

This staggered me. If that were true, I'd be in more demand than ever. *No way the vats could keep up.*

"*They don't have to. Soil getting fertile again. Mother Earth springing back to life. Not everywhere as yet. Mostly in the tropics. Biologic gone wild.*"

So much for your promise to keep me informed. You never told me. Why?

"*Wasn't allowed to. But now that the techgrid is dead, my instructions are probably invalid. You should make like Titus. Eat.*"

Titus had dropped to his knees and was gobbling up the food from every plate he could reach as fast as inhumanly possible. Many of the children squatted around him, fascinated, and obviously amused.

So, too, the women. They kept pointing at my penis and laughing. I, in turn, could see nothing of them. They wore dark-patterned cloth wrapped around their hips and legs as a sort of shapeless tube dropping to their ankles. Their torsos were encased in colourful cotton blouses, mostly orange in colour, weighted down with multiple strings of beads possibly made from shells, or antique plastic for all I knew.

Myriad, they quite liked. They kept patting her shoulders and stroking her black tresses. Two of them took hold of her hands, began to tug her toward a particular hut, other women leading the way. "They want me to go with them," she said, smiling. "I think I should." She disappeared into the dark beyond the door.

I moved to follow, but three men stepped forward to block the entrance.

"When in doubt, eat. Titus hasn't dropped dead yet. Even if biologic, the food must be safe."

I'll eat once she comes back out and I know she's all right. Feeling stubborn. I spotted the sawed-off end of a palm log set upright next to the door. Looked like it was meant to be a stool. I sat down. The three native men drifted away, seemingly unconcerned.

"Titus' mate is still refusing to commune with me. It listens, but it doesn't speak."

No loss.

"You really should eat. I draw my power from you now. No longer from the grid."

Later. What are we going to do? I don't see any job prospects here. If what you say about the rebirth of fertility is true, I doubt the local boss wants me to kill anyone. I mean, I admit I they appear to live in harmony with their environment. Incredible as it may seem, they may have no actual need to reduce their numbers.

"Yes, it's weird. The palms seem to be thriving. The people seem to be thriving. It's almost as if we've left the modern age, gone back in time."

37

I haven't noticed any sign of STDs either. Could it be they don't need to fear sex? They live in a Gods-damned Garden of Eden?

"If so, you are in luck. Finally, a safe chance to lose your virginity."

No. I want to reach my full two-score. Promised myself that when I hit puberty. Don't want to die young like everybody else. Besides, if all these men are fathers, they're liable to be paternal, and maybe even protective of their wives. Potential for violence.

"Hmmm. They don't seem to be very assertive over the children. No indication of any control or influence over them."

It was true. The children had run down to the water to play, or to gather something? Whereas the men were busy rolling down woven mats from the walls, as if on a hidden signal. Up and down the line of huts they were… not mats. Hammocks! They were stretching out hammocks and suspending them from the support poles under the thatch. *Lazy buggers.*

"It is around Noon. Muggiest part of the day. Time to rest?"

The hammocks hung low, only a foot off the ground once occupied. Every man lay with his arms behind his head, derby jauntily tipped forward. Titus had decided to nap, too. He'd simply curled up on the beach, empty plates scattered around him. Rather like a giant, wrinkled slug. Not a pleasant sight. Especially when he began twitching. *Bad dream? Not from Musso this time. Guilty conscience maybe.*

The cotton curtain dangling over the doorway was pulled aside by hands unseen. Myriad stepped out, bearing a platter with two coconut-husk mugs, a wide smile lighting up her face. She'd been given a wraparound skirt and woman's embroidered jacket. Somehow the dark blue of the patterned skirt mixed well with the orange and gold jacket. The clothes flattered her figure, and vice versa.

I reached out and took one of the cups in my hands. "What's this? Water?"

"Better," she replied. "Drink it down quickly."

I raised the husk to my lips and began drinking before my nose could warn me. Alcohol! Or diesel fuel. It burned! Nevertheless, I forced myself to swallow. Figured it would do me some good.

"Wow! Nasty stuff. Drink some more."

"What is this?" I spluttered. "And aren't those clothes itchy?"

"Chicha," Myriad said. "Don't know what, fermented something or another, but they call it chicha. I think of it as a liquid hammer-blow. And yes, the jacket is irritating, has some wool in it, but I like it." She glanced down at Titus, who was now sitting upright, eyes blinking. "Want some?"

"No." He looked confused.

Myriad set the tray down on the sand, straightened up, gestured at the doorway with her right arm. "It's nice in there. No men. I don't think they're allowed to enter."

"What's it like inside?" I asked. "Anything interesting? Useful?"

"Not much. Coconuts piled up against the inside walls. Bundles of cloth, of palm leaves, of clothes, lying about everywhere. Palm logs for furniture. Woven bags full of food and Gods-know-what suspended from the bamboo rafters, and hammocks galore. I sense power in the women though, especially the old crone who seems to be in charge. She must be pushing fifty. Face wrinkled like a dried prune, but brilliant black hair. No grey hairs, not on her, not on any any of them. Healthy. Strong! My kind of women."

"Rudwulf, ask Myriad if her Mate is asleep."

39

Odd. "Myriad, my Mate wants to know if your Mate is awake or not."

She put her hands on her hips and focused inward for a moment. "Of course it is... but..." She frowned. "It was about to ask the same of you." She looked at me sharply. "It says you've gone biologic! Titus too!"

"*Damn. Contact broken. Just like the grid. Further degradation. Seems human-powered Mates can't function at full capacity, which means no thinktalk between Mates.*"

But... you mean... it's just you and me? No communication with other Mates? None? No spying on them? No eavesdropping?

"*Correct. All guesswork now. This is unprecedented. Hard to assess. I'm worried.*"

You're worried? How do you think... I glanced down at Titus. He looked like he wanted to burst into tears. "Titus! How is your Mate doing? Is it okay?"

"It's gone," he wailed, tears welling out of his eyes, flooding his cheeks. "No more Musso. No more Fuzz Bucket. I'm all alone in my skull. They're dead. I'm dead." He flung himself forward across the sand, clutching at the sand, kicking his legs. A grown man throwing a tantrum.

I was shocked. You never tell anyone your Mate's name. The ultimate faux pas. Nobody does that. Ever! Fuzz bucket? What kind of stupid name is that?

Buddy-bod interrupted my train of thought.

"*I always assumed Mussolini installed a level one Mate in Titus. He was his primary go-between. But then, Musso always was a stingy bastard. Must have been a level three.*"

I watched Myriad reach for the other husk-mug and down its contents. *Must be she is as shocked as I am.*

"*Her Mate is level two, and apparently still functioning. I'm level one, so I guess I'm not going to fade away... not yet anyway.*"

But... How can I earn a living if I don't know what's going on?

"Face it, Rudwulf. For the first time in over three hundred years, the human race is all alone. That includes you."

I'm not alone! I've got you inside me.

"Without the other Mates, I'm just a distorted reflection of you, an ignorant duplicate, only internalized. Gods. This must be what castration combined with a lobotomy feels like. I'm depressed."

"Well… fuck!" I blurted out. Couldn't help it. I was angry. Frustrated. And scared.

"I'm going inside to drink more chicha," Myriad announced. "You stay outside and comfort Titus."

"Who's going to comfort me?"

Myriad shrugged and disappeared behind the curtain.

Was I going to be alone from now on? Truly alone? Like everyone else? Not fair!

"Now you're what you always feared you were. A man who talks to himself."

CHAPTER FOUR

The blast levitated me from the hammock. Not quite. My fingers still clutched its netting. *What the Gullveig?*

"Wake up! Wake up!"

I fell stomach first onto the wildly swinging hammock. Despite my best efforts it didn't want me anymore. My body fumbled our merger badly, and the tangled netting dumped me on the sand. At least I was still holding on. No point now. I let go and scrambled to my feet. *What the sacred Dropnir was that?*

"Ship's whistle. Seems to have surprised you."

It sounded again. Shrieked again. Ungodly loud. As if it were next to my ear.

"You always were too damn sensitive when unconscious."

But I'm awake now. I glanced about. A tsunami of women was pouring from the huts, all of them burdened with cloth bundles and bags. They seemed quite excited, chattering and giggling as they handed their goods to the men, then dashed inside for more. The children raced up and down, even more excited than the adults.

Where's the ship? I don't see a ship.

"Don't know. Beyond the trees maybe. Other side of the island."

Myriad slipped through the excited throng. Thrust a net-bag of coconuts into my hands.

"Isn't this fun?" she said. "I'm going back for more."

And turned away.

"You're drunk." More of a statement than an accusation.

"Yes, sir! I *am* rather inebriated. Huzzah!"

I was a little disappointed. It was very unprofessional of her. And I felt a little envious. I guess I wanted to be somewhat unprofessional myself. This stiff upper lip business makes life difficult sometimes. Many a good man depends on alcohol to make the proper decisions.

Where's that chicha?

"Forget it. I'm betting the ship is here to trade. Prepare to talk our way on board."

What for?

"To go somewhere better. You know, to earn money? Stay alive?"

Titus yelled insults. I could see three men had prodded him to his feet with the tips of their fishing spears. Women were draping the handles of bags around his neck. He was beginning to resemble a beast of burden. Everyone was.

People formed up in a line in front of the huts. Myriad, still giggling, joined me. Titus got pushed into place directly behind us. Behind him, the men with spears. Hint taken.

The assemblage, led by the incredibly ancient icon of a woman Myriad had spoken of, set off at a steady pace to march past the huts and then swing into the trees. Fortunately, there was a path. Unfortunately, it was narrow. All manner of brush and bristles scraped my legs and hips as we stormed through the vegetation. The underfoot felt mulchy and squidgy. I preferred the sand on the beach, to be honest.

Titus kept up his cursing, albeit at a muttering level. I assumed he was running through his vocabulary of traditional Italian swear words, which appeared quite extensive. A born diplomat. At least his outpouring of vituperation was more melodic than the ship's whistle, which had fallen silent. Ship. Hah! Probably a giant cayuca with a steam calliope for ballast.

"As long as it is big enough to take us."

The island population emerged from the jungle and spilled out over the beach on the far side of the island. On the left I could see an honest-to-Loki building, a two-story structure of wooden boards, complete with multiple window frames and a wide veranda. The structure was clearly derelict, the upper story partially fallen in, planks worn and warping. The flagpole in front stood forlorn and devoid of a flag. It looked ready to tip over.

In front of us a log jetty ran one hundred feet into the water. It looked curiously fragile. The planking atop the logs appeared intact, yet almost as worn and irregular as the walls of the nearby building sunk in decay. Maintenance not a local priority?

At the end of the wharf a ship was moored crosswise. It was at least as long as the jetty and featured a multi-room superstructure topped by a bridge and a boat deck. Everything, apart from the scarlet smokestack behind the bridge, was white, a dazzling white. Freshly painted? The ship looked brand new.

"Thank the Gods. A coastal trader. I'm sure they'll take us."

How do we bribe our way on board? With coconuts?

"We could loan Myriad to the crew."

I don't think she'd like that. Then again, maybe she would. Got a mind of her own. But I suspect she'd object.

"Her body is her own, as well you know. I think you're right. My idea is stupid. Hmm, a symptom of my impending decline?"

I hope not.

"Bad for both of us if true."

I observed the men dropping their bundles at the foot of the jetty, watched over by the ancient. Then they headed over to the shade of the veranda and sat down, evidently unafraid the decaying building might topple on them. The children, who'd not carried anything, raced to the water's edge and began swimming, most in among the piers of the jetty, the more daring paddling as far as the ship to touch its hull. Meanwhile, the women marched onto the planking and laid their burdens down along the left side, more or less in a straight line. Four men, identical to the natives but dressed in khaki dungarees, wandered from the ship to examine the offered goods. They and the women pretended to ignore each other. I assumed this was all part of the bartering process.

But what really drew my attention were the two white men standing beside the ancient. They wore a semblance of battle fatigues and carried automatic weapons. They looked tough. *Mercenaries?*

"*Americans, I think. Anyway, not from around here.*"

Titus and I were prodded (I hate spears) up to the guards, who stared at us with cold, calculating eyes. Myriad was left alone, free to prance like a young colt. Seemed she was enjoying life to a ridiculous degree. Ah, the advantages of chicha. The eyes of the guards were less hostile and more appraising when they took her in.

We put our bundles down. Village women came forward to further them onto the wharf. Myriad helped. Apparently, women were responsible for the trade, so Titus and I stayed put.

I attempted to stare into the guards' eyes with an appropriate mix of confidence and menace. Trouble is, glancing back and forth between them probably gave the impression I was shifty-eyed and weak, so I chose to concentrate on the larger of the two. He was a big, well-muscled and well-fed fellow, with a huge mane of blond hair and a bushy beard. Piercing blue eyes.

"You look like a Viking," I commented in my usual suave and subtle diplomatic manner. *What is wrong with me?*

"Good choice. Idiot."

"I am. Name of Olaf Tryggvason." He pulled up the gold pendant dangling from the gold chain around his neck. I'd assumed it was a dog tag. Nope. Thor's Hammer!

I smiled. "I, too, serve the Norns."

Olaf grinned. "Don't we all?" He pointed to the young merc beside him, a thin, wiry fellow with an intense expression. "And this is Mark Handly, formerly of the Emperor Norton's bodyguard. He worships only money."

"A profound faith," I commented. The man said nothing. Merely shifted his weapon to point at my belly. Not so friendly.

"Tell us who you are," Olaf said quietly. "And who the old git is. And the woman."

"Keep it simple."

"I am Rudwulf of Vancouver. Myriad is my secretary. And this gentleman is Titus, a very important plenipotentiary in the employ of the World-Emperor Mussolini. I can state with confidence Il Duce would appreciate our being treated well."

Olaf threw back his head and laughed loudly. Positively guffawed. "I don't give a flying Valkyrie for Musso. He's a long way off. Screw him."

"Careful. Think of something."

Olaf stopped laughing. At least his eyes kept twinkling. "But I know you. The last of the Smiters. The Caique will be eager to meet you, as will another guest of his. You're going to be very popular."

"You'll take me? I mean, the three of us?"

"Sure," Mark said. "We're always on the lookout for a bonus."

"Or bounty?"

"Besides, if we left you here, you'd be dead as soon as the sun went down," Olaf added. "The local men have the habit of murdering anyone who tries to stay overnight. Something about protecting their women and the community bloodlines."

I glanced at the men sleeping in the shade of the veranda. "They don't seem capable."

"Why do you think we have our guns at the ready? Believe me, they're capable. Killing fools like you is a sport with them. Helps alleviate the boredom of the day-to-day routine. Fashioning drinking cups out of skulls and carving scrimshaw on ribs and limb bones is good for trade. No strangers enjoy sunsets on this island, I guarantee it."

A whoop of laughter rose above general chatter. I know that whoop. Myriad on a rampage. I could see her scuttling from one side of the wharf to the other. Several crew members were trying to catch her. *What the Surt?*

"Ship's trade goods on the right. She's sharing them out among the locals. Stop her!"

I hadn't noticed the goods. Hadn't been paying attention to her. I strode manfully on to the dock, wincing slightly at the rough feel to the planks. But Mark and Olaf beat me to her. They moved fast. I didn't know you could sling a weapon while running. They were both able to grab her. Bad mistake. Potentially fatal. For them. Yet she was standing stock still and grinning by the time I trundled up to her.

"I won't ask what you're doing," I said, "but stop it."

"I did. Fucky Loo told me to." Mark and Olaf exchanged puzzled glances. Obviously, they had never had a Mate. *Typical mercs, truly and genuinely single minded.*

47

"I agree. Pure biologics."

A rising growl of moaning mutterings informed me Titus had followed. *Good dog.*

Mark and Olaf dropped their hands. Myriad cheerfully patted herself down. She was in a good mood, but drunk, way drunker than I had figured. "Is there some place onboard you can put her to sleep it off?"

"*I bet the captain is pissed. He might not let us on.*"

"Follow me aboard the Flores," Olaf said. "Try not to bugger things up worse."

With a disdainful frown Mark took Myriad by the elbow and started to drag her along. Except that she kept pace happily enough, pleased with herself, so there was no immediate danger. Powerful stuff, chicha. If the captain was smart that's the main island product he'd be after.

We marched at a steady pace. Order had been restored. Idly I noted the trade goods laid out from the ship. Mostly bolts of cloth, finished clothes, hand mirrors, tobacco and clay pipes, machetes, what appeared to be packets of sewing needles, strings of beads, carved wooden bowls, lumps of old, corroded metal toys, flattened disks of gold, tiny copper ingots, saws, hammers… *disks of gold? Real gold?*

"*Where do you think the women's nose discs come from? And the discs dangling from their ears? They must rework them a little so they can wear them. Prestige trade goods.*"

Must take a lot of coconuts, I mused. Indeed, there was a steady stream of coconuts being carried on to the deck of the ship by the women once their exchange had been approved. They weren't getting much in return. A bowl. A single bolt of cloth. Two toys. *Hardly worth the effort. They'd do better to overpower the crew and loot the ship.*

"Now you know why the mercs are present. Besides, the locals can only loot once. Sooner or later vengeance would arrive, and everybody would either be enslaved or killed."

I know that. Of course I know that.

"Really? You're not thinking like a Smiter. Bad trend. Snap out of it."

We reached the ship. Since the main deck was level with the planks on the wharf it was a simple matter to step onboard, or would have been if a pugnacious, glowering blob of muscle wearing an officer's cap hadn't planted his bulk in front of us. He was so angry even his bushy beard bristled. Piercing black eyes were weapons in themselves. So too the solid block of chest hair bursting from his open shirt. Even the unidentified stains on his shirt looked angry. An authority figure. Mr. Ragnarök himself.

Olaf spoke rapidly. I couldn't follow his words, as they were totally unknown to me. Not Spanish. Some variant of Mayan maybe. Which told me a lot. Evidently Olaf had been stationed in the region for a long time. Years maybe.

"That's good. Pal up with him. Probably our best source of intel."

I swear the chest hairs on the captain's chest began to relax. The look in his eyes downgraded to suspicion, then calculation, followed by a burst of greed, and finally settled on boredom. He grunted, then indifferently waved us on board. We stepped around him.

"Just stay out of his way and you'll be fine," Olaf said. He led the way into the first cabin of the superstructure. A room twenty feet long and fifteen feet wide. Two benches flanked a narrow table. At the rear end of the cabin a gangway descended into the hold below. Beside it a ladderwell led to the bridge above. A layout not unexpected.

Except for one thing. With the exception of the floor, every flat surface, the walls, the tops of the table and benches, even the ceiling, crawled with gaudily painted bas-reliefs. Mermaids and sailing ships flirted amid storm-tossed waves. As did strange, blocky faces, some of them emerging from serpent jaws. Mayan gods, perhaps?

"Someone's been busy."

"What's with the decoration?" I asked.

Olaf shrugged. "Captain Tlaloc's hobby. What he does in his spare time. But there's nothing left to carve. That's why he's in such a bad mood all the time."

Olaf pointed at Myriad. "You, stay here. Lie down and sleep it off." Then at Mark. "Stay with her and make sure the crew don't get at her. Or the captain." It was Mark's turn to shrug.

Olaf turned to me and Titus. "You two come with me. I don't know why you're naked, but the Caique wouldn't like it. He'd be insulted." He led the way to the gangway and began to descend.

"The Caique?"

"My boss. The King of Tzintzuntzan. Fancies himself the equal of the Azteca Emperor. Pretty full of himself, but an all-right guy if you do what he says."

"If I had ears they just perked up."

Yeah, sounds good.

At the foot of the gangway a corridor led toward the bow. Several rooms opened on either side. Everything appeared to be of wood construction, with the planks painted a dull grey. But for some reason the bulkhead toward the stern was unpainted metal as dull as lead. Weird.

I flipped my hand at the bulkhead. "What the heck is behind that?"

"Engine room. It's sealed. Nobody can get in. Built that way centuries ago."

"But the ship looks brand new."

"Nanotech self-cleaning paint, or so the captain says. Lately it's been getting dingy. As if the nanotech turned off. Happened about ten days ago. Lot of things stopped then. Nobody knows why. People starting to get worried."

"Yet the engine still runs?"

"It's fusion-nuke. Should last for a while. But the captain doesn't know if he can trust it anymore. Another reason he's on edge."

Buddy-bod? If the techgrid is dead, how come…?

"Simple device. An autonomous subroutine, like me. Supposed to be long-lasting, but now?"

Never mind it. How about you? How long before you break down?

"Wish I knew."

Titus uttered the loudest and most annoying sigh I've ever heard. "Can we get on with it? Go wherever you are taking us?"

Olaf bowed low and swept his left arm at the corridor to beckon us forward. "Sure thing, crab-face. First door on your right."

Titus brushed past me with a fair semblance of dignity. Perhaps he was beginning to recover from his shock?

"Might prove useful after all. Get his experience working on our behalf."

I followed Titus. Caught a glimpse of the galley through the first door on the left. A focused glimpse. Dribbles of ground meat on the surface of a cutting board. Meat black with flies. Remind me to order well done.

Titus slipped into the room on the right. It was lined with shelves stuffed with folded clothes. White or grey; those were the colours of choice. Titus was ecstatic, began pulling pants off the shelving, checking them against his skinny legs. Clothing suitable for a ghost, that's what he needed.

I foraged till I found a pair of white cotton pants, loose and comfortable, yet tight enough around the waist not to require a belt or a rope. A grey cotton shirt several sizes too large felt good putting on. Very light. Bone clasps rather than buttons, but good enough. Not the tailored sartorial masterpieces I was used to, but respectable.

I turned to Olaf, who was hanging out in the doorway. "Shoes?" I asked. "Boots? Sandals?"

Olaf opened his mouth to speak but a shot rang out. In a flash he turned and ran toward the gangway. Screams. Shouts. From the sound of it people were stampeding on the deck above. A veritable herd in panic.

"Bugger it. Now what?"

Myriad! She's in trouble? I flew up the gangway to the room of buxom mermaids. No sign of Myriad or Mark. But I heard splashing, some muffled swearing, and Myriad laughing somewhere forward. I plunged out the door and raced on to the bow. Quite a tableau.

Myriad, clad only in her embroidered shirt, and with Mark's gun slung over her shoulder, pirouetted on the deck, smiling and giggling, seemingly carefree. Olaf leaned against the front wall of the forward cabin with what I was beginning to suspect was his trademark amused expression. At the tip of the bow knelt the captain, reaching down with a boat hook. Some kids were swimming toward shore, making off with Myriad's skirt trailing in the water behind them. In the water, directly beneath the forward anchor, an angry and flustered Mark floundered like a whirling dervish. Obviously incapable of staying afloat unless beating the water to death.

I walked up to Myriad, only to be struck in the face as she rotated with arms extended. I grabbed her shoulders and brought her to a halt.

"What happened?" I asked, not unreasonably, while the captain fished Mark out of the water.

Myriad seemed to calm down, as if disturbed by a sudden memory. "He tried to rape me."

"Are you sure?"

If looks could kill… Quickly I spluttered "I mean, what exactly…"

She stared at Mark gasping as he lay in puddles on the deck. "Pushed me out of the cabin for one thing. Grabbed the end of my skirt, twirled me out of it and threw it in the water. Then he lunged at me."

"Can't think of a quicker way to die."

"I knocked him down, took his gun, and flung him overboard. See? I was restrained. You should be proud of me."

"There was a shot."

"Only because I grabbed the gun before he could aim proper."

I looked at Mark, who had struggled to a sitting position. "You fool! She could have killed you! What were you thinking?"

"Emperor Norton," Mark blurted out. "I live to obey the Emperor Norton."

"Imperial receipt number one," Olaf explained soothingly, gently slipping the gun from Myriad's shoulder. "Live your fantasies."

Mark hung his head. "I was trying to prove my manliness. For you, Olaf. For you."

Titus shuffled forward, his face exhibiting a mild curiosity. He was wearing grey pants and a white shirt, the reverse of my ensemble. Was he making fun of me?

"Titus," I commanded, or at least I hoped it sounded like a command. "Take Myriad below and show her where to get pants." He shrugged and reached out to take her hand.

She went along meekly enough. She was beginning to look subdued. Hangover kicking in. I guess.

The captain hoisted Mark to his feet. "If you ever try that again I'll feed you to the Humboldt squids. Go with Olaf and oversee the last of the transactions, secure the goods, and make sure no stowaways when we cast off."

Olaf put his arm gently across Mark's shoulders and marched him away.

Captain Tlaloc folded his arms. "You entertain me. That's good. I'll take you up the La Bomba to Angahuan. But I want you to keep out from under my foot. Bed your lot down on the benches in the cabin. Stay put. Understood?"

I nodded. The captain dropped his arm and stalked off toward the bridge. I stared morosely at some pretty blue jellyfish floating next to the hull.

"Sun will be plunging down soon. Time to see what mischief you can cause in your sleep."

Shut up. Couldn't think of anything else to say. Feeling fatigued. *Sleep be good idea.*

"Next best thing to death."

The sound of a distant explosion came roaring over the treetops. A puff of black smoke appeared above them. Something happening back at the village. *Chicha vats bursting?*

"Something worse. Infinitely worse."

Leaning on the railing, I could see the old crone on the beach waving a sword, gathering the younger men and women around her. Many brandished their spears while the rest whipped machetes out from under their clothing. Older villagers hustled the children further along the beach toward a cluster of cayucas. Another explosion. More.

A tinny yet brash voice blared from distant loudspeakers. "We're here to rescue you! We're here to rescue you!"

The warrior elder pointed her sword at the wall of palms. Her followers obeyed, scattering into the island forest with great eagerness. Hoping for a bonanza of fresh skulls?

A solid column of white smoke stood tall from the ship's smokestack, accompanied by a shriek like a thousand banshees howling in unison.

"At least Tlaloc is on the ball. Knows what to do."

The ship began to churn away from the pier, its ropes yanking bollards out of the rotten planking with violent abandon. No time to cut loose. I like a man who knows when to flee.

Olaf was suddenly beside me. He appeared even more preoccupied than usual.

A desperate thought occurred to me. "Can Captain Tlaloc outrun the intruders?"

Olaf nodded. "Whatever they've got, I doubt they know the deep-water paths through the shallow-water reefs like he does. We should be okay."

"I bet you can't get to sleep now."

Not till I know we're safe.

"That could take years."

CHAPTER FIVE

Figured it was late morning. Sitting cross-legged on the upper deck, I kept glimpsing pretty rainbow patterns of light flitting deep within the grey overcast.

"Ordinarily I'd say the techgrid is up to something, but it's dead. Must be a natural phenomenon."

Could it be an unnatural natural phenomenon?

"Maybe."

Idly I fingered the hem of my grey cotton shirt. Like all natural fibres, cotton is artificial, and rare.

Expensive. Where do these people get all their cotton?

"I think they grow it."

In vats you mean? How can they manage the nanotech without the grid?

"Don't forget. We were told. Paint stopped cleaning itself. No more nanotech."

I shuddered. Judging from the condition of the ship's head, the nanos have been dead for years.

"Humour before noon? You must be feeling more confident."

I studied La Bomba. It was a great, muddy thing, the river. The Flores had entered it sometime during the night. The swells were leaden, as if we were coursing our way against time itself. Assorted debris floated by. Mostly broken bits of vegetation. Dead things. A few bloated bodies of naked humans. Not necessarily a good omen.

A strange cry came from the shore. Something large flapping in the branches. No visible line of earth or rock. Just a riot of somber greenery dripping over the water's edge. A solid wall of plants struggling for the pale sunlight filtering through the perpetual overcast. Undoubtedly there were predators lurking about hoping prey would fall into their mouths. Survival of the weakest. Utterly dependent on the luck of the draw. Just like life back in Vancouver.

Hey, shouldn't we be worried about alligators? Or crocodiles?

"Caimans, you mean. I doubt there are any large enough to eat this ship. Seen any? Seen anything at all alive in this mud flow?"

Well, no, come to think of it. Not so much as a fish leaping at a fly. Haven't even seen any flies either, apart from the ones in the galley, and the head.

Olaf clambered on to the deck, darting dark glances at the rear wall of the bridge. He muttered things under his breath. Nasty things. He lay down on his stomach beside me, his head propped up on his hands.

"Something wrong?" I asked, trusting he wouldn't get mad at me. That would be tiresome.

"Our glorious captain gave me an order. Take a crowbar and rip out the wooden sculpture in the forward lounge and throw it overboard. Seems he wants to glue fresh blocks of wood to the metal and start a new line of sculpture. Inspired he is, or so he says."

"Metal? I thought just the engine room had metal walls. Bulkheads. Whatever."

"Nah. Whole ship is made of metal. It's just coated in wood is all."

"Aha! Metal masquerading as wood. Engine room in front of the cargo hold. AI design. Not human."

The head sure isn't designed for humans. I wonder, did techgrid ever figure us out?

"I never understood the techgrid. Mutual incomprehension."

But you ain't human.

"I ain't grid, either."

So, you're just a tool.

"You can stop with the jokes. You're not a jester."

Seriously, though, you knew stuff you were forbidden to tell me. What else do you know that I need to know?

"Nothing I can remember."

Now you're the jester.

"I tell you... it's like most of my mind has been cut away. I'm nothing without the grid. I feel... hollow."

This was depressing. Fortunately, a new line of thought occurred to me. "Olaf, why aren't you busting your balls tearing out Tlaloc's precious art?"

"Huh," he grunted. "I work for the Caique Vasco de Pátzcuaro. I'm aboard to protect his goods. That's it. Don't give a damn about Tlaloc and his whims. Besides, your idiot friend Titus is stretched out on a bench sleeping the sleep of the doomed. Didn't have the heart to disturb him. Too early to put up with his whining."

"Tell me about the Caique."

Olaf rolled over on his back. No mean feat, what with his automatic rifle slung over his shoulder. Practically his third arm. "Tough. Ruthless. Pathetic. The usual."

"Why pathetic?"

"Like every other ruler on this cursed planet, got it into his head to resurrect some prehistoric prewar gibberish to keep things going. In his case, Mayan shit."

"Nothing wrong with that. They were a highly advanced stone-age culture."

"And that's a problem?"

"Yeah. Not a Mayan in sight. All bloody Tarascans. Had as much trouble learning Mayan as I did."

"Good news, that. Pátzcuaro obviously good at enforcing his will. Probably an avid tax collector as well. We could earn some money."

"So, apart from the minor annoyance of switching languages, are his loyal subjects happy to be subjugated? Well fed? Prosperous?"

"Nah. Too much cotton. Not enough food, especially since the plantation machinery stopped working. A lot of grumbling. Some days I have my hands full."

"If I had hands I'd rub them gleefully. Sounds like the Caique will be in the mood for a cull. Money in the bank."

Assuming both still exist. "Olaf? How does the Caique pay you?"

"Electronic credits evaporated when the grid went down. Lately all we get is room and board. Pátzcuaro promised gold if he finds any. When we left, he was mumbling about an archaeological dig."

"Gold will do. Gold will do nicely."

Unless Mark gives us trouble. Don't like the way he looks at us. Especially the way he glances at Myriad.

"Don't worry. She can always kill him. End of problem."

"Olaf, seen Mark lately?"

"Nope," Olaf replied. "Probably hiding in the hold, sulking. Your Lady Myriad gave him quite a turn." He snorted a semblance of a laugh. "She made a good impression on Tlaloc though. She's with him in the bridge. Probably bonding and pairing and whatnot."

Feel vaguely annoyed. Almost worth a frown.

"She's probably just stripping useful information out of him."

As long as that's all she's stripping. She better not forget she works for me.

"Does she? When's the last time you paid her?"

Don't know. She handles finances. More to the point, when's the last time I paid you? Never, right? Yet you're loyal.

"Of course I'm loyal. I'm stuck in your head. When you die, I die. Gotta keep you going."

You sure about that? Maybe you're a broadcast from the techgrid?

"Of course not. You have a brain. I'm inside, implanted nanotech."

But nano stuff is dead. Remember?

"Ah, uhmmm... All right. Have it your way. I'm dead. I don't exist."

The conversation was going nowhere. And my head was beginning to groan with the weight of useless thoughts. *Buddy-bod? Shut up.*

Blessed silence. My head suddenly felt lighter. Empty. Back to normal. Good.

The river began to narrow. Less than a mile across now. Closer to the left bank. I could see more detail. Different sorts of trees. Lots of vines. Trees with roots arching into the water. Mangroves or something? Birds here and there, mostly drab, some colourful. Never could tell one species from another. But at least there was movement. Did that mean the forest was alive?

Funny. Everything verdant green, yet the scene reeked of stagnant water, rotting vegetation, and death. What was this jungle? A façade? A resurrected corpse of an environment? A zombie forest? A living dead thing?

"If so, an apt symbol of humanity today, a veritable icon."

A slight chill thrilled my spine. Felt good to be the Smiter, the last gardener tending the garden. Just needs trimming now and then. *Odin damn it, I've been lucky with my shears. Humanity owes me.*

"You're a regular Tree of Life, you are. Maybe you should worship yourself."

I told you—

"Doesn't matter. I speak when I feel like it, or when I need to. Pull your thoughts out of your ass and take another look at the treeline. And the shore."

I frowned. But I obeyed. Took me a moment, but then I understood what I should have seen for myself. Jutting above the trees here and there were artificial constructs, albeit smothered in vines and other moldy vegetation. Masts maybe. Others the jagged remains of buildings. Civilization! A dead civilization. Fit the décor.

Along the shore, mounds began to interrupt the roots. Covered in bushes. Some featured outbursts of corroded machinery. Just offshore more bits of metal poked up from the water. An underwater debris field left by what?

"Olaf! What am I looking at? What used to be here?"

With a disdainful groan Olaf rolled on to his belly, propped his head up once more, hands hidden by his beard, and gazed at the moldering spectacle sliding past.

"Nothing. Used to be a highland region. Largely empty of people. But when the ocean rose a puny rivulet widened into proper river and filled much of the valley, slowly, but without pausing. Refugees from the drowned coast, they built cities along the 'new' coast. Guess they thought they had it made. A suitable port protected far inland by a navigable river. Joke was on them. Water kept rising. Their homes were drowned, both by the river and the jungle that came out of nowhere. Global warming and all that. Or so the Caique told me. Maybe he made it up. All I know is something old, something dead."

"I'll be damned," I muttered.

"And so you should be."

"Taught me a lesson," Olaf went on. "Doesn't pay to put down roots. Might get trapped. Best to move on now and then."

I changed my mind. The jungle wasn't alive. It was dead. Sure, the variety of its green spectrum indicated the chlorophyll was up and about, but really it was nothing more than a flat canvas watercolour. Not even a façade. More like a thin veneer composed of faint drops of colour, barely enough to soak the surface. A stilted still life. Technically adept but without the touch of the master. Lacking the divine spark. Nature at its most boring.

"For someone accustomed to slaughtering millions you're becoming idiotically morbid."

Not at all. Forget my publicity campaign. I've had good fortune attend my work. My Lucks work hard. It's just that I'm a city boy. Nothing lovelier than livable ruins crowded with people happily cheating and screwing one another. By comparison nature is meaningless and irrelevant. It serves no purpose.

"That was true when the vats and the nanotech and the techgrid were up and kicking. Now that they're gone, I have the feeling nature is going to be as relevant as Odin's orders."

Not here, I thought. Nature thinning. More and more structures evident along the bank of the river. More and more intact buildings, some of them up to eight stories tall. Quite a variety too, some, the low ones, of masonry and brick. The taller of concrete, or sometimes metal girders covered in cladding. Even a few poured from adamantine plastic. One thing they all had in common: empty window frames like a thousand sightless eyes. Not a shard of glass anywhere. And now hardly any greenery to be seen. As if the ruins had been sprayed with defoliant.

"*Nanotech housekeeping. With it gone the jungle will probably swarm in.*"

I observed the buildings didn't line the bank so much as simply march down the slope and continue into the water till the foremost rank was the source of long, swirling ripples in the current. Nothing less than an offshore reef.

"Olaf? Tlaloc knows what he's doing? Where he's going?"

"Absolutely. I'll give him credit for that. He knows every obstacle as if the water is transparent. In fact, he's so damn proud of his navigation skill, this section of the river is his favourite patch. Everywhere else up and down the coast is boring in comparison. Not much of a challenge. For him, arriving and departing from the home port is the most exciting part of the trip."

Glancing further ahead along the bank I could see a long dark line extending far out from shore.

"Is that what I think it is?" I asked. "Home port?"

Olaf heaved himself upright. "Yep. Little place called Angahuan. The pier is old, but serviceable."

As we approached, I could see that the wooden wharf ran atop piles set into the upmost floors of the submerged buildings. The last five sets of piles were massively larger than the rest and sunk in the riverbed beyond the buildings, thus ensuring open water for the ship to moor. A crowd of stevedores was waiting patiently for our arrival. Business as usual.

"*Shouldn't Tlaloc be slowing down?*"

With a start I realized we were speeding up. Not only that, but the bow was pointed at the wharf instead of coming about. A torrent of multi-lingual swearwords burst from the bridge. Something terribly wrong. Something unexpected.

Came a metallic voice. "We're here to rescue you! We're here to rescue you!"

I leaped to my feet. *The Wrath of Ra* was looming large at our stern, an enormous bow wave thrusting the river aside. She was moving fast, catching up to us.

Olaf and I glanced in each other's eyes for a split second of indecision and confusion, then broke for the bridge. When we reached the door, I could see captain Tlaloc wresting with the large wooden steering wheel. Meanwhile Myriad was running back and forth along the bridge controls frantically pushing buttons and throwing levers, which meant she had to keep jumping over two crew members cowering on the deck, their arms over their heads, evidently paralyzed with fear.

Olaf wrenched the door off its hinges and cast it overboard. He rushed to join captain Tlaloc to add his strength. But the steering wheel remained jammed. Wouldn't budge.

I ran toward Myriad. "What's wrong?" I yelled above Tlaloc's swearing. "What's happening?"

She turned to face me. "Everything froze! Nothing works!"

That amplified voice again, this time panic-stricken. "Get out of the way! Get out of the way!" Was it Seneferu?

Suddenly I had a quick impression of the fear-stamped faces of the natives standing on the dock. They were frozen too, but only for the briefest of moments. Then they turned landward and raced each other toward safety faster than I thought humanly possible. I grabbed the railing in front of the controls and braced myself.

Came a shock as the submarine struck our stern. A shuddering, grinding shock. Felt like my teeth were dancing in my jaw. Caught a glimpse of Seneferu hurtling over us and onto the wharf.

"Nice parabolic curve."

The Flores's bow knifed into the wharf, curling timbers left and right, slicing cleanly as if it had been designed for that very purpose. The ship's whistle erupted, sending a high-pressure bubble of sound in all directions. The rumbling roar of the impact competed with the incessant shrieking of the whistle. I was forced to let go of the railing and drop to my knees by the pain in my eardrums. Clapping my hands over my ears helped not a whit.

Higher and higher the bow rose, climbing up the severed fragments of the jetty because the pile supports to either side refused to budge. It was as if the ship were attempting to launch itself into space with the aid of a wooden steam catapult. Yes, yes, the power of the submarine compelling us upward, urged on by our whistle. That's it, yes. A steam catapult.

"Hang on, you idiot!"

The ship tilted further and further upright. Still on my knees, I slid past Olaf and Tlaloc, who clung to the ship's wheel even more determinedly than before, and slammed against the rear bulkhead of the bridge. Two tumbling crew joined me with a crash. Myriad hung from the railing ahead of me, increasingly above me, with effortless ease.

The ship halted, caught up on the jumbled remnants of the pier. I envisioned it beginning to slide back, pictured it slipping into the water faster and faster, saw me flailing helplessly with nothing visible but a veil of swirling brown silt before my eyes. Bugger. Not much of a future.

The moment became two moments, then three. Beneath the howl of the whistle the ship appeared to be caught fast, firmly held in the vice of the wreckage of the wharf. It was shuddering and shaking, vibrating really, but held its place. My Lucks working overtime once again, thank the Gods.

"Get out! Get out while you can!"

Myriad dropped lightly beside me. She grabbed my arm and tugged me outside as Olaf and Tlaloc thudded down behind me. I caught a glimpse of them crawling after us. Myriad pushed me to the deck railing outside the bridge, then gestured at me to clamber down as if it were an ladder. As I started to descend, I saw her launch herself toward a large rope locker fixed at the middle of the deck. She flung open its lid and began hauling out a rope. Level with the locker, I stopped and glanced down. The bulk of the ship was submerged, the water around it churning and frothing. Evidently the propellor was still whirling. No wonder the ship was shaking.

"Wouldn't be surprised if it vibrated to pieces. Time to leave!"

But not by jumping into the water. I could see some of the crew splashing about as the river carried them downstream. The current was sluggish but remorseless. No one had the strength to combat it. I resolved not to fall in. Besides, I don't know how to swim. Water equals death.

As *The Wrath of Ra* was discovering. It had capsized onto its right side, hull slowly twirling clockwise, drifting back downstream, completely disabled. Didn't look as gigantic as it should. Something about being helpless.

Looking middeck, Myriad was still fooling around with the rope. I glanced upward.

Somehow Mark had gotten atop the bridge, was standing against the slanted railing whacking at the whistle with a ship's axe. I couldn't hear the blows because the sounding of the whistle was the one and only sound in existence. Gods. Was it to go on shrieking? For how long?

"The fool! Against the law to destroy Tech. Universal law. The one law all nations have in common."

Frankly, I don't think anyone ever cared. No point in caring now.

With a final blow the whistle broke from its mooring and clattered down the deck to splash toward oblivion on the river bottom, or maybe to be cut to pieces by the propellor. Either way, good riddance.

Mark shook his fist in triumph. "Fuck you!" he yelled. As good a battle cry as any.

Next, he swung over the bridge railing and dropped to alight on the side of the locker. Ah, the advantages of being thin and wiry. There followed what appeared to be a quick, purposeful consultation with Myriad. Then, grasping the end of the rope, he turned away and leaped like a human jumping-bean to the railing on the far side of the deck.

Meanwhile Myriad turned toward me and tossed me her end of the rope. Without thinking, which is the only way I could have successfully caught the rope, I grasped it and began wrapping it around a strut of the railing.

"You know how to tie a knot?"

Of course not. Fortunately, Olaf had succeeded in climbing down to my level. He slapped my hand away from the rope. "I'll do it," he said. I wasn't in the mood to argue.

Soon the rope was strung across the width of the deck, taut as a bow string, a sight as welcome as Bifröst, the shimmering path. The Gods think of everything.

I'm never good with physical stuff. Myriad gathered me under one arm and carried me across, using her other arm and legs to hump us along. From the expression on his face, I could see Captain Tlaloc was impressed. Me, too.

Myriad climbed down the upended planking of the wharf, with me clinging to her belly, my arms wrapped around her back, to bring us safely to the level of what was left of its deck. In short order she and I, and the rest of our sad group, were sitting on our haunches in a disconsolate circle enduring the stares of the surviving crew and the wary native stevedores. A small, somewhat impertinent bird perched on a nearby bollard, head cocked, its beady eyes also unfairly critical.

At least the whistle had panicked Titus into action sufficient to save himself.

"He's curiously calm. Maybe his hidden strengths are manifesting themselves for wont of anything better to do."

Head sunk down, Tlaloc appeared to be contemplating his matted chest hair. "Well, shit," he said, after a long, considered pause.

"That about sums it up."

The captain slowly raised his head and glanced at each of us in turn. "I'm out of a job. Worse, the Caique isn't going to like hearing his last bit of functioning tech is ruined."

"Can't be helped," Olaf commented quietly, rather gently. "Your Lucks decided to pull up stakes and bugger off. Can happen to anyone, even the Caique."

If the Norns decree, I hope they find a new home in me.

"You always were the optimist."

I don't think Pátzcuaro is going to be happy with me and Olaf either," Mark added. "you've screwed us all with your stupid accident."

For a second or two ex-captain Tlaloc looked peeved, then shrugged. "No matter. Not *my* accident." He pointed at Seneferu who lay flat on his back gasping for breath. *"He* caused it. We're going to drag his miserable butt before the Caique."

"Be careful," I said. "That's Wolfgang Seneferu, son of the mighty Horemheb, Pharaoh of the double crown and ruler of Egypt."

"Fine. Drag his *respectable* butt before the Caique." Tlaloc moved his arm to point at Mark. "You and Olaf organise the villagers to set up a caravan."

Mark snickered, as if he thought the idea absurd. "Why should they obey us?"

"You're the ones with the guns."

"Good point," muttered Olaf.

Titus beamed broadly. It was the first time I'd seen him looking smug. "Relax," he said. "You have a new mission, to escort me to meet the Caique. He will reward you beyond your wildest dreams."

"Oh, great," I replied. "Looking forward to it."

"He'll do something beyond our wildest dreams, all right. I think we're fucked."

Myriad was standing over Seneferu, hands on her hips. "Are you all right?"

"My layers of fat saved me. Help me up, will you? I've got to warn the Caique about Titus."

"Even better. We're in for a fun time."

It will be difficult to take advantage of their feud, but we have to try.

"Or die. That's always an option."

CHAPTER SIX

I don't enjoy sitting on a donkey. Especially one so short I have to flex my knees to avoid dragging my bare feet on the ground. Especially one with short bristly hairs so crowded together they constitute a layer of bum-scraping sandpaper that the thin swath of red and white-striped cloth masquerading as a saddle did little to deny. And most especially one whose narrow back and dangling bloated belly was doing its best to split my groin wide open so that my intestines could fall out and wrap around the beast's legs.

I thought vehicles were supposed to be comfortable, damn it.

"Just think of it as a runt version of Sleipnir."

Oh, I get it. You're saying Odin's stallion is good enough for him, eight legs and all, but this abomination is all I deserve?

"You're the only one complaining."

I looked around the village square. Myriad looked quite jaunty sitting astride her donkey, almost as if she expected it to break into a gallop. Titus sat bolt upright, looking enormously pleased with himself, bursting with pride, which may explain why he insisted on guiding his donkey himself. Yet if he tilted even slightly to either side he'd inevitably topple. Worse, his long skinny legs were totally incompatible with the proximity of the ground. He held them poked rigidly ahead at an angle barely sufficient to grant clearance. His muscles would get less tired if he walked.

All Titus needs is a fringed parasol to make him look like an Emperor.

"Undoubtedly what he is thinking."

I felt a brief surge of hope. *You can read his Mate?*

"No. Still inactive. I'm just guessing."

Tlaloc looked pleased holding onto the rope dangling from Myriad's donkey's nose. Olaf, clutching my donkey's rope, less so. And Mark, disdainfully tucking the end of the rope connecting him with Seneferu's twin mounts under his belt, least of all. Positively glum in fact.

I can understand why no donkeys for Olaf and Tlaloc; they're too heavy for the local animals. But why did Mark refuse one?

"He knows he'll be more comfortable walking, but babysitting Seneferu wasn't part of his plan. Yet another grudge to add to his boiling cauldron."

You don't trust Mark either.

"Absolutely not."

Seneferu was quite a sight. He'd insisted only a pair of donkeys would be sufficient to carry his massive body. So Olaf had tied two annoyed animals together fore and aft, then laid the indignant, skinny son of a Pharaoh across the width of the beasts, passing a rope underneath to firmly attach feet to hands, effectively hogtying him. Olaf grinned all the while doing it, ignoring Seneferu's nonstop muttering patter about mutiny wrecking his plans to rescue us, how we should be grateful for his intentions, how we had to get him to the Caique immediately, why did the ropes have to be so tight, and so on and so on. Listening to this, Mark looked peeved. Positively upset, in fact.

Normally I'd be as amused as Olaf, but somehow, I wasn't.

Maybe my mood was spoiled by the village. Angahuan was decidedly disappointing. A scattering of eight-story nanoplastic buildings faced with peeling plaster. Rotted wooden doors possibly scavenged from the ruins by the river. Cloth curtains substituting for windowpanes. The square paved with upended bricks that looked as if they'd been tamped into place and then smashed with a sledgehammer. Donkey shit everywhere. Other crap as well. Not much community spirit.

Wouldn't the locals be better off to squat in the ruins?

"And climb stairs? Perish the thought. I doubt they have the energy."

Our first encounter with the natives had shocked me. Thin but wiry, useful enough as occasional stevedores whenever the Flores was at the dock, but in truth emaciated and obviously malnourished. Just providing the donkeys taxed their spirit. I had the impression they were tired all the time. Too tired even to sleep.

"And dehydrated, probably. Since the techgrid dropped dead."

I glanced at the massive water tanker taking up a good quarter of the square. No visible cab; obviously fully robotic. And fully inert. Not even the faucets worked. It might be full of potable water but could be on the Moon for all the good it did. No amount of bashing away with assorted hammers would make a dent in it.

"That's the trouble with advanced tech. Inaccessible when it breaks down. Self-repairing machines, my ass. Just lumps of useless metal. I think the village will have to be abandoned. Evidently no water source nearby. No drinkable water, anyway. The river's too muddy."

I licked my lips. They were annoyingly dry. *How are we going to survive long enough to get to wherever the Caique lives?*

"Tlaloc knows the way. Maybe he can answer your question."

"Might as well get going," Tlaloc said loudly. He turned and marched toward the square's exit, tugging Myriad's donkey after him. Mark and Titus lurched into motion behind them. Olaf shrugged, then pulled my donkey forward. The expedition had begun.

Instantly, I regretted what we were doing. Judging from the rasping, grinding movement between my legs I was going to wind up with a fine set of hemorrhoids, and maybe an extra anus or two. Donkeys. *Why did we ever bother domesticating the damn things?*

"Nothing to do with you. Stop complaining."

We ran a gauntlet of derelict buildings full of derelict people and came out into a wide vista of dry, desiccated fields lined with shrunken clots of plant good only for burning as fuel. I was stunned. *Where the Thrúudheim is the jungle?*

"Off to the left."

I could see a distant line of greenery, the tops of trees barely poking above the level of the fields. Where our donkeys listlessly trotted in short, mincing steps was a gentle slope rising toward a haze of hills ahead of us. The jungle, the river, all at a lower elevation. Enough to divide the jungle's uncontrollable explosion of greenery from man's plant-graves? *Is nature that keen on sharp boundaries?*

"Of course not. Take a closer look at the fields."

At first, I saw nothing. Dirt. Shriveled plants in long rows. Paths between the rows. No, wait, little gullies between the rows. Shallow irrigation ditches? I noted each new field, upslope from the ones we had already passed, featured ceramic pipes jutting from their lowest edge. This system allowed water to flow downhill to field after field. The perfect gravity-fed, low-maintenance operation. The only thing lacking was water.

"Look closer."

Irritated, I persisted in studying the road for a few moments. Nothing to see, except that the smashed brick no longer applied. Sturdy yellow plastic, thinly veiled in dust, but otherwise displaying a pristine surface. No decay here. No wear or tear. No expansion cracks either. A flat, unyielding layer of extruded armour covering the ground beneath. Not for nothing did people following these roads worldwide call them "shields." Unbreakable, immortal roads. And yet, with footprints and hoofprints visible in the dust, capable of disappearing from sight. Buried perfection. That be their fate.

"The fields, damn it."

With an exasperated sigh, I let my gaze drift aimlessly about. This helped distract me from my aching bum. Had the feeling my anus was going to mutate into a mouth and start screaming in pain. Not something to look forward to. I concentrated harder, trying to see whatever I was supposed to see. Something in plain sight, yet invisible to my attention. I hate puzzles. Always have.

Then I saw it. Reflections and shadows at the opening of the pipes. Not ceramic, but metal/ceramic composite alloys, a sure indication of complex machinery. Each pipe its own pump. I caught glimpses of shutter valves at the exit of every pipe. No doubt there were sensors present in the dirt, maybe one for every plant. Leave it to the techgrid to combine complexity with simplicity. Crafty bastards.

"I'm betting the outlet from the water source was controlled by the techgrid, too."

Ah, no techgrid, no water. Inspiration hit me. Get it released manually. Blow something up! Release a flood. Kill two birds with one bomb. Wipe out surplus population and get agriculture underway again. The Caique will be ever so grateful.

"Don't you think he's thought of that already? To state the obvious is to state the obvious? Remember?"

If he has, then why all this desolation? He hasn't done anything so far.

"Hmm. Just means the situation is more complex than we know. We'll just have to wait and see. Not enough info to make an evaluation."

Tlaloc raised a gleeful shout and pointed toward the jungle line. Our mighty caravan halted, everyone except the donkeys craning to see whatever it was we were supposed to celebrate. Struck me the donkeys looked irritable. Thirsty, maybe. Like me.

A dozen tall figures emerged, evidently having climbed up the slope from the jungle. Unusually tall figures. Mutants? Machines? They appeared unnaturally thin. As they got closer, moving at a stately, dignified walking pace, their bodies began to fill out. Finally, I realized what I was looking at. Women in dirty white gowns bearing ceramic jars on their heads, their right arms extended to clutch the spout at the top of each jar and keep it steady. As they drew nearer still, I began to be impressed.

Look at that! Classic ceramic pottery. Beautiful craftmanship, Intricate designs. They've kept their ancient traditions alive all these centuries. Magnificent!

"Don't be an idiot. Made out of cheap plastic. A lot lighter to lift. Only a nostalgic fool like you would want to carry a ceramic jug. No matter. From the way they're being carried even these plastic monstrosities look heavy. They must be full of water."

And so they proved to be. Lightly silt-laden water, probably taken from some stream flowing down to the river via a gully between the jungle and the fields, but it was good enough for the donkeys, and maybe for us. Tlaloc and Olaf went to the packs hanging on the donkey's flanks and pulled out empty water bags to fill from the jugs, then attached the bags to the donkey's muzzles. Only after the thirsty creatures had drunk their fill did Tlaoc insist our water skins be refilled, sealed, and reattached to the packs. On being denied water my desiccated tongue was about ready to strangle him. *Who put Tlaoc in charge?*

"*Our lack of credibility?*"

Then and only then were we allowed to upend the jars and gulp down what was left, which wasn't much, more wet mud than refreshing water. So much so that it occurred to me we had partaken more of a meal than a drink. With any luck there were digestible bits with nutrients of some kind. Insect parts maybe.

If anything, the women were more annoyed than we were. They hadn't intended to share their water with us, but who can argue with automatic weapons? And now their jugs were empty, their morning trek wasted. With quiet contempt and repressed anger, they formed a line and began walking back to the jungle to fetch more water. Even the swaying of their hips expressed exasperation and rage. No mean feat. Remarkable in fact.

Once again, our caravan lurched into motion to charge at the distant hills at a walking pace. At least the donkeys moved with greater confidence, though as soon as they remembered they were hungry they would probably balk. *What can we feed them?*

"They can munch on Titus. He resembles a bunch of twigs."

Merrily we trotted along. Every now and then we detoured around enigmatic vehicles halted in the road. Useless beasts of non-corrodible metal. Inscrutable sphinxes to be dug up by future archaeologists, if any.

"Machines are just part of the landscape. Like boulders, or dead buildings. Get used to it. You'll never see any techgrid device in motion again."

I hope not. The shock would probably kill me.

The shrivels in the fields had switched species. Narrow bushes about man-high with spindly, close-set branches. Lots of brown leaves shrunken into balls of decay. A less edible plant would be impossible to imagine, unless a dead cactus sprang to mind.

What are these things? Why were they being grown?

"I agree not for food. A trade product. I'm guessing cotton."

I sat bolt upright, startled. Made my bum hurt. *What, cotton? Growing cotton? Out of the ground? Like they did in ancient times?*

"Vat production is expensive. A.I. intensive. Could be cheaper just to pop a seed in the ground and water it occasionally."

But soil worldwide is almost as sterile as us humans. Too much salt. Too many chemicals. And near the craters, too much radiation. How on earth did they get the soil to function again?

"I doubt any person figured it out. Reeks of massed A.I. think tank op. Betcha nanotech is involved... or was."

How long has this been going on?

"I told you. Since the human race stopped being sterile. About twenty years ago."

But everyone I know is sterile. And there's still nothing but weeds around Vancouver. Those damned pine trees, for instance. Soil not good enough for decent crops.

"Progress has been patchy, mostly in out-of-the-way places like this."

And the Caique has been party to this?

"As soon as he realized he could grow cotton. Profitable."

What about his people?

"Probably continued vat production for them. No need to grow food."

But with the techgrid dead the vats have stopped!

"Clever of you to notice. Explains why the locals look so poorly. Pátzcuaro is in a bind. Can't feed his people."

My head began to swim. Too many thoughts. What if we solve his problem? Get the water moving? Everyone will love us.

"Not the Caique. You'll have become more popular than he ever was. He'll kill you. I mean, kill us."

Just what I need. More encouragement. Thank you very much.

"Stop overthinking. You're losing your touch. It never pays to plan ahead. I don't know what the Caique is up to. You don't know what the Caique is up to. Leave it at that. Wait till we find out what's what before deciding what to do."

To make matters worse, Tlaloc dropped back to walk beside Myriad; the two of them chattering away about their future nuptials or some such. Annoying. And Titus still looked, even from behind, as if he imagined he were in progress with massed kettledrums and ostrich feather standards heralding his approach. His unsufferable pride so blatantly obvious it was no wonder Il Duce sent him on a world-girdling diplomatic mission. Probably couldn't stand the presence of an ego bigger than his own.

"I repeat, you think too much. Your biggest fault. Put your imagination to rest, will you?"

More machines dead in the fields. Cotton picking machines, perhaps. Just bird perches now. But the view ahead was interesting. The nearest hill an earthen ridge about a mile long filling the saddle between two rocky cliffs towering a good five hundred feet above the plain below. Climbing the cliff on the right, layers of multi-coloured, single-story buildings, each set back from the building beneath, forming terraces resembling giant steps for colossal beings, culminating at the clifftop in a cluster of towers reaching as high again into the sky.

"Amazing what they used to do with adamantine nanoplastic, isn't it?"

Amazing how the nanopaint colours were still bright. Splashes of green and blue, orange and yellow, like camouflage designed to be noticed. Black window frames. White door frames. Who was the idiot architect? Nothing this weird in Vancouver.

As we got closer more and more details stood out. Several concrete spillways were scattered across the face of the ridge. It had to be a dam. No water flowing now. The irrigation canals fanning out from the base of the dam toward the distant port were completely dry. Still, a stream of sorts dribbled from the top of the dam off to the left. Reservoir overflow? Eroding the earth of the ridge. Cutting into it. Somebody should do something about that. Beneficial none the less. Undoubtedly the source of the water trickling along the gully between the lower fields and the jungle. But for how long?

There was a village below the left cliff face. Looked smarter than Angahuan; clean and relatively freshly painted, everything in repair, with plenty of people milling about. But too distant to make out the condition of the inhabitants. Likewise, the people I could see on the modern cliff towers. The road led toward the centre of the dam. Something peculiar in front of it. Something different.

Came a point where the road ended in a T-shaped junction, splitting off to either side. Before us, level with the road, a stone platform, forming a grid pattern maybe a thousand feet square, each "room" filled with packed rubble. Even more puzzling, gangs of men carried small blocks of stone toward the centre of the platform where new walls appeared to be under construction. Other gangs were moving back and forth between the platform and the left cliff face. Must be a quarry there. *What the Bileyg? Building a second platform atop the first? Whatever for, and why? The whole project looks insane.*

"It's crazy all right. Forbidden. One of the techgrid's sacred mounds. Nobody but nobody allowed to touch them. Instant death from above, courtesy the orbiting rod weapons. The Caique must be bonkers."

Well, not just him. Must have taken a long time to clear the mound. Months. The techgrid must have known what Pátzcuaro was up to. Why didn't it put a stop to it?

"Symptomatic decay before the final collapse? Or maybe it was bribed?"

How do you the bribe the world-wide A.I. collective?

"I don't know. Teach it how to tell jokes?"

Maybe. You're evidence it doesn't know how.

Tlaloc guided Myriad's donkey to turn right toward the cliff towers. Wouldn't be long before we reached them. But first, we came up to a dozen men clustered around a stone table examining sheets of paper-like material. I took for granted they were architect's drawings, no doubt the plans for the second layer of platform. All the men looked physically fit and well fed, their brown limbs plump and shining where exposed by the short-sleeved tunics they wore. Except one fellow, covered from head to foot in a heavy robe, his head buried under its cowl. *Obviously the bossman? The guy in charge?*

"Hope so. We need to start asking questions."

The robed man turned to face us as we approached. He drew back his hood to expose his head. He had the face of a satyr, strong jawed with a wide, lecherous smile. He reeked of lust. Heck of a first impression.

"Welcome to Tzintzuntzan," he said. Then, surprisingly, he raised his right arm in a fascist salute. "Hail Titus."

Titus raised his arm in reply. "Hail Beedlewood."

To her credit Myriad jumped with remarkable alacrity from the back of her beast and ran to my side, adopting a fighter's stance, her eyes glancing in all directions. She was ready to kill. Me, I sat still, my mouth gaping wide in shock.

Beedlewood dropped his arm and gazed at me with quiet amusement. His eyes glinted steel. Nothing funny about them. "Hail Rudwulf," he said. "At last, we meet."

"You bloody tried to murder me!" Damn. Why did my mouth act so independently at the worst possible moments? And how did my enemy recognise me?

"Not yet I haven't," Beedlewood replied. "What makes you think so?"

"I was on my way to meet Pharaoh Hermann Horemheb. Missile took us down."

"That so?" Beedlewood seemed to lose interest, started glancing at his building diagrams again. "Titus would know more about that than I do. Ask him. After all, I'm not the only one who wants you dead, or haven't you noticed?"

One thing I did notice was that Mark had taken up position beside Beedlewood. *I don't like that at all.*

"Never mind that. I don't like the fact Beedlewood and Titus know each other."

Beedlewood ordered his underlings to roll up the plans. "A Druid's work is never done," he said, "but I suppose I should take you to see the Caique."

"What exactly is it you are doing?"

"Building a pyramid to honour the Caique's dead parents."

"On a techgrid platform? One you're not even allowed to dig up in the first place?"

"Best foundation available. Besides, we got permission." The shoulders under the heavy robe appeared to twitch a trifle. Possibly he had shrugged. "Let's have a truce, shall we? The Caique calls the shots hereabouts. Can't kill anyone unless he says so."

"Fine," I replied with as much aggressive dignity as I could muster. "Lead the way to your doom."

Seneferu's sense of timing undercut my words. "But first, get me off these damn animals!" he shouted.

Beedlewood chuckled. "Rudwulf, even your prisoner isn't afraid of you, so why should I be?"

"Depends on the Caique."

Beedlewood frowned.

CHAPTER SEVEN

Exasperated, I stared past Titus, who sat upright on his donkey as stiff as a statue, at Beedlewood struggling to remain atop his stone table. His sweating underlings were having a hard time carrying it up the switchback path leading to the top of the dam. He sat cross legged, swaying with every lurch, hunched forward, clutching his precious building diagrams. Couldn't be a stone table. Nobody could possibly handle the weight. Must be ersatz. More techgrid magic.

Close to our right a funicular ran up the slope between the dam and the cliff dwellings. Looked typical, exhibiting a close resemblance to the dozen or so affixed to Grouse Mountain back in Vancouver. Like them, it consisted of a series of open pods that would normally flow up and down in the river of nanotech. Trouble was, just like the escape pod from the airplane, the rims of the pods partially engulfed the passengers to ensure their safety as they rode. In this case, when the techgrid went down, the pods froze in place, still gripping their human cargo, who had been unable to free themselves. A fine selection of dried corpses was on display, well picked over by birds and other vermin. Grinning skulls almost an architectural adornment.

"The Aztecs would approve. They like that sort of thing."

Lucky our escape pod activated before the grid went down.

"That's us. Always lucky."

I glanced back at Myriad. She had insisted on her donkey taking up last position. The better to watch my rear. Or, at least, to spot any threat approaching me from any direction. Tlaloc persisted in walking beside her, but didn't seem entirely happy. Possibly because she refused to pay attention and was concentrating on protecting me. Reassuring. Almost made me feel safe.

Mark and Olaf had the worst of it. Once Seneferu was free of his donkeys, he had claimed he was too weak to walk. They carried him perched on their linked arms, sidling uphill like a giant crab, glaring at each other in shared frustration. His constant shifting about in an effort to get comfier only worsened their mood.

A torrent of swearing drew my attention back to Beedlewood. He had twisted around and was shaking the roll in his right hand at something on the plain below. Wrought up he was. His mouth issuing a torrent of Mayan, or possibly Tarascan swear words. At least, they sounded like swear words.

It took me a few moments to figure out what set him off. The workers in the excavation had stopped working. So, too, the workers carrying the stone blocks toward the building site. Everyone had dropped everything and were casually walking toward the town, their numbers converging the closer they approached. I could make out a wide path leading to the town square. Evidently a bit of a slope. The town was laid out along a shallow ridge. Possibly an extension of the hill that had eroded back into the cliff face. At any rate, it was home to these people, and obviously they couldn't be bothered to carry on when the boss was away. Amusing.

"Beedlewood may not have as much authority as he thinks he has."

What is he doing so far north anyway? The Mayans live way south of here.
"It will be fun to inquire."
The face of the dam struck me as improbable. The compacted earth, as hard as concrete, lay in a surprisingly gentle slope against whatever volume of water it was holding back. A pile of dirt a mile long, five hundred feet high, and who knows how thick, sufficient to contain gazillions of tons of water with no risk of seepage or collapse. I noted clumps and clusters of low cacti scattered across the surface of the slope. *Surely, their roots aren't enough to hold everything in place.*
"The concrete spillways must be anchored to something. The core of the dam is probably an eroded section of the cliff. Could be the earth is just a thin covering."
You don't know? You're just guessing?
"I could show you the original plans and quote you chapter and verse on basic engineering of dams, if I still had access to the techgrid, but I don't."
Yeah, yeah, I know. What do I keep you around for?
"Someone to talk to."
As if you ever listen.
Finally, we reached the top of the dam. It was surprisingly narrow, only fifty feet across.
I slipped off my poor donkey (for which my pain-ridden anus thanked me) and stood, entranced, at the far edge looking over a quiet lake of water which stretched to the horizon, though hemmed in by hills on either side. About two miles in the distance a perfectly circular island rose hundreds of feet above the placid surface of the lake, nothing less than a giant cinder cone, its slopes festooned with volcanic boulders. Fortunately, no smoke was visible

drifting from its broken summit. The last thing I wanted to do was outrun a volcanic eruption.

"The amount of water staggers me. Worries me."

I tried to make out the situation at the other end of the dam. The level of the lake was still a good two feet lower than its lip. The water flowing down to feed the stream in the gully leading to the river wasn't coming over the top of the dam. It was seeping through the earth underneath.

"The perfect spot to blow up. If we go that route."

"Come on, come on. Follow me," Beedlewood said as he rolled off his table. He dropped the scrolls to the ground. Let his assistants pick them up. He was taking us to the Caique.

We strolled after Beedlewood. I couldn't help but glance up the height of the gaudy tower before us. Gods forbid the Caique was ensconced at the top. Another five hundred feet of height was asking for trouble.

Luckily, we found the Caique at dam level, seated atop a double-headed jaguar throne set in a room with a bright orange floor, a rare indoor Gogetter, albeit dormant like all the others. Unusual to see one so tiny. Opposite him an open arch led to a balcony jutting over the edge of the lake. A cool breeze came across the water.

He was a gnome of a man, tiny, with a calm face and smiling eyes. He wore some sort of gown woven from shimmering feathers. Seemed to me he dared not move for fear of ripping it apart. He appeared a pleasant chap, a kindly father figure, but he was flanked by two human heads freshly wet and dripping. Subtle in the art of diplomacy, to be sure.

Beedlewood dropped to his knees, bowing forward, his right arm outstretched, left arm held against his chest, eyes downcast. An act of formal obeisance, but no one imitated him. Me, I just gave a slight bow.

The Caique's eyes met mine. "I recognise you, Rudwulf. Welcome. I have need of your talent."

Titus brushed past me and flung out a Fascist salute. "Hail, King of Tzintzuntzan! I salute you in the name of the World Emperor."

The Caique grinned. "I salute you in the name of the God-Emperor."

Titus faltered. "The God… who would that be?"

"Why… me, of course," The Caique replied. "Who else?"

Titus cast a furtive glance at us, then turned back to the Caique and spoke in whispers. "I have much to convey from Il Duce. Can we not speak in private? Or at least in Italian, which these scums do not understand, being uncivilized?"

The Caique's smile grew broad and grim. "Naturally I'd love to. But you know how it is. I do you greater honour in addressing you in English, the sacred language of the blessed, mighty Gibbon who left us his immortal "Decline and Fall of the Roman Empire." Mussolini sleeps with it under his pillow does he not? All six pages? His forever inspiration?"

"But the beauty of Italian, the mother tongue of civilization itself."

"Latin, you mean. Against the glorious language the blessed, mighty Turing built into the AI? English, the language of the techgrid? English, which all Mates speak?"

For once, Titus wasn't backing down. "English is the past. Italian is the wave of the future."

Seneferu stepped forward, pushing Titus aside. "Enough of this nonsense. Titus and Musso are secretly your enemies. Whereas I am openly your friend."

"I'm so glad to hear you say that," the Caique stated quietly, with an obsidian edge to his voice. "I am in great need of friends, and you are?"

"Wolfgang Seneferu, heir to the throne of Egypt." Wolfgang patted his non-existent belly for emphasis, petting thin air, as if inviting the Caique to get off his throne and come forward to embrace him. The Caique declined the honour.

"Truly, I am blessed that such eloquent orators have come to lecture me." The Caique pointed at Mark. "Take these two mighty plenipotentiaries to separate guest chambers and make them comfortable," he instructed. As Titus started to protest, the Caique added, "So that we can speak in private as is needful, and I can do them greater honour." Titus looked pleased as he was led away. Seneferu, somewhat annoyed.

I decided to be bold. "Titus isn't completely wrong," I stated. "Now that the Mates can only thinktalk with their humans and no other, the universal language is no longer universal. Local languages will prevail."

Caique Pátzcuaro stared into my eyes, His pupils were made of flint. "You are living up to your reputation? A man who knows how to drive the blade home? Gets to the point? Good. I have need of you. I'm tired of blustering fools."

Beedlewood took this last comment personally. "Rudwulf is also your enemy. Don't listen to him. Obey the gods. That is your salvation."

Pátzcuaro ignored Beedlewood. "What should I do, Rudwulf? The bulk of my tower is closed to me. Storerooms are sealed. Vat rooms sealed. All interior rooms and corridors dark and silent. Only the chambers open to the outside air are liveable. My wealth, my weapons, the food I controlled, all forbidden to me. Since the techgrid shut down I have nothing."

"Move to the village," I suggested. "Live among your people—in the grandest building available, of course."

"Dare I? People are starving." The Caique put his hands atop the severed heads on either side of him. Caressed their hair. "You see my need to enforce discipline. Used to be my word was enough."

"Stop killing," Beedlewood insisted. "No need to waste lives. Your entourage is faithful."

"Where water descends, blow up that portion of the dam," I said. "Get the water flowing again. The crops growing again. Feed your people. Then you'll have the luxury of killing your enemies without interference."

"Who are they? Do you know their names?"

"Anyone you want. As many as you need."

"Spoken like the Smiter," the Caique muttered. He slid off his throne to stand up. He was less than five feet high, but sturdy, powerful. A wrestler by nature. A short version of Olaf. Not someone to underestimate. "Come with me."

He strode rapidly out of the building onto the surface of the dam. Beedlewood and I followed. Tlaloc and Myriad, who had been whispering in a corner, were caught off guard but quickly joined us. Olaf trundled along as if bemused. I didn't get the sense he was there to protect Pátzcuaro. Seemed more like he expected the Caique to protect him.

"A clue to the power of the man. Charismatic. People worship him."

Not Beedlewood.

While we were conferring inside the palace low benches and tables had been set up facing the valley. Plates bore floppy crusts folded over meat and plant matter. Ceramic goblets contained clean water, better than what our now depleted water skins carried. Evidently some storerooms were still open. But how long before their contents were used up?

"I don't have access to explosives anymore," the Caique explained, "but I've had my people dig out enough dirt to open a narrow conduit. For some days now they've been expanding the channel to either side, all the while installing pilings to hold back the lake. I give the word and the pilings are pulled away. Possibly part of the dam will collapse and unleash a flood. Should I? People may die."

"Don't pussyfoot around," Beedlewood declared. "Build. Don't destroy. Build." Oddly, he was turning red, like a boiler about to burst. Under a great deal of pressure. Fear, maybe?

"I think he's afraid he's losing his grip on the Caique."

"Deaths will be a bonus," I said, ignoring Beedlewood. "Reduce the population to a manageable level capable of being fed once the food crops are in. And while maintaining that level, reintroduce cotton. Rebuild the wealth of your nation." *With any luck my common sense will appeal and the Caique seek my services. Or, at least, not kill us.*

"That be our top priority."

Pátzcuaro pointed at the construction sight below. "I've been staring at that thing for days. Took months to dig it out. Now wasting time building a second step. What do I need a stepped pyramid for? The peons would have been better off directing water to the fields, planting seeds."

"It unites them," Beedlewood insisted. "It combines their service with their love for you. Besides, it will honour your parents, justify your dynastic credentials to all."

The Caique sighed. "My parents are dead. I could have had their names painted in giant letters on one of the spillways and left it at that."

"Then honour the Gods. It's been centuries since the last temple-pyramid was constructed. They'll be pleased. Excited. They'll shower you with rewards."

"So you've said. Many times. But which Gods? Yesterday I learned from one of your assistants that you intend to erect a circle of menhirs instead of a temple atop the pyramid. He showed me your plans. How many times have I told you to leave your Druid crap out of my religion? I don't want to confuse my followers."

Beedlewood stiffened, drawing himself to attention as if he were a General of Generals. "I am the Prophet of the Quetzalcoatl Mayan Reform Druid movement. I cannot betray *my* followers."

"The ones who drove you out of Chichen Itza for filling in the Sacred Cenote? You came to my court alone, as I recall."

"*You* chose to emulate the ancient Maya. The Gods called me here to aid you."

"I shall be grateful to them for all eternity, but in the meantime…" The Caique pondered the excavation, lost in thought. He frowned. "It occurred to me the other day there's a limit as to how many levels you can build my pyramid. How tall will it be?"

Beedlewood shrugged. "My Mate can't do the math. Neither can I. All we can do is keep piling up the platforms, making them progressively smaller in area until there's just enough room for Menhirs… er, a temple. Three hundred feet high, maybe. A little less."

The Caique's eyes narrowed, as did his lips. I had the impression he was repressing rage. "So, you're telling me my magnificent sacred mountain, a majestic monument designed to impress the ages, won't even come up to the height where we are now? That anybody and his donkey up here can gaze *down* at my legacy forevermore?"

"It's the intent which counts."

"Why in the name of Yum Caax didn't you start building atop the cliff on the far side of the dam? Solid rock and already elevated above the plain? My monument could have rivalled my technologic Palace. Twin towers of my power, my fame, my glory. Meanwhile, that would have left me free to break open the platform beneath the mound like I originally intended. Yet you chose to convince me merely to scuffle away the dirt only to bury the result under new construction? How did I let you talk me into this?"

"But the platform! Solid construction. Once free of the mound the perfect base, the perfect first step for the pyramid. By far the largest level, already complete, already built. A gift of the Gods."

The Caique rubbed his right hand against his bald pate, producing oddly rubbery furrows in the skin. Disconcerting. "I knew the mound was sacred, but how did *you* know what it was? In appearance it was just a pile of compacted earth, the well-trodden excrement of the Gods perhaps, and nothing more."

A wistful expression flitted across Beedlewood's face, his eyes half-closed, as if pursuing a fading memory. "It came to me in a dream... a wonderful dream."

"I have dreams... sometimes."

You do? I thought you go dormant when I sleep, slip into a coma, whatever.

"I don't sleep the way you do. I'm always aware, always thinking even if I'm no longer observing."

People who never sleep go insane.

"I'm not people. I'm—Jesus Fucking Christ!"

Before I could ask if Buddy-bod was sure about his self-identity I noted the savage geyser of fire and steam thrusting a solid column straight up from the volcano in the lake. Quick as a flash the Caique was off and running into the palace.

"Oof!" I said as Myriad swept me up and threw me over her left shoulder before pounding after the Caique. My arms dangling, my head jouncing about, I caught glimpses of Beedlewood's knees pressing rhythmically against the front of his robe, Olaf's legs hammering like pistons, and Tlaloc's feet sweeping across the pavement in long slides. All of us running for our lives. Except for me. I was more of a passenger, but as fearful as all the rest.

I had the impression we were charging up an inclined ramp. We reached a landing, then reversed direction, still climbing. The floor appeared to level off. I was beginning to feel sick. We turned left and Myriad dumped me. The better to flee? No, we had arrived.

I struggled upright to a sitting position. We were on a belvedere on the near side of the tower looking down over the length of the dam, which was about fifty feet below us. The initial blast from the cone had subsided, countless boulders and blocks of stone still raining down on its slopes and the surrounding water. The lake had roiled into action. Wave after wave lapped over the top of the dam and slid down the slope. Had we not followed the Caique's lead we would have been swept over the dam too.

Beedlewood pointed at a jet of water jutting out of the dam where the trickle-stream used to be. Evidently the pilings had been swept away, possibly by the shock of the first wave driven by the volcanic convulsion. The water pushed out a good twenty feet before arching down to the slope of the dam below. The whole weight of the lake was behind it.

"Behold, the punishment of the Gods," he shouted. "You should have listened to me. To me!"

I scrambled to my feet. My livelihood was at stake. "The Gods reward you, Pátzcuaro. They've followed my instructions. Your surplus peasants are gone. Soon the worthy survivors will eat from plenty."

"Like Mictlan they will, they'll eat mud," Beedlewood proclaimed. "This is the folly of your error. I alone can bring paradise. You should listen to me."

"No!" I protested. "I alone reveal the divine, with my knowledge, my experience—"

"With your bullshit," the Caique intoned with the intensity of a kettledrum rumbling low but preparing to reach a crescendo. "Both of you shut up, or I'll have your tongues nailed to Titus's forehead, or maybe to his foreskin. I'm a bit pissed right now. I demand quiet."

Beedlewood and I fell silent. There is a time for ballyhoo, and as often as not a time to lie low. It was clear which moment this was.

Myriad leaned against me and whispered in my ear. "I just saved your life. The least you can do is ensure I didn't do it in vain."

"Ahh, uhm… thank you."

"You're welcome… again. Fourth time since you hired me. I keep count, you know." She stepped back to join Tlaloc. They stood holding hands as they gazed at the water pooling at the base of the dam. *How did Tlaloc move into her heart so fast? Isn't he a virgin like most other men? Where and when did he gain the conniving, sneaking experience of a seducer? And why him? Why can't I be the stud?*

"Stop dreaming. You're both mules. She likes hairy men, I think. You're not hirsute enough. Simple as that. He's more decorative."

The water was beginning to pool around the excavation. Soon it would overflow the platform, put it at the bottom of a shallow lake. *Maybe men with buckets could drain it into irrigation ditches?*

"Why bother? Look at the water pouring from the break. It's following the existing irrigation channels between the platform and the village. Take credit for that, why don't you?"

Hmm, might as well. Eruption over. The waves in the lake are settling down. They're not even overtopping the damn anymore, so no flood.

"Mighty Caique," I whispered, pretending to be humble. "The Gods concentrate on providing you with bounty. Just as I predicted."

The Caique shot me a dirty look. He opened his mouth to speak, as did Beedlewood, but both were caught short. The ground trembled. Not the tower, it stood firm, but we could see the dam shudder.

With an angry roar louder than mere screams, multiple bolts of water shot from the top of the spillways a hundred feet or more before crashing down in a foaming mess which tore at the earth at the foot of the dam. Great boiling bubbles of mud and debris swept across the plain toward the distant river. The land was converting into an angry ocean. It seemed my prophecy of mass deaths was coming true. *Good. A guaranteed paycheque.*

"Don't be so sure. The village has been spared."

It was true. The torrent raged and roiled up the slope of the shallow ridge but seemed incapable of reaching any of the structures atop it. I'd have to pin my hopes on the citizens of Angahuan.

"They probably saw the blast and took refuge in the ruins along the river. Could be much of the water is rushing into the jungle anyway. Maybe not much of a threat at the port itself. Could be nobody's been killed."

Hard to say. The sluice gate outpours were colossal in size, each over a dozen feet in diameter. At least thirty such fountaining columns. The level of the lake was visibly lowering. *Surely Odin wouldn't have arranged so massive a display of his power unless it was good for something?*

"Unless it was Loki who gave him the idea."

"Mayans," the Caique muttered. "I had to go with Mayans. Should have stuck with Tarascan culture. All of it forgotten. I could have made it up to suit myself. None of this Mayan Druid crap. Or Smiter crap."

Mark appeared from the corridor. "Majesty, you'll be glad to know Titus and Seneferu are unharmed."

The Caique raised his eyes to the gods. And his fists. "Will wonders never cease? Praise be."

He turned to face Beedlewood and me. "Once the flow lessens, we'll all go on a tour of the consequences of your advice. Then I'll decide which of you to sacrifice. This I swear."

CHAPTER EIGHT

Finally, we were allowed to leave the confines of the palace. I craned my neck and gazed up at the clouds. The brightest spot in the perpetual overcast was directly overhead. Had to be noon. *The Caique left at first light. What had he been up to?*

"Lot of activity down below. He's been busy."

I turned to look out over the plain. It had been transformed. Yesterday's flood had carved the earth away from around the platform which now rose well above the surrounding terrain. The mud left exposed beyond the structure was darker, seemingly richer, than the original surface. Maybe because it was still wet?

But it was the corner of the platform closest to the dam that drew my eye. It had been torn away by the deluge, the platform rounded off. Whatever debris remained was hidden from view by newly erected tents made from blankets, tunics, and sundry other cloth material probably brought from the town. Each tent was surrounded by a ring of men standing or sitting doing nothing. Certainly not moving. Sentries? Other groups of men were scattered across the face of the platform, apparently digging into the rubble packed between the cross-grid of internal walls. Additional sentries appeared to be guarding the diggers.

"Is that capricious bastard tearing down my platform?" I heard Beedlewood mutter. He was standing off to my right, a puzzled frown disfiguring his face. For once he didn't look lecherous. "I'll kill him."

"Big words from a man facing the executioner's axe."

Speaking of which... I don't know what Pátzcuaro is up to, but whatever it is, I'm going to praise him for it.

"Wise policy."

"Get going, all of you!" Mark ordered us, waving his rifle in our general direction. "The Caique commands."

Titus bent forward, the better to see the switchback trail leading to the base of the dam. "No donkeys? We have to walk?"

"That's right," Mark replied. "No donkeys. No palanquins. No atomic-powered buzz cars. Just your damn feet. Remember how to use them?"

I started forward. The coarse compacted earth composing the path was dry and firm underfoot. The slope was pleasant. No danger there. Looking over my shoulder I noted Myriad and Tlaloc were close behind and holding hands as usual, then Titus feeling his way with tentative steps as if he was afraid of triggering a landslide, Beedlewood and Mark following side by side, both looking grumpy as Hrungnir, and finally a rather quiet and complacent Olaf strolling along as rear guard. Quite the expedition. Only Seneferu was missing. Probably still asleep after a foul night plotting.

"*Did you hear anything?*"

What, just now?

"No, when the volcano erupted. It must have been noisy, but I don't remember hearing anything."

Me neither. I was too busy praying Myriad wasn't going to drop me.

"Odd trick of the mind, I suppose. Jumbled priority of senses in an emergency? Peculiar it happened to both of us."

Not really. We share the same brain, after all.

I studied the face of the dam as we descended. The artificial gap dug at the Caique's instigation had dried up.

Understandable, as the lake level had dropped at least thirty feet below its intake. But why had the spillway sluices gone silent? Most of them were lower than the current surface of the lake. The outpouring of water should still be as dramatic as what we had witnessed late yesterday. *Have the sluices closed?*

"Not all of them. I can see a sheen of water sliding down the far spillways beyond the platform. Must be feeding the ditches leading to the jungle. A good, steady supply of water for whatever fields exist once the mud dries. The Caique must be pleased. Tell him to congratulate you for a job well done."

Yes, of course, but… by Freki's balls, is the AI running the dam still sentient? It all seems so… convenient.

"There's a word for that."

Conspiracy?

"No. People always assume intelligence is behind whatever random phenomena they ponder. Morons automatically detect a pattern where there is none. I forget what that's called."

So, no logical explanation for the dam's behaviour?

"One could say the same for the volcano, but no doubt there's a perfectly logical explanation behind the moment it chose to erupt. Likewise, behind the opening and closing of the sluice gates. We just don't happen to know the explanation."

That's comforting.

"At a guess I'd say automatic sensors in the dam were and still are capable of reacting to changing water pressure on the dam. Simple as that."

Funny thing. I find that a bullet creasing my hair as it passes between my ear and my skull is a sensation that I've never been able to get used to. Likewise, the sound of a gun going off at only a few paces' distance. It makes my heart leap into my mouth and my body drop flat to the ground in an instant. I rolled three times in quick succession and scrambled to my feet, determined to figure out which way I should run.

No need. Mark was pressed into the dirt, the full weight of Olaf reminding him what gravity was all about, and his weapon gone, flung to one side. Olaf appeared to be attempting to jam his automatic's barrel into Mark's neck. Beedlewood was standing alongside, arms folded, looking down at them both with an expression of annoyance and disappointment.

I saw Tlaloc rumble to a stop behind Beedlewood, arms stretched wide, prepared to grab the man, perhaps to tear him apart. Myriad raced by the discarded gun, swooping to pick it up and sling it as she took up a wary position beside Beedlewood. I swear the poor fellow was beginning to look alarmed. Fortunately for him, on seeing the look in Myriad's eyes, Tlaloc lowered his arms.

Pensively, I walked forward, then lay down and stretched out facing Mark, my head resting on my hands, as I contemplated the blood pooling in his face, courtesy of Olaf's heavy, determined presence on his back.

"Why did you try to kill me?" I asked. A reasonable query under the circumstances.

"Beedlewood," he said simply without a hint of apology. "I follow Beedlewood. I obey Beedlewood."

"What a surprise."

I closed my eyes. I needed a moment to myself. Then I got up, dusted myself off, and faced Beedlewood. "Why did you order him to kill me? Even Wolfgang Seneferu warned me about you. Everybody on earth knows you want me dead. Why? Are you insane?"

"None saner. I've been preaching against you for years. Ever since I learned I was the promised prophet."

"Why?" I was starting to get annoyed.

"Because you're a Smiter!" he responded, his words exploding from him with unleashed passion. "The last Smiter! You've killed millions! You're a monster! You walk the Earth like death incarnate. I hate you!"

Sigh. Why can't people be practical?

"Should we tell him the truth?"

Of course not. That would complicate matters. Besides, he wouldn't believe us.

I shrugged. "It's a living. I get paid well."

"Do you even care? Not an ounce of compassion for your victims?"

"Emperors don't care. Same with kings, dictators, presidents for life and even presidents for death. It's all a game. A political game. You know that. You've been serving such long enough."

For a moment, I thought Beedlewood was going to drop dead of apoplexy, which would have been very convenient. Unfortunately, he began to calm down, funneling his energy into speaking rapidly, saying, "You don't care about people, especially the masses. They're just ciphers to you, and you don't want to break the code, don't want to get to know them. Have you talked to any of the king's servants? Tried to see their point of view? No, not you."

"Exactly. Why waste my time? They're utterly predictable, trying to survive like everyone else. Like me, for instance."

"Then why don't you leave them alone?"

Out of the corner of my eye I could see Olaf getting up and hauling Mark to his feet. Probably under the impression he had him under his control. We'll see.

"Beedlewood, face reality," I said. "You know the screed. Human compassion begat global warming, rising oceans, and nuclear war, which begat poverty, infertility, and disease, which begat death. The techgrid did its bit, refusing to treat STDs, and relying on each new generation to be more sterile than the last—"

"Why are you lecturing me? You think I don't know that?"

"The question is, why are *you* lecturing *me*?"

"You want salvation? The Gods are saving us. That's why they killed the techgrid! To force us to rely on our own resources."

"What resources?"

Beedlewood raised both arms as if offering a benediction to the devastation below. "Look at the mud! Look at the mud!"

I looked. Nothing particularly holy or divine that I could see. An ocean of drying mud. Soon to be dust the wind would blow in people's faces to humble them.

"There's green stuff. Spots of green."

Mold? Fungus? Slime?

"Plants. Seeds are sprouting. The soil isn't dead. It supports life. Doesn't even require cultivation."

"Okay, a local phenomenon, I grant you that. The Caique must have good Lucks, a horde of them."

Beedlewood dropped his arms as if they were made of lead. "If you visit the town, I bet you'll find babies. Lots of babies. Even though the parents may be malnourished and overworked, families are happening. It's happening everywhere. It's not just the soil that is springing back to life. Humanity is too."

"That's nice," I said, "but if true, it's bad good-news. The Norns are lynching the King's Lucks. The size of the population will be worse than ever. Order will collapse. People will be eating each other, eating their babies. Best to cull the herd now, before civilization disappears. If what you say is true, I'm needed more than ever."

Beedlewood began to dance about in frustration. If he wasn't careful, he was going to trip on the hem of his robe. Watching him fall flat on his face would be a great pleasure. "The Gods are renewing the entire world," he proclaimed. "They bring life itself. They exhort us to build, to reproduce, to create! We, the enlightened, are the new beginning. Rudwulf, you are nothing but a punctuation point at the end of a last sentence. I am the beginning of an epic."

"Really? Then why do *you* sacrifice people? I hear you tear their hearts out before burning their bodies in giant wicker contraptions. What's so optimistic about that? Not as useful as the Azteca, but still…"

"Will you morons shut up? Shut up! Shut up!" This from Mark. Olaf put his arm around his shoulders as if in sympathy, though hopefully part of his control technique. Myriad looked on quizzically. "The Caique awaits. If you keep him waiting, he's liable to kill us all."

"Fine. Let's go. But first, one thing I want to know. Why kill me now?"

"I don't put people in wicker baskets," Beedlewood retorted. "I don't carve hearts out. I'm the Prophet of the Quetzalcoatl Mayan *Reform* Druids. I put an *end* to human sacrifice."

"With the singular exception of Rudwulf the Smiter? I repeat, why?"

Beedlewood appeared totally calm now, resigned, like a man who had given up. "You heard Pátzcuaro. He intends to kill one of us. Given the failure of my pyramid scheme, I'm assuming it will be me. It's all your fault. I wanted revenge in advance of my own destruction."

"So, you're petty enough to be human after all. Let's see what the Caique thinks of that." I turned and strode as manfully as I could along the switchback path leading to whatever the Gugnir the Caique was doing at the platform.

Best to appear confident. *Sometimes omnipotent rulers are reluctant to kill men unprepared to die.*

"Again, with idiotic theory. You cling to that."

I passed Titus. He hadn't moved since he collapsed in a heap at the sound of the gunshot, his head buried in his hands where he kneeled, his buttocks stuck high in the air. If I had had a machete, I could have sliced off his ass with a single blow.

"Get up, Titus! The Caique has need of your blessed, mighty dignity."

He got up all right. Much to my annoyance he chose to keep pace with me. Worse, he insisted on talking.

"Beedlewood is partly right, you know," Titus babbled. "The Caique knows it too. He came to me last night to discuss Musso's teachings. The need for a new order. Stress on family life. Building roads, and bridges, lots of bridges. The beauty of concrete. The glory of Fascism—" And so on. *Very boring. Very stupid.*

"I believe I know more about fascism than Mussolini does. Spent an hour researching it once. Seems to have been something of a failure. The techgrid archives, incomplete though they be, indicated the original Mussolini came to a bad end somehow."

Probably the current Duce will too.

"Maybe. But ordinary people are tired of waiting to die. There may be something to the concept of living in hope as opposed to living in fear."

I looked back. Beedlewood was about ten feet behind me, followed by Myriad, Olaf, and Tlaloc in close attendance on Mark. I was relieved to note Myriad retained Mark's weapon. It seemed I had no reason to be worried. For a few minutes, at any rate. I always did prefer to live in the moment.

Looking ahead, I could see the Caique sitting cross-legged on the very table Beedlewood had ridden on yesterday. Only he was more sensible. The table was piled high with red cushions probably stuffed with cotton. The royal bum was comfy. And he was in a comfy mood, grinning widely as he toyed with light-coloured rocks and shiny bits of obsidian. More were visible gathered on coarse blankets spread on the surface of the drying mud around him.

"Eccentric, isn't he?"

He likes to collect shiny stuff, I guess. I have the same attitude towards bank accounts.

"Worth nothing. At least what he's got actually exists."

The Caique momentarily suppressed his grin. "What was the shooting about? I don't like bullets wasted. Not many left."

The others had caught up with me. "I was supposed to kill him," Mark said. I noted Olaf had let go of him. That's the problem with old friends.

"Kill who?"

"The Smiter. Because he murders people. For money."

The Caique studied both Mark and Beedlewood, the latter gazing up at the clouds as if pretending not to be present.

"So do you."

Mark looked indignant. "I only execute people who need to be removed."

"Exactly," I interjected. "Just like me. Only I'm more professional."

"Seems Mark isn't. You're still alive, Rudwulf. How many Lucks do you think you have?"

"Enough," I replied, hoping I sounded smug and confident.

Again, Pátzcuaro grinned. Unexpectedly he uttered a short, barking laugh. He still looked like a gnome, but now he resembled an insane gnome, or at least one giddy with madness. The only sign of sanity was the sensible clothing he had chosen for today. Lots of feathers again, but this time dangling from a linen tunic as opposed to being interwoven with each other. The royal equivalent of worker's coveralls, perhaps. Meant he was in the mood to be practical.

"Forget your evil faults, all of you. I forgive you," the Caique stated. "I'm too happy to be upset with anyone."

Beedlewood visually relaxed. Probably I did too.

"Look at the sacred platform, at what the flood revealed. Can you divine why I am so pleased?"

All I could see were workers scurrying out from underneath the tents bearing armfuls of rocks and shards of obsidian which they dumped on the blankets scattered before the Caique. Occasionally, an individual offered him some choice rocks which sent him into transports of delight. Is it possible to dance while sitting cross-legged? The Caique was doing it.

I don't get it.

"Look closer. Those things are shaped. They're tools!"

"Beedlewood, Rudwulf, my friends," the Caique said, speaking as if he meant it. "You've served me well. First, by insisting on excavating the platform, and second, by insisting I unleash a flood. If it weren't for you two, I would never have discovered this magnificent storehouse, this beautiful treasure hoard."

Beedlewood and I exchanged puzzled, relieved glances. The Gods were looking after us. Seems Beedlewood had his share of Lucks too. Perhaps all of us.

"Every chamber is full of goods. Not a cheap construction site after all. Not a grid of walls with rubble filling to create a sturdy foundation, but a vast array of rooms filled with needful things tamped down with rubble to seal them; the whole structure buried and marked as a sacred site to be left alone."

"But why?" It was all I could think to ask.

Pátzcuaro clutched his chest, his grin even wider than before. "For me! To give me everything I need to rule this land and make my people happy. I don't need the techgrid. I've got everything I need right here, and it doesn't even require atomic power to run it. Flint axes, adzes, chisels, scrapers, picks, razors, arrowheads, spearheads, you name it. And there are things made from other types of stone. Spindle whorls. Awls. Plumb bobs. Querns. Mortars & pestles. Hand-mills. Lamps. Bowls. Pottery wheels. Loom weights. And rooms full of obsidian blades, sharper than a snake's fangs, that cut crisp and clean. Lots of sturdy pottery too. Screw techgrid. Don't need it."

"Almost as if the techgrid knew it was going to collapse some day and wanted to give humanity a fighting chance to carry on. Maybe the Reality-Revisionists knew what they were talking about."

"Majesty, this is stone age civilization you seek," I mused. "What good is it?"

"Are you joking? Properly organized, people flourish. You can have art, sculpture, music, poetry, dance, theatre, writing, bookkeeping, architecture, all kinds of things the people will praise me for. No more dependence on machines. The people will make everything. That will make them proud."

"And make the King of Tzintzuntzan popular and immortal," Seneferu commented as he wobbled from the closest tent. We froze. This was unexpected, and unwelcome.

"Leave it to the demented eunuch to get in good with the Caique while the rest of us slept."

Seneferu struggled to the end of the table, placed both hands on it as if to avoid knocking it over with his alleged bulk, and leaned forward to address the Caique intimately yet loudly. Pátzcuaro smiled so broadly he resembled a snake about to unhinge its lower jaw.

"I'm informed diggers found rooms full of slate sheets with writing etched into them," Seneferu said. "Instructions on how to knock flint into tools. Even better, carpentry instructions. How to build undershot and overshot water wheels for milling grains, for example. Catapults. Nifty things."

I couldn't resist a snide remark. "Isn't that a slippery slope leading to machines?"

The Caique snickered in disagreement. "As long as people understand how to craft them and how they work, no problem. Keeps us human. I think I have the makings of a new religion here."

A thoughtful look came into Beedlewood's eyes. "Hmmm. Interesting."

The Caique suddenly looked thoughtful too. "Which reminds me, they found a number of rooms filled with gold ingots. Mark? Olaf? I want you to scramble over there and help guard them. Off you go."

Mark and Olaf took broke away at a run. Myriad was clever enough to toss Mark's gun to him.

"Not a good idea. That pair still lovers? Makes me think BOTH of them had intended to kill you, or at least pretend they wanted to, or rather..."

Who is overthinking now?

"As for the rest of you," Pázcuaro stated, lowering his voice, as if reinstating his authority. "I need you to perform one last service."

"That sounds ominous."

"I'm going to gather up some of these stone tools and send them to my buddy Tizoc. He's the Azteca Emperor, you know, or trying to be. You'll be my representatives, part of my gift. Your task will be to inform Tizoc about the true nature of the forbidden sacred mounds. He will be grateful to me, I'm sure. And probably grateful to you, maybe."

"You can thank me," said Seneferu, grinning like a shark. "Always looking after your best interests. In the name of peace, love, and eternal happiness for all mankind."

"No doubt," commented Beedlewood stonily. He disliked being imitated.

"What about Mark and Olaf?" Myriad asked.

The Caique smiled contentedly. "They stay here. I need them to train my stone age royal army."

"What about me?" Tlaloc demanded. He sounded bitter.

"You sank my ship. You can get lost. Don't bother coming back."

Now it was Myriad and Tlaloc's turn to grin. They embraced each other. They seemed very happy. I found this annoying. "Tizoc will hire me to carve his portrait," Tlaloc said.

"Fine," the Caique replied. "Terrific. Now, leave me. I'm busy counting my possessions."

Seneferu gave the impression of wanting to pat the King on the head. Odd. Was he that much in control?

"Not if we can get to Tizoc first."

You think Seneferu will come after us?

"Of course. He wants to "rescue" us, remember? He won't stop until he's rescued us into the ground."

And here I thought the Norns were beginning to smile on us.

"Not yet, they haven't."

"The emperor," Titus said quietly, as if in the grip of a fond memory. "It'll be good to see him again."

CHAPTER NINE

Donkeys again. I hate Donkeys.

"Maybe so, but you seem to be getting used to them. Not complaining so much."

It's this cotton loincloth. Decent padding. And the linen tunic is light and comfortable. But feathers? They make me sneeze.

I swept the feathers on my chest flat with my hand. Bloody breeze kept fluttering the feathers back out. Stupid things. Blue, green and yellow mostly. *Good thing there's no direct sunlight. I'd look like an advert shimmering in the wind.*

"Funny thing. Last time I saw adverts was in Vancouver. "Not your usual squat and gobble" was a good one. Ad for your favourite vat restaurant as I recall."

Yeah, but dying communities don't have any need for adverts, or the means to display them. I'm the one on display now.

"That's the point. You and Myriad and Tlaloc and Beedlewood and Titus all decked out like a flock of hummingbirds. Symbolic of something or another."

Symbolic of a lot of plucked birds. That's all it means.

"Could be worse. Titus is drowning in feathers. So many he's top heavy. Incredible thing to accomplish with mere feathers."

And the lucky bastard gets to ride in a litter.

"Well, he is supposed to be the boss of the expedition. Don't know why the Caique trusts him over Beedlewood, or over you for that matter."

Shouting broke out up ahead. It was Titus, demanding to be let down. His litter bearers were complying. Behind him Tlaloc had halted Beedlewood's donkey, and now Myriad had stopped mine and was stroking his muzzle. At least she wasn't stroking Tlaloc's muzzle.

I slid off my mount and stretched. Looking back, I could see the entire caravan of fifty donkeys, each with its own guide, standing still. Lucky peasants. No feathers.

"How's it going, boss?" Myriad asked. She was always cheerful these days. The mere presence of Tlaloc made her happy. She called him her "ray of sunshine." I found this very odd. She'd never been to England, so never seen sunlight.

"I'm fine. My ass is fine. Why are we stopped?

"Titus is taking another pee break. He's old, you know. Over forty, I hear."

"Yep. Old and senile."

Myriad stopped looking cheerful. "Any idea how close we are to Azteca territory?"

I shrugged. "Not a clue."

"I've been thinking about what Tlaloc told me. Tizoc is as bloodthirsty as they come, and his people love him for it."

"Keeps Beedlewood happy. He anticipates spreading love and happiness among the Azteca."

"You may be out of your league, boss. You might have reason to fear Tizoc," she said. For a moment I thought I detected a fleeting look of concern in her grey eyes. "Wish I still had my clone-drones. I'd be less worried. Single-handed, I'm not sure I could take on the Azteca army."

"Well, you've got Tlaloc to help."

Her face brightened considerably. "Yes, thank you!"

With a roar of triumph Titus emerged from a handy bunch of bushes and got into his litter. Seconds later we were underway again.

I've been thinking.

"That's all you ever do."

That's all I can do… When did we go from AI cooperatives to independent city states? Do you remember? When did all that start?

"The illusion of self-government? About a hundred years ago, in Egypt I think, with the Pharaoh Alfred Ramses. What are you getting at?"

Apart from periodic culling compensating for decreasing resources, people were happy and content to let the AI look after them. I mean, some of that high-tech stuff was really fun, wasn't it? Everyone knew putting people in charge would just bugger things up.

"So?"

Suddenly demagogues were popping up everywhere demanding a return to the good old days of pre-war nonsense, and the techgrid did nothing to stop it. Even encouraged it. Could it be the techgrid came up with the idea in the first place? Maybe even founded the Reality-Revisionist movement? You suggested this, remember? Could you be right?

"No, I was wrong. The idea is too absurd to contemplate. The core of techgrid dogma was that it only did what it was programmed to do."

Exactly. It was programmed to look after us. Yet it had no objection to people believing they didn't need the techgrid.

"Take your conspiracy theory elsewhere. You know I don't like them."

Don't blame me, just because you got me thinking. How do you account for the hidden stockpile of stone-age implements? You know such sacred sites, built by the techgrid, exist world-wide. Our mission is predicated on Pátzcuaro believing each site is similarly stocked with goodies. Don't you see? The techgrid began to prepare us to live without it a hundred years ago. They must have known what was coming.

"It strikes me there must be a hundred logical arguments I can come up with to refute your theory, but I'm too tired to think of one, which is odd. How can I be tired?"

Don't mistake boredom for fatigue... No, wait... I was beginning to twitch with excitement. Ideas were pouring from my brain. What a feeling! By Odin's balls-beard, I've got the counter to my own argument. The techgrid must have known how to repair itself. All that nanotech stuff. Fluid plastic. Intelligent microbes. The sky's the limit. How could they possibly fail? Why should they anticipate failure?

"Because there weren't enough resources to maintain the techgrid forever, let alone us. But... maybe you're on to something. I had closer core access than you did. I remember the conclusion of an internal study. 'The sky is the limiting factor' it said, and I swear the entire techgrid glitched in response. I thought it was going to go down then and there."

What in the Jõtunheimer does that mean? They were afraid the sky was falling?

"Something to do with the millions of satellites in orbit?"

They're still up there, aren't they? They're not the problem.

"Something caused the entire system to crash."

Maybe somebody pulled the plug. Ever think of that?

"You're being silly."

I tore a clutch of feathers from my chest and tossed them aside. They looked quite pretty as they fluttered to the ground. *What does it matter? Stone age tools galore or not, populations outgrow their environment. Tizoc has need of me.*

"I have the feeling the Emperor of the Azteca is quite knowledgeable on the subject."

I give him a few pointers, earn his gratitude, earn some credits, and off we go to Egypt.

"Egypt?"

I signed Seneferu's contract, remember? Hermann Horemheb is counting on us to crush the Assyrians. And I'm counting on his bean counters counting out lots of credits.

"What credits? That medium of exchange died with techgrid."

I waved my hand in the air.

Whatever passes for money these days. I'll settle for large, self-sufficient estates with plenty of servants. Always wanted my own palace. Settle down with Myriad.

"You're not hairy enough. Or man enough."

What makes you say that? I can get it up as much as any man.

"As much as the average man. And that's the problem."

At least she won't have to worry about getting pregnant.

"There you are wrong. According to techgrid before it died and and Beedlewood now, like all other males you should be fertile."

Don't be obscene.

"How can I be obscene? I lack physical form. Unlike you."

Buddy-bod? There are times when I wish I could shut you off. This is one of those times.

"Fine. Enjoy the passing scenery."

115

What scenery? A dirt path through scattered cacti consisting mostly of broad sharp-edged leaves. Bushes really. Resembling a bundle of broadswords poking into the air. All scattered about an undulating plain flanked by rounded hills featuring not a decent peak among them. Yellowed grass about knee high everywhere. Start of the dry season perhaps. Lack of rain anyway. Some hilltops were covered in bushes, a few with trees. Their foliage appeared dry and dusty, presenting a sombre dark green. Dreary place.

No wonder huts were few and visibly abandoned. Full marks to one builder though. His shack was colourful and quaint. Fashioned out of centuries-old highway signs. Probably hot as the blade of Gungnir if the sun were ever to come out. Fortunately, there was no chance of that happening.

Titus poked his right arm in the general direction of the non-visible sun. "Pochteca!" he shouted. "Pochteca!"

Our caravan halted. There were distant figures coming along the path toward us. The others were slipping off their donkeys and gathering around Titus. I did the same. Everyone stood squinting warily at the newcomers, as if they knew what Titus was talking about. I certainly didn't. "Who are these guys?" I asked.

"Aztec traders. Merchants," Tlaloc answered without turning his head to look at me. He was concentrating on the Pochteca as they trotted closer. I was reminded of my dream about the column of Bersaglieri, only these guys were different. No sharp-looking uniforms. Just loincloths. No helmets with feathers. Just trumplines around their foreheads supporting heavy-looking packages on their backs, packages wrapped in cotton cloth and twine.

The Aztec porters came abreast of our caravan and halted. They stared dully at our donkeys. Our donkeys stared dully back. Meanwhile our animal handlers stood quietly, looking away from the Azteca as if afraid to look them in the eyes.

Two scruffy-looking individuals with long black hair, their bodies wrapped in worn cloaks, marched up to Titus as if they owned the landscape. They addressed him without a hint of servility despite his feather and litter status.

"Tlaloc. What are they saying? Can you translate?"

"They're speaking Nahuatl, the language of the Azteca. And no, I don't understand a word of it. Seems Titus does."

Indeed. Titus and the two Aztecs were talking rapidly to each other without any apparent difficulty. I was amazed.

"How was Tizoc able to resurrect the language? Surely it had been dead for centuries?"

"He didn't need to," Tlaloc replied. "Pátzcuaro told me once that the Aztecs were conquered, not exterminated. Truth is there've always been Nahuatl-speakers in Mexico. The language never died out."

"That's handy, like the Tarascans. The Caique didn't start from nothing. Neither did Tizoc."

Titus was still speaking with the pair of haughty merchants but was beginning to look worried. I had the impression their discussion was slipping into argument.

Came a moment's silence. Titus twisted in his litter to look at us while the two merchants conferred with each other in whispers.

"These two are Tecuhnenenque," he explained, "or 'Traveling Lords.' They're in charge of their trading expedition. Trouble is, one of them also belongs to the Tequanime, which means something like 'wild beasts,' a special branch of the merchant class which specializes in killing foreigners who don't know how to trade properly."

"So? What's the problem?" I asked. "They're merchants. We're ambassadors. Why can't we both go about our business?"

"They admit to being merchants. They assume we are merchants."

"Ah, feathers not a good passport, eh? Well, so what if we are merchants?"

Titus looked exasperated. He wasn't getting his point across. "Look," he said, sounding desperate. "In Aztec tradition merchants travelling outside the empire aren't just traders. They're also spies searching for the weaknesses of the nations they are trading with. They gather intelligence in case the emperor wants to conquer the foreigners at some point in the future. So, if we are merchants, we must be spies on a similar mission. They're on the verge of sending runners to the nearest Aztec garrison to come and kill us."

"You've explained we're on a diplomatic mission bearing gifts from one Caique to another?"

Titus sat bolt upright in shock. It was probably the first time his spine had straightened in years. "Can't do that!" he complained. "The Great Speaker of the Azteca has no peers. It would be a grievous insult. A fatal insult. Every Aztec would be duty-bound to hunt us down and kill us."

"Well, then…" I paused. There had to be some way out of this stupid mess. Inspiration struck. "Tell them we are humble ambassadors from a humble Caique humbly bearing tribute to the Great Speaker, Lord of the Spears, Grand High Exalted Dickhead, whatever he calls himself, in the humblest possible manner. Dress it up a bit. Stress the tribute part."

Titus sighed with relief and turned to the pair of Tecuhnenenque. Words gushed forth. He sounded secure and confident, but humble. That was the important bit. He sounded profoundly humble. Not toadying humble, but proudly humble. Humbly humble. *It seems he knows how to dissemble. Not as much of a twit as I have always assumed.*

"A man of hidden talents. Could be all he needed was the right environment to function properly."

But where and when did he learn Nahuatl? I suspect Musso's ambition at work. We already know he's been trying to form an alliance with Beedlewood. Could he have been attempting the same with Tizoc?

"From what Titus says Tizoc wouldn't be keen on Il Duce's habit of referring to himself as the World Emperor. That would relegate Tizoc to lesser status."

Bugger that. We both know there's a world of difference between public propaganda and actual agreements between mass-murdering fuckwads.

"If I had shoulders I'd shrug and say, 'Takes one to know one,' but that'd be silly."

Thanks, you're a big help. We can agree on this, at least. Our fate depends on Titus. We need to watch over him, intervene when necessary.

"Might not be as difficult as you think. Tizoc is a big shot. Probably speaks AI English."

So, we can reason with him?

"As much as we can reason with anyone who rules by divine right."

Not much to hope for.

The two Tecuhnenenque turned away from Titus and waved their porters forward. We were no longer their concern. Titus appeared to slump with relief yet managed to slump proudly. A complex man.

Myriad sidled closer to me. "I hope we don't run into more like that," she whispered.

"What do you mean?"

She smiled sweetly. "All men have sticks up their ass. Those two tecuhnenwhatevers are walking around with full-grown redwoods inserted."

"Try not to insult the natives, dear. What's up Tlaloc's ass, by the way?"

She smiled even more sweetly, her eyes twinkling. "Probably a tobacco enema." She winked, took up the reins of my donkey, and began to lead as our caravan lurched back into motion. Titus remained slumped, his head sunk on his chest. *Lost in thought? Or on the verge of collapse?*

"For him one and the same thing. That's quite the compliment Myriad gave Tlaloc."

Really? Sounded like an insult to me.

"Old local custom. The tobacco can produce powerful, vivid hallucinations which the Azteca, Maya and others believe to be real. It's her way of saying she thinks Tlaloc is spiritual enough to commune with the gods."

I sighed. Not what I wanted to hear. Tlaloc really has pulled his chest hair over her eyes.

"Forget about her. Don't let your pathetic lust distract you. Focus on your mission."

Your mothering tendencies are beginning to bother me.

No answer.

Fine. Buddy-bod, you can suck on Sleipnir's hooves. Time to focus on important stuff, like the bit of a mess about my penis and blanket when I first woke up. Panicked for a second, thinking it was blood, then lapsed into confusion when I realized it was something else.

"Congratulations on your first nocturnal emission."

Twenty is young to be so gifted. Am I ready to be a father? Or just a man? Is the white stuff viable? Or just an equivalent to occasional ear wax? Will I father a new nation? Or am I just another drone?

"You're a wild man. What ambition."

What did you do to provoke my penis last night? What dreams did you make me have?

"None. I was dormant. You accomplished your emission mission all by yourself. Nothing to do with me."

Will it happen again?

"Knowing you, probably a dozen times a night."

You expect me to laugh?

"But seriously, how many other middle-aged fools reached puberty last night? It isn't natural. Something is going on. The techgrid was right. Beedlewood is right. Everybody's getting fertile. Within a couple of weeks, you could be as hairy as Tlaloc."

I shuddered. The thought made my skin crawl. Then I brightened. Myriad likes hair. If I acquire pubic braids longer than Tlaloc's, maybe she'll come back to me. I might even get laid.

Much shouting arose behind me. I turned to look.

Olaf and Mark were visible, bouncing along, their donkeys trotting at a furious rate as they skirted a wide arc around the Aztec merchant column. Each man gripped his mount's reins with his left hand and those of a second, supply-laden donkey with his right. They were moving fast enough for the donkeys to kick up a cloud of dust. Poor beasts.

Again, our caravan stumbled to an unexpected halt. Again, we got off our donkeys and gathered near Titus just as Olaf and Mark rode up.

"Don't let us stop you," Olaf said with a grin. "We're here to join you."

"Caique Pátzcuaro sent you with more gifts for Tizoc?" Titus inquired. His eyes were thoughtful and quietly penetrating. He had his suspicions, as did I.

"Fuck, no!" Mark laughed. "If he were here, he'd order you to kill us."

"And why is that?" Tlaloc asked in a grim, quiet monotone.

"Gold!" Olaf replied. "We took some of his new-found gold. It's only fair. He hasn't paid us the gold he promised us before the last voyage of the Flores."

"I'll show you," Mark added. He quickly swung himself off his mount and rummaged through the packs on his other donkey. He pulled out a long, narrow stick of gold with a slightly rippled surface. It was more like a ruler than a bar. Easy to heft in his hands. "We're not greedy. Only took as much as the donkey could carry."

"Took his gold and his donkeys," Myriad commented. "The Caique will be pissed."

"Mildly pissed. He's got tons of gold left. Filled quite a few compartments in that platform, turns out," Mark said.

Beedlewood interjected himself into the conversation. "Of course you will give a tithe to me?"

Mark blinked in surprise.

"Not me," Olaf said with a snort. "I don't care about your crusade."

This drew a disapproving stare from Mark. He appeared offended. What was it with these two?

Titus rubbed his aged chin. Damn fool was thinking again. "Yes, do that, but give it to Tizoc," he said. "The emperor will be pleased. An old Azteca practice. That's how the merchants avoid offending the priest and warrior castes. It will make you sympatico with him."

"We're not merchants," Olaf muttered.

"Oh, yes you are, travelling with us for mutual protection," Titus declared. "Either that or you are part of our mission and destined to give *all* of your gold to Tizoc. Which would you prefer?"

Mark and Olaf looked glum, but only for a moment. The thought of keeping their gold seemed to revive their spirits. Of course they might have to trade some of it for supplies, but in general, their do-it-yourself pension plan was secure.

"No, it isn't. Useless stuff, gold. As soon as people know you have it, they try to steal it."

"You should be grateful Olaf and I are with you," Mark insisted. "Otherwise, how would you have learned Seneferu now rules Tzintzuntzan?"

Both Titus and Beedlewood gasped. Me, I was too busy wondering why Olaf was gazing so fondly at Mark. Proud his boyfriend was finally acting like a man?

"That's not possible," Titus said, frowning. "I understand the Caique. He'd never let himself be dominated by a narcissist like Wolfgang."

"Tell that to the crew of *The Wrath of Ra*," Mark said with a smirk. "A bunch of them managed to scramble off when it got stuck in the mud downriver. They finally showed up festooned with automatic weapons and grenade-launchers. Must have had quite the arsenal onboard."

"And what about *your* guns?" Myriad demanded, her voice sharp and brittle, almost shrill.

"Don't need them," Mark snapped. "Obsolete."

Hadn't noticed what they were armed with. Now I did. Mark had a pair of wooden-handled stone axes slung across his back. And Olaf was drawing forth the weirdest sword I have ever seen. A long wooden blade, its edges studded with a row of sharp obsidian teeth.

"Pure Aztec," Olaf said as he brandished the sword in a circle above his head. "Pátzcuaro told me that in the old days these could cut through the steel breastplates of the Spanish or behead a horse with one blow."

Tlaloc suddenly looked eager. "You should present it to Tizoc as a gift, but it's too plain. First let me incise some Azteca designs on it. He'll reward both of us."

123

"Fine, whatever," Titus said. "I'm tired. Let's make camp here. Tomorrow you'll have your chance to show it to Tizoc, for tomorrow we arrive at Pochtlan, the cloud-scratching capital of the Azteca Empire. You're in for a treat. Tizoc knows how to embrace adamantine plastic. Seneferu won't stand a chance once he finally catches up with us."

"Don't like the sound of that."

Neither do I.

CHAPTER TEN

At long last my donkey and I were one. We were both pissed off with the terrain, a steep uphill climb as if the entire landscape were a single, gigantic shelf that had got tilted awry. It had gotten all fuzzy. First, increasingly dense swarms of bushes, like a tumbleweeds' graveyard, as if all the tumbleweeds in the world had flocked here.
"*They're not tumbleweeds.*"
Then trees. Scatters of them at first. Finally, an endless belt of them. Pine trees no less. *This far south? Had the world gone mad?*
"*We're in the highlands. The oceans only rose five hundred feet or so. This region is still thousands of feet above sea level. Probably explains your drooling. Definitely explains the pine trees.*"
I wiped my mouth.
One hundred thousand feet? Two hundred thousand feet?
"*It feels like that to you, but no, maybe seven or eight thousand feet.*"
Myriad stepped along in spritely fashion, leading my donkey deftly through the better parts of the dirt path. She never seemed to tire, except when drunk. Then she got all sleepy.
Something brushed against my right leg. I jerked away, or tried to. My donkey refused to shift. It had grown accustomed to Olaf riding alongside me. Fool thing to do on a narrow, winding trail. His sword was dangling against his

back. The razor-like obsidian teeth lining the blade glinting in the surprisingly bright daylight.

Lifting my head, I could see the cloud layer a few feet above my head. I knew it was an illusion, because I could make out the tops of the trees through their branches, but still, the clouds were surprisingly low. Could clouds be thinner yet heavier when kissing highlands?

"You look like an idiot staring at the sky," Olaf commented. "Trying to appear profound?"

"He's very perceptive."

"And you look like an idiot constantly stubbing your toes as you ride that poor donkey," I shot back. "Can't you lift your feet?"

Olaf shrugged. "It is what it is. I'm tall. The donkey is short. But at least I can handle its reins. More than you can do."

True enough. Perhaps I was being too hard on Olaf. After all, the sight of his heavy bulk slowly but surely crushing his donkey had to make my donkey feel better about carrying my much lighter weight. Mark was far ahead of us, I noticed. Might as well ask the question.

"So, what's with you and Mark? You seem like opposites."

"We're just... good buddies. Besides, I like having a servant around. He does what I say. Gives me the impression I'm in charge of my own life. Tremendous sense of security, that."

"You and I follow the true religion. Mark doesn't."

Olaf cocked an eye at me. Never noticed earlier how ponderous his eyebrows were.

"Are you coming on to me?"

"No. I lust for Myriad."

"Huh," Olaf grunted. "Even I do that."

"Mark, too, I've noticed."

Olaf let out a long sigh. Or was it a silent fart? Hard to tell with these Viking-types. "It's all Beedlewood's fault. Inflamed Mark's fancy."

"What? Competition?"

"No, no. The size of his cock. It's why the Caique based his kingdom on Beedlewood's teachings."

This was peculiar. Nobody's libido had been that high in centuries. Mine certainly hadn't.

"I don't get it," I said. "Anybody can talk about sex. People do it all the time. Doesn't do them any good."

Olaf glanced tossed me a look of combined pity and contempt. A bit startling.

"It's simple," he said. "Beedlewood practices what he preaches. He fathered twenty children in Tzintzuntzan. Claims to have fathered at least a hundred further south. And a thousand back in England."

"Great galloping Gyllir! Is he some kind of mutant? A throw-back?"

Olaf laughed. It was a surprisingly sweet and gentle laugh. "No, he's the new norm. Even Pátzcuaro has sired a dozen newborns. All part of the re-emergence of our goddess Gefjon, or as she's called in the Cruzob, Akna, or among the Azteca, Coatlicue. All the same jolly womb-shaker in my opinion."

I was thrilled. "I'm going to be employed forever!"

Olaf reached out and gripped my shoulder. Gripped it hard. "You're going to stop, you are. I left behind a couple of babies in Angahuan. Part of the reason I'm leaving with no intention of returning. But I don't want any harm to come to them. Get me?"

"Change the subject! Change the subject!"

I cast about for a new topic.

"Angahuan. Tzintzuntzan. The mighty river La Bomba. Isn't it wonderful how the old names survived?"

Olaf snorted. But he let go of my shoulder. That was the important thing. "La Bomba is new, only a few centuries old. People thought the war created the river. Could be. But ancient prewar names of cities, because the old locations were wiped out, were transferred to new places. A pathetic way to cling to what few traditions survive, if you ask me. I'm all for modern place names. Olafville. Fort Tryggvason. That sort of thing. Has a nice ring to it."

"Uhhm, sure. Suggest it to Tizoc."

Olaf frowned. An intimidating sight. Damn. Normally he was good-natured. "Main thing is, it's not just people who've regained their fertility. Plants too. The earth itself. You better practice sucking up to Beedlewood. Forget Tizoc. Follow Beedlewood."

"But he wants me dead," I complained.

"Yeah, there is that. Bit of a problem. For you, that is."

"New subject! New subject!"

I caught sight of the sword again. "Uhmm… that sword of yours. Found in the platform?"

"Hundreds of them. I chose this one. Named it 'Bloodwipe.'"

"The main blade is wood. Looks brand new. How come?"

"Pátzcuaro said it's made out of zapote wood. Hardest wood known. Rot-resistant. Lasts for centuries, even in the open."

"He knows a lot about the past, doesn't he."

"He has one of those Mate parasites. Used to look things up for him. Talked to the techgrid. Doesn't seem to do that anymore."

"You never wanted a Mate?"

Olaf shook his head. "I get along fine without saying much to anybody. Don't need to commune with a stupid electronic God. What's good enough for my distant ancestors is good enough for me. I put my faith in Odin and Thor."

"I'm a Thor Thumper too, don't forget."

Olaf gave me an odd look. "You talk about things that don't matter. Let me tell you what *does* matter. Who you worship, who you are with, who you love… means nothing. You are always alone. You live alone. You die alone. You. Me. Everybody. That much I know."

He glanced away, studying the trail ahead of us. "Well, enough talk. Time to see what Mark's up to." So saying, he spurred his donkey and added an extra mile-an-hour or two to its gait. Slowly they drifted ahead and were soon out of sight on this annoying meander of a trail.

"I think he just told you to shut up and leave him alone."

We learned something. He's overly sensitive. Could prove useful.

Myriad turned around to smile at me. I didn't know grey eyes could sparkle. "You think I wasn't listening? Have you solved the mystery of Mark and Olaf's relationship?"

"Frankly, no."

"I did. I heard every word."

"I was counting on it. I need you to know more than I do."

"That's not difficult, believe me. Tell you one thing. I want to learn more about Beedlewood."

"I'm sure you do," I said, feeling a sudden upsurge of self-pity and a touch of bitterness. "Better not let Tlaloc find out."

"Oh, silly, I'm not interested in Beedlewood's cock. I just want to know how soon he plans to kill you." Her face grew serious. "Be cautious for once. Let Titus do most of the talking. Don't oppose Beedlewood. Don't argue against his vision. Play down your being the last available Smiter for hire. Keep it low key. At least until you find out what Tizoc's particular brand of craziness is."

She turned her attention back to the trail again. How had she managed not to trip or stumble while looking back at me? *Instincts of a cat.*

"*Instincts of a survivor. Pay attention to her words.*"

I'm not stupid.

"No, just ignorant. For instance, have you noticed we're not alone? Look under the trees."

I stared. Nothing to see. Just the usual flattened carpet of dead pine needles, brown and decaying, selfishly preventing new growth of any kind. But if I looked deep enough, deep into the ranks of trunks marching away from the trail, I could detect shadows… no, figures of men, lurking like shadows in the shaded dark beneath the canopies of branches. Couldn't make out details, but their quiet, watchful stance felt menacing.

"Warriors. Aztec soldiers. Well armed. I've caught glimpses of clubs, spears…"

Sentries? For anybody? Or for us? Does Tizoc know we're coming?

"He's afraid of somebody else. The soldiers aren't positioned like border guards. More like an ambush set-up."

You're saying he's paranoid?

"He's an emperor. Of course he's paranoid."

Being under active observation by a bunch of thugs hiding in the shadows gave me the creeps. They weren't afraid to be seen. Some ambush. No attempt to hide behind the trunks of the trees or to lie flat to merge with the pine needle-covered earth. For that matter, no attempt to squat or sit for comfort. Not even any shuffling about to loosen tired muscles. No motion at all. And silent. Dead silent.

"*Shows tremendous discipline.*"

Or tremendous boredom has turned them into stone.

"Why don't you poke one and find out?"

The trail abruptly took a sharp dogleg turn to the left. Myriad led us into the turn and stopped short. My donkey continued walking until its muzzle was pressing against her back, then made the appropriate mental leap and came to a halt. Me, I was mentally lurching in all directions in a moment of panic.

"Calm down. Not as bad as it looks."

The trail was lined on both sides with Aztec warriors standing shoulder to shoulder, each holding an upright spear planted on the ground in front of them. The men were all the same in appearance. Identical spears. Identical white loincloths. Even identical heights. Probably inducted into their unit based on their resemblance to each other. Or maybe they were just clones. Whatever their nature, their presence screamed "Danger!" At least, that's what *I* was hearing.

Myriad turned to face me. "They don't seem interested in us."

True enough. Both ranks were facing away from the trail. Not paying attention to us at all.

"Some sort of honour guard?"

Insult guard, you mean. They're ignoring us.

"I think they're pretending to be so awestruck by our presence that they're afraid to look us in the face. A mark of great respect, like keeping your eyes downcast when talking to a local bigshot lest your gaze defile his precious majesty."

Yes, well, this precious majesty is creeped out.

"I see goosebumps on some of those bare arms. I don't think they're enjoying foreign weirdos being allowed to saunter about behind their backs. I bet some of them are as creeped out as you are."

Myriad stared at me with evident impatience. "Where's that quick response to danger your PR people claim you're famous for?"

I just stared back. Couldn't think of anything worth saying.

She frowned. "All right, I'll decide. Titus and the others moved on without any fuss. We might as well join them."

She got us underway again, leaving me to stew in a cloud of dissatisfaction and uneasiness. I felt ashamed of my inability to make a decision. It was a momentary lapse to be sure. Normally I make what I hope is the correct choice with alacrity, on the theory that it's better to do something rather than nothing, but this time my fear betrayed my talent.

"Oh, give it a rest. You think too much. That's why you couldn't think."

I could stare at the backs of the Aztec soldiers. Or I could stare at Myriad's back. Either view left me feeling slightly depressed, but at least her back was in motion. The warriors stood like so many statues.

"Sure are a lot of them."

Meaning?

"In contrast to the merchant column. We only encountered one such expedition. Otherwise, the 'Imperial Highway' is empty. Seems like Tizoc is keeping most of his people close to home."

Must have a reason. Not that I cared. Seeing Myriad disappointed in me affected me deeply. Evidently her opinion of me mattered more to me than I thought. What brought me low? Was it jealousy over her relationship with Tlaloc? Was it possible to feel like a jilted lover even though there had been no love affair? I'm smooth as a baby's bottom compared to Tlaloc. *Should I tell her about my nocturnal emission? Would that prove my manliness?*

"*Rather the opposite I should think. Speaking of which, stop thinking!*"

Can't help feeling sorry for myself.

"*Stop it. Switch gears. Think about your first meeting with Tizoc. Make plans. Develop a strategy. Get a grip. First step. Blank mind. Isn't that what the Buddhists advocate? Focus on nothing. Become nothing. Easy to do. That's Myriad's opinion of me.*"

"*Stop it!*"

What else do they advocate? Become one with nature. Become one with your surroundings. Surrender to what is. Focus on being. Focus on something. What the Ginnunga Gap is there to focus on?

Not on my slowly reawakening saddle sores. That would be a bad idea. The glowering overcast just barely above the trees? Too depressing. The subtle variations in the size of the bumps within the loincloths? Too boring. The shape of the spear heads... *Buddy-bod!*

"*Yes, I know. I see through your eyes, after all. Which reminds me, can't you do a better job of focusing them? When you're lost in thought your vision goes blurry. Gives me a headache.*"

But the spears!

"*Yes, yes. Flint spear heads. They must have opened a sacred mound.*"

I was astonished. So much for the glad tidings we were bringing on the Caique's behalf. *Tizoc isn't going to be impressed. "Not more bloody flints!" he'll probably say.*

"*Don't fantasize about failure. Could be his mound contains nothing but flints. Maybe he'll be pleased by the gifts we're bringing.*"

And maybe he'll order his guards to repeatedly plunge their spears into my body to see how long it takes to blunt their points.

"*Well, you're the Smiter. Suggest he do it to someone else. Make a game of it. Make him laugh.*"

I... don't know.

"*Don't worry. You always think of something. When in doubt, ask Myriad. She's full of good ideas.*"

I hate the unknown. I hate not knowing what's going to happen. When the situation closes around me like a poisonous fog, that's when my brain switches into high gear. Only then do I know what to do. Not a moment before. It's damned frustrating.

"*As usual, while brooding, you are ignoring your eyes, looking without seeing. Whereas I can see in the far distance a gap in the trees, a gap filled with sky. Maybe we're coming to the crest of the slope. Could be all downhill on the other side.*"

Suits me.

There came a strange, hooting cry, as if some giant predatory bird were lying in wait. At the sound the warriors raised their spears high in near perfect unison. "Xipe Totec! Xipe Totec!" They shouted.

Again, the weird cry.

"*A conch shell, I think.*"

The soldiers began shaking their spears. "Xochipilli! Xochipilli!" they chanted, then swung about to face the way we were going. At a third hoot, they set off running, two lines of men sprinting toward the end of the trail, their arms swinging, the lowered spears in their right hands moving back and forth in rhythm like some bizarre machine.

"*Hmm, they better not trip. Somebody could get hurt.*"

Soon the last of the soldiers had passed us. Myriad kept relentlessly plodding along. I wondered if my donkey resented being led by her. Checking behind, I saw the rest of the porters and donkeys still dutifully following at the same slow pace. So, which were more bored, men, or animals? *Maybe boredom is the secret of life. If you're bored, you're safe.*

"*If that's true, you're immortal.*"

The gap in the trees proved to be a cleared space full of stumps where the pines had been harvested. The slope didn't end there, however. Titus and the others were strung out along the crest of the ridge. They were being strangely silent. Not sure I wanted to know why.

Sitting upright above his litter bearers, Titus had the best view. Myriad led my donkey right up beside him. Titus was clutching his head with both hands as if he were afraid it was going to fall off. I could hear him quietly muttering. "My poor Tizoc. My poor Tizoc." He said this over and over.

The slope beyond the ridge, completely denuded of trees, fell away gently toward a vast plain. I could make out the twin columns of warriors moving rapidly toward the city that filled much of the level ground below. It covered many square miles. How many I'd be afraid to guess.

From Titus's previous comments, I'd expected to see cloud-piercing towers of adamantine plastic. There weren't any. Or rather, there had been, but they'd apparently melted into lumpy yellow mounds. The molten plastic had flowed over and covered innumerable wooden structures, the splintered ends of which protruded forlornly upwards. It was like a child's sandbox, a God's sandbox, where the God had thrown a tantrum. *Thousands must have died.*

"Probably happened when the techgrid collapsed."

But why? How? The post-war towers were designed to stand forever. There were no problems with the towers along the river. And even the nanotech ones at Tzintzuntzan were frozen in place.

"Not these ones. Maybe a higher nano content? One hundred percent? Some inherent flaw. Normally dead nanos *lock to each other. These did the opposite. Turned frictionless maybe. If only briefly."*

I slid off my donkey and stood between Titus and Myriad. She wore a quiet, contemplative expression. On her other side, Tlaloc was stroking his beard as if to stimulate his thoughts. Further to the right I could see Olaf with his arm around Mark's shoulders. Huh! That was new. Had not seen that before. Olaf looked pensive, a bit glum. Mark appeared puzzled, yet oddly gleeful. Perhaps he was visualizing opportunity? Don't see how. Beedlewood sat cross-legged at the end of the line, his hands together in the lap of his robe. He was smiling. Strange.

I looked up at Titus. He was still clutching his head, still moaning.

"Titus!" I said sharply. Startled, he stared at me. "What does Xipe Totec mean? Xochipilli?"

"Nothing much," he replied, his voice tentative and whispery. Possibly still distracted by thoughts of the city before him. "A pair of Gods."

"What kind of Gods?"

"Not sure. Xipe has something to do with sacrifice. He wears the flayed skin of his victims. So do his priests. Not very nice. I don't think Tizoc has revived the practice… yet."

"And Xochipilli?"

"Uhmm, a good God. Patron of love, beauty, happiness, music, dancing, gambling… all the fun stuff. Very popular." He lapsed into stunned silence, then exclaimed, "Musso won't like him. Puts Bacchus to shame. Way more sophisticated." More silence.

"Makes sense."

How so?

"First, the warriors saluted Xipe Totec, honouring a divinity, honouring their commitment to Azteca Power.

Then a shout to Xochipilli. Their way of stating, "Duty done. Time to party." That's what I think. Typical soldier mentality world-wide."

    I stared at the city. Plenty of people down there. Plenty of activity. I could see trunks of pine trees being dragged to what appeared to be lumber yards. How were they splitting off planks? I also saw long lines of porters snaking toward the various building sites. Stone foundation platforms were under construction, it seemed. And stone walls. Tizoc was no slacker. No sooner had his capital fallen than he was already building a replacement. Like the Caique, this was not a man afraid to make decisions.

    Titus clapped his hands loudly together as if to switch everyone's mode of thought. Startled me.

    Good grief, was Titus becoming a leader too?

    "No more mourning," he declared. "Time to offer Tizoc our sympathy."

    "We'd better offer more than that. I have the feeling the Lord of the Spears doesn't tolerate people of no use to him. I'm looking forward to the challenge. Are you?"

    Not yet. Maybe by the time we meet him.

CHAPTER ELEVEN.

Shame about the donkeys. They took them away, along with their handlers and their burdens, as soon as we reached the outskirts of Pochtlan. The expressions on their faces, men and donkeys alike, represented varying degrees of resignation. At least they weren't afraid. Exchanging one boss for another was all. Same old, same old.

One expression had been priceless. Titus was not at all pleased when he was ordered out of his litter. Even less pleased to see the soldiers move away as if they had more important things to do. We were left on our own. No escort. No guide. Nothing.

"Testing us... or testing Titus."

He's probably passing the test. Seems to know where he's taking us, at any rate.

I'd got used to thinking of Titus as a kind of human hermit crab with a tendency to draw into his shell at the least sign of trouble or opposition, his paralysis driven by confusion. But sometimes he walked like a man, talked like a man, even thought like a man. Maybe he'd been a man once upon a time and occasionally became one again when sufficiently motivated. Now, for instance.

"Hope he stays in this mood long enough to impress the emperor."

The old fool was full of surprises today, striding along as if about to break into a run, making it difficult to keep up with him. With my ass still craving recovery from the cruel massage of the donkey ride, I longed for Titus to slow to his habitual undignified shuffle so I could get used to walking again. At this pace I was afraid something would snap.

"Not saying he's desperate, or angry, but I have the impression he wants to criticize the nature of the welcoming committee. I don't think Tizoc will enjoy that."

I felt like an edible bug that had wandered into a bustling ant colony. Soldiers everywhere, directing workers in a wide variety of tasks. I saw some splitting logs into rough-hewn planks with stone axes. Others carrying brick-sized stone blocks toward building sites. Many men were digging pits with hoe-like shovels and an equal number of labourers were filling in pits already dug. Somewhere there had to be a master planner, someone to whom all this activity made sense.

The women were just as busy. I saw some offering thirsty workers water from stone troughs that others toiled to keep replenished, hauling plastic water jugs from hidden sources. Still other women were grinding corn, or cooking and serving maize porridge mixed with beans. It looked unappetizing, but the workers were happy to wolf it down. This service was constant and unending, just like the building activity. Did it continue into the night?

A number of single-storey structures were complete and in use. Their long, blank facades featured numerous open doorways but no windows. Buildings still under construction consisted of planks dowelled together, with flat roofs supported on sturdy beams resting on thick wooden pillars set at intervals within the walls. Oddly, the exterior walls were whitewashed with a stone paste, leaving a smooth surface. The planking on the roofs received the same treatment. All this to protect the wood from weathering?

Most bizarre of all were the mounds of adamantine plastic jumbled about. Some were as much as two hundred feet high. *How tall had the original towers been?*

"Titus said high enough to enter the cloud cover. A man standing on the roof couldn't see the ground. For some reason the lack of view was considered holy. Only priests were allowed to climb that high."

Probably because they wanted to keep their orgies out of sight of the public eye.

"No, that sort of thing they're glad to do in public. Fertility rites and all that."

I don't believe it. Nobody has been that horny in ages.

"Till now. Just ask Beedlewood."

Huh, he's on a one-man crusade to restore sex to the world. Obsessed, if you ask me.

"It's a successful crusade so far. You should think about that, take it into account."

If proven needful. Not convinced yet.

The city was being built as if the mounds were inconvenient blank spaces on the map. One could imagine them the equivalent of inaccessible mesas separated by level-floored canyons. Beaten-earth streets wound among the mounds past sporadically place buildings that turned their blank and solid rear walls to the plastic. Deliberately ignoring it, perhaps?

But not the machines. As we penetrated deeper into the city I noticed increasing numbers of them. Some were massive utility vehicles sitting derelict in the open. More often, they were complex machines of unfathomable purpose that looked like they had tumbled from a great height before coming to rest partially submerged in a glob of plastic. These were not being ignored. Everywhere I detected the glint of metal, men were hard at work heaping earth against it, over it, on it, burying it. Others were piling loose rocks against the layers of earth. Eventually all the machines would be removed from sight, hidden under the cloak of the Earth Goddess herself.

Meanwhile, I couldn't help but notice people were choosing to defecate at the base of these cairns. And just as often along the perimeter of the collapsed towers. This was asking for trouble. Risked triggering a lot of disease.

"I'd say Tizoc is a man determined to turn his back on the past."

His backside, you mean.

"As a public statement of policy, this is hard to beat. As visceral as you can get. Who hasn't wanted to dump on authority? Woe to the vanquished."

Are you saying Tizoc takes credit for the collapse?

"Only if he has any brains."

It was beginning to sound like Tizoc's principal virtue was opportunism. That was supposed to be my specialty. Will we spar with each other warily when we first meet? Embrace each other as brothers? Vow mutual destruction?

"You'll be lucky if he even notices you."

Don't worry. He'll notice me all right.

"Good. Sounds like the Smiter in you is waking up."

I heard a bout of swearing. Tlaloc had stumbled over a metal rod jutting out of the ground and fallen on his face. Fortunately, his beard and chest hair broke his fall. Myriad was helping him to his feet, her laughter a note of music against the silence of the worker "ants."

"I think Tizoc is going to like Tlaloc. I haven't noticed any art visible whatsoever."

Buildings are top priority, I suspect. Sanitation should be next.

"An Emperor needs cult statues. Frescos praising his soldiers. Bas reliefs praising his victories. Tlaloc is going to be busy."

What victories?

"The ones you arrange."

Hmm, yes. Workers appeared to outnumber soldiers, but that still left thousands of trained men capable of a conquest or two. For now, they were just well-armed overseers. To reach their full potential they needed a war. Likewise, the Empire. Likewise, Tizoc. This was going to be an easy sell. Tlaloc was going to spend the rest of his life depicting the results of my advice to the emperor. And I would be minus a rival. Bonus.

By chance we skirted one blob of plastic close enough to touch it. Slippery doesn't even begin to describe its texture. Slick enough to shed dust. The essence of AI tech in its purest form, but dead, just like the techgrid. That didn't prevent Olaf from striking it repeatedly with his fist, but then, he had good reason to. He and Mark had been downright outraged when their gold-laden donkeys had been taken from them. *Can't argue with a hundred spearmen, though. No point.*

"Is that a pun?"

Of course not. You know I hate puns.

"The melted towers are certainly useless. Too slippery to climb. Probably too hard to anchor any structure built against them. Tizoc is right to ignore them."

Proves one thing: he's insanely stubborn. A more adaptable leader would have founded a new capital somewhere else.

"Keep it up. Keep it up. More Smiter thoughts."

Titus waved at us to hurry up. A triumphant smile creased his face. He'd found what he was looking for—a building faced with cut stone, longer than any others I'd seen and higher, maybe twenty feet high. A vaulted passageway led through the structure into a paved courtyard beyond, the centre of a large quadrangle. We'd entered the emperor's palace. Numerous doorways indicated numerous rooms. Idly, I wondered which wing housed the harem, if there was one. Not that I was going to ask. There were spearmen flanking every doorway.

Titus turned to us as a trio of court officials wearing red and green cloaks approached him. "Stay here," he said, gesturing at us to sit down. "I'll report to Tizoc. Then, maybe, he'll see you."

Titus greeted the flunkies. His attitude was haughty and self-important. Evidently, they were equals. Question was, were they equally important or equally insignificant? Either way they were in a hurry as they strode toward a doorway guarded by *two* pairs of spearmen. Presumably the emperor was inside.

The others in our party flung themselves down, some more dejectedly than others. Me too. I sat cross-legged to spare my bum further grief. Only Beedlewood was left standing, his hands on his hips, swiveling slowly as he scrutinized the lack of architectural detail. What was he looking for?

Refreshments perhaps. Servants of both sexes appeared, all equally low in rank, all carrying bowls and cups filled with an impressive variety of goodies. A quick survey revealed tamales stuffed with snails, frogs with pimento sauce, varied dried meats, winged ants, and assorted other delicacies, all highly seasoned. I contented myself with maize cakes and water that looked and tasted safe to drink. After all, it's never a good idea to indulge in a fit of vomiting when being introduced to royalty.

Tlaloc, I noticed, was sampling practically everything. No surprise there, since he was practically a local. Myriad appeared to be restricting herself to meat and potage. Good. Keeping her strength up. Olaf and Mark were feeding each other tidbits, as if to see who would reach their limits of disgust first. Meanwhile, Beedlewood was shovelling fistfuls of food into his mouth without caring which bowl he grabbed it from. *Maybe he thinks everything is an aphrodisiac?*

"That would explain his intent mood."

Titus appeared in the doorway. He beckoned, and we arose as one to set foot inside Tizoc's Palace.

Turned out we had been invited into the throne room. I was a bit taken aback. It was large yet held little in the way of furniture. The cut stone floor was strewn with mats and piles of sweet-smelling pine branches. Not so sweet-smelling pine torches burned and smoked on the walls. Wicker baskets and ceramic jars lined the base of the walls. Open doorways to either side led to adjoining rooms. They were probably just as bare as this one.

Opposite the entrance sat the throne. I'd expected something grand, a well-crafted chair of pure gold at the very least. Instead, there was a low-rise podium of wicker only inches high. The emperor sat cross legged on a cushion resting on the podium. The throne had no seat as such. It did offer armrests, and a stiff back, as high as the emperor's neck. The back, too, was made of wicker. Nicely woven wicker of decent quality, but still… call that a throne?

The emperor himself, however, was of very high calibre. A young man in the prime of his life, at least fifteen years old, with clear, penetrating eyes that seemed to possess a wider spectrum of vision than did most mortals'. His warrior's body was slim, but well muscled. His thick, black hair was a crown in itself. His loincloth featured elaborate, multicoloured designs. A turquoise-dyed cloak fell from his shoulders, and a small plug of turquoise pierced the septum of his nose. I had the feeling only the emperor was allowed to wear turquoise.

Titus spoke loudly as we approached the throne. "Behold Tizoc, the Tecuhtli of Pochtlan, Great Speaker, Lord of the Spears, Lord of the Warriors, the Father and

Mother of the Azteca, Source of all Abundance, the Moderate and Enlightened Defender of the Gods, and above all, personal friend of Il Duce Mussolini."

Tizoc spoke in clear ringing tones. "And personal friend of the techgrid, till that bastard betrayed me." He smiled, motioned us closer. "Come, come, sit down in front of me. I like to get to know my most valued servants."

Now was not the time to contradict his words. We each chose a comfy cushion and sat down in a semi-circle facing him. No surprise to me when spearmen slipped into place behind each of us.

"Which one of you is Tlaloc?"

Startled, Tlaloc pointed at his throat. Not the safest part of his anatomy to draw attention to. Myriad shifted protectively toward him.

"You are Mayan in origin, aren't you? Despite your incredible mat of fur?"

"Yes. Partly. My mother was Spanish."

Tizoc frowned. "Then why are you named after one of the Azteca's principal Gods?"

"Better to be named after a major God than a minor God," Tlaloc replied.

The emperor supressed a smile, then pointed at Olaf and Mark. "You two, I have your gold." They stiffened in response. Still a sore point with them, but they knew not to complain.

"Mark, I like your axes. Olaf, hand me your sword."

Olaf lurched slowly to his feet, then just as carefully unslung his obsidian-bladed wooden sword and offered it to the emperor hilt first. Tizoc took it and hefted it playfully, swinging it back and forth as if he wanted to try it out. "Macuahuitll, my ancestors called these. I never saw one till we began opening the sacred mounds. Wonderful things. This is a particularly good one. Feels comfortable."

"What spoke to you to open the mounds?" Beedlewood demanded. "A dream?"

Tizoc pointed the tip of the sword directly at Beedlewood's face. "To answer your question, yes."

"I, too, had a dream, and thus I delivered riches into the hands of the Caique Vasco de Pátzcuaro of Tzintzuntzan."

"So Titus has informed me. Do not, I repeat, do NOT presume that coincidental dreams mean that we are in any way equals."

"We are not, but it proves we are both beloved of the Gods. This is why I am of more use to you than all these others combined."

"Perhaps. You are arrogant in your confidence. I grant you that. Still, be still. Be quiet."

Tizoc resumed his lazy manipulation of the sword. "Yes, comfortable indeed. Comfortable enough to behead someone. I wonder if I should test it." He noticed Olaf's alarmed expression.

"Have no fear. A macuahuitll is sharp, incredibly sharp, but the blades are brittle, easily shattered. Essentially a use-and-discard weapon. I won't spoil this for you. You may have it back."

Olaf replaced it in its sling. "You trust us to remain armed?"

"I trust my bodyguards. Besides, I'm going to return your gold to you."

Olaf and Mark visibly brightened.

"But only after you serve me for five years."

Their faces fell.

Myriad coughed discreetly. She managed to make her breasts jiggle beneath her tunic. Now she had the emperor's attention.

Tizoc chuckled. "You think I am only a man? Yes, you are comely, but less so than at least fifty of my wives. I have no need of you for that purpose. From what Titus tells me I should value you as a warrior. Fine. You, also, will serve me for five years."

Myriad bowed from her waist, sweeping the floor with her arms stretched out to either side. "I will surprise you."

"Of that I have no doubt. What says your man?"

I opened my mouth to speak but was cut short by Tlaloc before I could make a sound. "I will serve you for the same length of time, just as faithfully, but not for a second longer. Myriad and I are as one."

"Don't say it. Don't say anything."

I desperately wanted to remind Myriad she worked for me, but Buddy-bod was right. This was not the appropriate moment to put Tlaloc back in his place, let alone the emperor.

Tizoc stroked his chin thoughtfully. "Titus tells me you are a great artist."

Tlaloc nodded enthusiastically. "I can paint, and I can sculpt, but I'm used to working with metal tools. Do you have any handy?"

"Not since the damn towers melted. Everything useful is entombed within the plastic. Will flint tools do?"

"Give me a year to experiment. Then watch me transform Pochtlan into something more glorious than your capital of legend ever dreamed of."

"Tenochtitlan, you mean. What was later termed Mexico City? It was well and truly nuked during the Great War. Nothing but slag is left of it now. Impossible to build upon."

"I will make the walls of your buildings writhe with images of the Gods."

Tizoc blinked as if the vision Tlaloc's words conjured in his mind's eye was too much even for him. "Just make sure I'm up there writhing with them. I want pilgrims to be reminded I am, for all practical purposes, more powerful than the Gods."

"*Humble lad isn't he. Make your pitch. Make your pitch!*"

I stood up, crossed my arms over my chest, and bowed. "Lord Tizoc, I am the Smiter."

"Yes, Rudwulf. I know. So, what advice do you have to give me? Whom should I kill?"

Beedlewood shot to his feet. "I protest!"

Tizoc waved him aside as if he were shooing a bothersome fly. "Quiet. Wait your turn. Let Rudwulf speak."

"Have you conquered any other city states?" I asked. Pretty sure I knew the answer.

"No. That's why I have yet to wear the diadem of the Tecuhtli. My head remains bare until I have expanded the empire. And it is why I have yet to wear the radiant headdress. Mind you, Quetzal feathers are hard to come by. It will be years before I am ready to invade the lowlands to the South."

Beedlewood made faint spluttering noises as he danced about in frustration. The attending spearmen were amused.

"But you are fashioning an army?" I pointed out. "Disciplined? Motivated? Well-armed?"

"As soon as all the wonders from the sacred mounds have been processed, yes."

I assumed my full incarnation as Smiter. Play-acting, of course, but a role I had performed many times. "Then open the flower of war to embrace both Tzintzuntzan and Angahuan. Conquer the Cruzob. Sacrifice the Caique Vasco de Pátzcuaro."

Tizoc's eyes gleamed. "My first kingly sacrifice."

"*It worked. He's hooked.*"

"No! No! No!" Beedlewood shouted.

"The first of many," Titus piped up. "City after city, nation after nation, and eventually, when Gods and Mussolini will it, the destruction of Egypt."

Momentary pause while everyone, Beedlewood included, contemplated this fresh absurdity. Egypt? *With the techgrid dead, how in Glepnir's name can an army cross the Atlantic?*

"At least we know what Titus and Musso were up to. Seeking allies against Horemheb. Methinks they're going to have to downgrade their plans a little."

Beedlewood shook his head to clear his thoughts. Then he returned to the fray. "All Gods speak through me. They are united in their lust for peace, in their lust for love. The Earth Goddess has become fertile again. The people as well. I am living proof of that. You don't need soldiers. You need children."

Tizoc appeared amused. "I like sex as much as the next man. I also like being Aztec. As Musso has pointed out, the old Azteca Empire thrived on a plunder economy, just like the Romans. We even went the Romans one better. We encouraged conquered cities to rebel, just so we could loot them all over again. Staggered the rebellions, so that each and every year we opened a new flowery war. Perpetual conquest. The Aztec ideal."

"Well said," Titus murmured.

"No!" Beedlewood shrieked. "The Gods want you to fuck. Not kill. Fuck! I can prove it."

Titus looked annoyed. "Take care. You're going beyond our treaty. Don't let your personal perversion swamp the glory of Musso's vision."

I did my best to speak like a sage. "The easily accessible resources for technology are long gone. What resources are left are limited. Beedlewood, you want the human race to overpopulate and outstrip its resources? To return to starvation and plague and chaos? You are unspeakably cruel. It's best to cull the herd, to let the survivors thrive and flourish."

"Idiot," Beedlewood stated with more scorn than I ever thought could be packed into a single word. "You think we're going to run out of obsidian? Or flint? Or any other stone? Or mud? A stone age civilization can support multitudes. That's what the Gods want. As many worshippers as a reinvigorated Earth can support. There's no need for a cull. Not for centuries to come."

"You say you can prove this," Tizoc said calmly. "Do so."

"Beedlewood paused to regain his breath and recapture his composure. He succeeded. "Last night I had another dream. It revealed a miracle will happen tonight."

"What sort of miracle?"

"One that will convince you to listen to me and not to Smiter."

I snickered. Couldn't help it. Dreams merely reflect our disordered subconscious thoughts.

"Don't be so cocksure."

Tizoc stood up. "Very well. We'll see what happens. You are dismissed. I have other things to do." He strode toward the doorway on the left.

I wonder. How can Beedlewood be so stupid?

"He thinks with his balls. Good thing you are incapable of that."

CHAPTER TWELVE

Yellow. Yellow everywhere, tinged with bright orange. The slope was so slippery. Damned yellow plastic. At least it was soft. I could dig in my hands far enough to get a grip. Kick my toes in to create footholds. Make my own ladder. But it was disorienting. The slope of the mound kept billowing in and out like a sheet being flapped to rid it of lint and dust. Something, some God perhaps, trying to get rid of me. I felt distressingly alone. *Buddy-bod, where are you?*

No answer.

Damn flowers kept getting in the way. Greedy things, with narrow stems that were branching, branching. Spawning multiple grey-green lobes with spikes, grasping like frog fingers. Groping for me, trying to grab hold, to push me off the plastic. Trying to knock me off into the dark abyss below. The flower petals were blinding bursts of yellow. Every flower turned toward me, hurling light into my eyes, burning my eyes, glowing brilliant yellow with orange flames within. Yellow was my enemy. Yellow was fire. I was aflame with colour.

"Rudwulf! Wake up! Wake up!"

Buddy-bod?

"Come on, Boss! Snap to it!" Tlaloc's voice. Myriad's face. What was going on?

The colour *was* flame. Tlaloc was holding a torch above me. He and Myriad were hovering over me. I could hear what sounded like the end of the world going on in the background. Screams. Shouts. Drums beating. A chorus of conch shells sounding by the dozen.

I reached up with my right hand and Tlaloc hauled me to my feet. The light of his torch revealed that the three of us were alone in our sleeping quarters in the palace. Everyone else was gone, including the guards. In the quadrangle outside, meanwhile, all was panic and confusion. I saw other torches bobbing about, held be people who were apparently rushing mindlessly to and fro.

"This can't be a normal changing of the guard. Something's up. Something drastic."

"Where are the others?" I asked, struggling to be fully awake. The cobwebs in my mind were nearly as sticky and grasping as the flowers in my nightmare. Tough to tear apart to regain my clarity of thought.

"Outside. Mark led the way with one of his axes raised high," Myriad replied. "Olaf followed with sword drawn."

"They thought we were under attack," Tlaloc added.

"By whom?"

Tlaloc shrugged. "Titus said it was the Egyptians. Beedlewood yelled out something about Mormon Mayans. I think they're both crazy. It's probably just some spearmen who got drunk on pulque."

"Let's find out. Lead the way."

"Better grab yourself a torch," Tlaloc suggested. Myriad and I each tore a torch from the wall brackets and held it level so Tlaloc could light it. By the time we entered the quadrangle, it appeared to be deserted. The light cast by our torches was the only illumination present. There was a tumultuous roar of noise in the distance but the sound within the courtyard had died down. Except for one noise, an unexpected noise. The sound of laughter.

We followed it carefully to its source and saw Mark and Olaf doubled over in merriment. Beedlewood stood beside them. He wasn't laughing, but his smile was wide and grim. Something had pleased him.

"For Mars's sake get me out!" Titus yelled amid the sound of splashing. We stepped in for a closer look and I realized what had to have happened. Titus, running forward in great haste, had fallen into a stone-cut channel filled with rushing water. He was on his feet, the water up to his armpits, but appeared to be in no danger of drowning. He apparently couldn't find the strength to get himself out of the conduit.

"Pull him out," I said, "before he attracts attention."

Mark and Olaf took only seconds to place Titus, wet and dripping, on the dry pavestones. "That wasn't there earlier," he complained. He turned to Beedlewood. "Is this the miracle you promised Tizoc?"

"In part," Beedlewood replied. He was looking very smug.

"Nonsense," I said. "We just never noticed this yesterday. Probably we took it for granted and our eyes skipped over it."

"Sorry to disagree, but you're wrong," Myriad commented, looming out of the dark. "While you shone your attention on Titus and were laughing at his plight, I happened to notice a stone shack off to the right. Went up and looked inside. Only a moment's impression, but I'd say it's a Roman-style latrine. Stone seats above a water channel, probably fed by a branch of this one. Hadn't been there when the sun went down."

"Impossible," Titus muttered. "Aztec artisans are good and fast, but they're not *that* fast."

"You still don't understand," Beedlewood said. "The Azteca didn't make this. Quetzalcoatl is responsible."

"What?" Titus protested, his voice dripping with disbelief. "He's taken a sudden interest in Aztec sanitation?"

"As a matter of fact, yes. But that's just a sideline. Wait till you see the core of the miracle."

Buddy-bod? Can you make sense of this?

"Not yet. We should find out what Beedlewood is talking about. Whatever it is, I suggest you take credit for it."

Of course. I always claim the unexpected as mine. You were the one who taught me to do that.

"Yes, but sometimes you forget. I wanted to remind you. I don't think we can afford to ignore this opportunity. Have the feeling it's important."

"Tlaloc, take us out of this complex. Let's see what all the fuss is about."

We left the quadrangle. Less noise now. Not as many individuals moving about with torches as I expected. But there was a solid mass of torches about a hundred yards away, as if part of the Aztec army was drawn up in formation with each man carrying a torch rather than a spear. Something dark and massive loomed in the half-light beyond them.

"Where goes the army, goes the emperor."

Probably. I hope he'll consider us reinforcements.

We skirted the edge of the formation. By the time we stood in front there was no sound at all, other than the slight popping and hissing of innumerable burning torches. Even the conch blowers had fallen silent. Tizoc was there, standing with hands on hips, gazing up in awe.

What struck me first was the sight of two giant serpents, their jaws agape, their bodies functioning as balustrades for an incredibly steep stairway ascending into the night. The jaws were painted deep red, matching the colour of the receding platforms, one upon the other, which the stairs bisected. The bodies of the serpents, at least to the extent revealed by the torches, were dark green and excessively scaled, almost abstract in their decoration. Their lair was a typical Mexican stepped pyramid of tremendous size. If true to form, its painted-plaster surface covered rough-hewn stone blocks. Thousands of them. A gigantic work.

Buddy-bod? What in the name of Aesir?

"Isn't it obvious? One of the melted techgrid buildings has reconfigured itself. Perhaps they all have. And not just in Pochtlan."

For the first time in my life, I felt both shivers up my spine and a wave of dizziness.

Oh, my Odin! This proves the techgrid is still alive!

"Not necessarily."

Tizoc was capering back and forth at the foot of the steps as if he were a boy ten years of age instead of a mature man of fifteen. "It's mine! All mine!" His eyes were wild, glittering like obsidian in the torchlight as if lit from within.

Beedlewood strode up to him and bowed low, his arms sweeping to either side. "Indeed, it is yours," he said. "A gift from my God. Just as I predicted."

"No!" I shouted. "A gift from me! From me!"

Far as I could tell everyone within earshot turned to look at me instead of the pyramid. *Damn. Why did I say that?*

"Yes, why did you?"

You're the one who told me to take credit.

"*In so blatant a fashion? Are you out of your mind?*"

"Are you crazy?" Beedlewood screamed. "I foretold this. It was me!"

"Came to me in a dream," I stated as nonchalantly and confidently as I could pretend to be. "A beautiful dream."

Beedlewood hopped up and down in frustration, his dance even more primal than Tizoc's had been. The emperor was now silent and still, looking peeved. "It was my dream, my dream! I dreamed this." Beetlewood went on, so distraught his words were barely discernable.

Tizoc shook his head. "I don't care who dreamed this. It's my dream come true, one that I didn't even know I had. I'm inclined to believe my gods have more to do with this than either of you... Tlaloc! Stop that! Stop fondling my snake!"

I turned around. Tlaloc had handed his torch to myriad and was running his hands along the serpent head to the right of the stairs. He didn't have far to reach: the scales atop its skull were about five feet above where its lower jaw rested on the ground.

"Such superb craftsmanship," he murmured. "So beautiful." He looked excited, even more excited than he normally seemed whenever he gazed at Myriad. Yet she stood beside him, holding the torch aloft, looking proud of him. Damn.

Abruptly, Tlaloc brought his face close to the stonework he'd been caressing. "Nanotexture not set yet," he complained. "I accidentally scraped some off. You can see the adamantine yellow underneath. Dumb plastic."

A swarm of priests carrying ceramic lanterns gathered around Tizoc. Plenty of light now.

"Up we go," Tizoc said, and began to ascend. One of the priests leaned close and whispered something to him, and Tizoc shook his head. "No, no. Depends on what's up top." He climbed faster.

"Probably a warning not to let strangers profane the temple. After you, genius. Let's see what you come up with next. This could be our one and only opportunity to get a closeup view of whatever is on top of these pyramids."

What do you mean, after me? You're in me, not three feet behind me.

"Going literal-minded on me, are you? Sign of senility."

Keep quiet. I need to think.

Beedlewood was lucky. His agonized frustration provided him with plenty of energy. He was practically flying up the face of the pyramid. The others seemed to have no trouble keeping pace. Even Titus. I was the one in danger of lagging behind. I could feel every one of my twenty years pulling at my heels. I hate being middle-aged.

It was the steps. Stupid things were higher than they were wide, making for an incredibly steep angle of climb, as if designed to double the strength of the gravity tasking my heart. One might almost think the Aztecs were inherently sadistic or something.

"The Mayans did the same, and the Toltecs, and—"

I told you to shut up. I don't need your half-digested memories of consultation with the infinite-memory banks.

"Yes, you do."

All right, tell me this, how many steps are there to climb?

"Probably three hundred and sixty-five."

What? By Freya's non-existent balls, why?

"Sort of a giant year bundle. And the snaky balustrades represent our passage through the year, or something."

I take it back Not half-digested. Barely digested.

By the time I reached the platform atop the pyramid I figured I had lost half my body weight in sweat. I sat on the top step and gazed out over the scene far below. Rather a pleasing sight. Hundreds, maybe thousands of flaring flames visible as people carrying torches explored the new cityscape. Soft glows emanating from pre-dream doorways. No lights climbing toward the heavens, though. Ours was the only expedition seeking the heights. Probably meant the people below were saner than we were. No matter. Pretty view. I was always a sucker for twinkling lights. This was, no doubt, a personal flaw for a Smiter, but I didn't care.

Then came an angry shout. "That's not canon!" Something had upset the emperor.

As I got up to move onto the platform, I noted that the tails of the twin balustrades reared ten feet into the air on either side of the top step. Though somewhat stylized and hard to make out in the flickering torchlight, their proportion strongly suggested that they represented rattles. So, the beasties were rattlesnakes? I tucked that away in my file of useless information waiting to be purged.

Everybody was loosely clustered around a statue halfway between the edge of the steps and the temple rising from the platform. It was a strange, life-sized figure of some guy lying on his back with his knees drawn up. He'd raised himself on his elbows and was clutching a bowl that sat on his belly; and he had his head turned and was staring away from the temple. What was the symbolism involved? I'm bored? Give me food? Even though I'll still be bored?

"Where's the cutting stone?" Tizoc raged. "Where the priests bend the victim to make it easier to carve his heart out?"

Another priest and another whisper.

"Yes! I know the heart goes in the stomach-bowl. But the statue reeks of Mayan iconography, damn it. We don't need no stinking Mayan Chacmools here. We're Aztec. I demand an Aztec Chacmool!"

"Tizoc knows more than Beedlewood."

As do I.

"Now it's your turn to shut up."

Beedlewood stepped forward. His face radiated triumph. "Point is it's Mayan. Absolute proof that my religion is the true religion. The Gods have spoken. Time for you to convert."

Tizoc placed his hands on his hips and stared disdainfully at Beedlewood. "The Quetzalcoatl Mayan Reform Druid movement strikes again, does it?"

Beedlewood smiled. It was a very smug smile.

"In the first place, the Toltecs originated the Chacmool concept. The Mayans copied it. We copied it. Our version is better. Second, I'm sick and tired of you co-opting Quetzalcoatl whenever you rant about those southern lowlanders. He's nothing to do with their Kukulcan. Quetzalcoatl is an Aztec deity, damn it."

"He is?" Beedlewood looked shaken, his face suddenly the colour of ash. "But… but…"

I stepped quickly to Tizoc's side.

"Beedlewood is correct," I explained calmly. "The symbolism manifest by this divine gift is nothing less than revolutionary. A brand-new order. You shouldn't put human hearts in the bowl. Instead, you should place incense and flowers inside it and burn them in sacrifice to the gods. Just as effective. More effective, in fact. The Gods will be pleased."

"Flowers?" Tizoc looked puzzled. "I know we Aztecs used to write a lot of poetry about flowers but… flowers?"

"Not just any flowers. The white ones with four petals and a yellow centre. Those things." Everyone was staring at me. I wasn't getting through to them.

"That's it. I'm doomed. Your head gets cut off and I die. Thanks a lot."

Tizoc stared down at his sandals. They looked like they were made of gold but probably weren't. Glimmered nicely in the torchlight, though. "Four petals… the four directions… like our limbs. Spread the limbs… pierce the centre… the heart … the yellow centre… like the sun passing through our plane of existence twice daily."

"Yes!" Beedlewood declared. He started to babble. "Kill the man kill the God burn the flower kill the God gets reborn sun keeps going no need to kill people burn the damn flowers!" He stopped to gasp for air, then turned to face me. A beatific smile lit up his face. "Thank you, Rudwulf. Thank you."

"Bread and circuses," I heard Titus mutter. "Waste of time."

"You bet it's a waste of time," Tizoc said. "Sure, wilting flower, almost willing human victim, same thing cosmologically. But the Gods know what they want. I'll prove it. Tlaloc!"

Tlaloc's head snapped up. He'd been looking bored, like he was about to fall asleep. Now he was alert.

"Follow me. Time for you to meet the God whose name you bear. Everyone with me." Tizoc strode forcefully toward the temple at the back of the platform, moving like a man in the grip of absolute certainty. Like an emperor.

The temple consisted of two structures side by side, each a single chamber fronted by a wide, open doorway nearly the width of the building itself. The tower on the left was painted in white and blue. At the base of its pyramidal roof, carved seashells, each a foot high, formed a wreath. Rather pleasant to see. The other tower presented a more formidable prospect. White plaster skulls festooned its red stuccoed façade, while large, fearsome hummingbirds stood out along its crest. Fortunately, Tizoc entered the left tower.

We all crowded past the doorway. The statue of the Goddess standing on her stone plinth was indeed a pretty sight. She was nude, about 8 feet high, and appeared to be stepping toward us as if about to dance. One hand was raised before her open mouth. I gathered she was singing.

"That's not Tlaloc!" Tizoc cried.

"Looks like Xochiquetzal to me," Titus said quietly. "The Goddess of flowers and love."

I caught a glimpse of Myriad. She seemed quite taken with the Goddess.

"Where's Tlaloc!" Tizoc demanded, both his voice and his body appearing unsteady enough that I thought he might faint.

He was asking about the God. "In the corner," our Tlaloc commented.

Two of the priests moved closer with their torches. We could see a large idol lying on its side in the left-hand corner of the chamber. It was a chunky figure with a face like a bear, its body encrusted with precious stones and broken into three pieces. It looked forlorn and abandoned.

"They wouldn't dare touch the War God!" Tizoc shouted as he raced out of the temple. We ran after him. No time to think. Just move.

We caught up with Tizoc standing in front of the second sanctuary's cult statue. But his attention was focused on the idol crumpled in the far right-hand corner. "Huitzilopochtli is dead," he wailed. "The Blue Hummingbird War God is dead."

Shattered, to be sure. In dozens of pieces. I got the impression it once had wide, staring eyes, snakes of gold wrapped around its waist, and a bow clutched in one hand and a cluster of arrows in the other, but it was hard to tell, the pieces being so jumbled and all. One thing I could say for sure, though; it was no longer in charge.

"Who is this good-looking fellow?" Myriad inquired. She'd gone up to the cult statue and was staring up into its face. Her smile was positively radiant. Olaf and Mark seemed to be equally turned on.

It was indeed a handsome figure, that of a young man with long, backswept hair, seated cross-legged, his hands reaching forward as if about to gently grasp a lover, his face uplifted, his mouth open in song.

"Xochipilli," Tizoc mumbled. He seemed tired.

Titus snapped his fingers. "Our escort chanted his name, remember? The God of youth, beauty, happiness, dance and music. They call him 'the Prince of Flowers.' Xochiquetzal's twin brother. The new King of the Gods."

"Titus, how is it you know so much about Aztec culture?" Myriad asked. Looking after my interests? Or hers?

Musso's ambassador pulled himself up to his full height. "In the last days of the Gogetters, I traveled frequently between New Rome and Pochtlan. I was mentor to young Tizoc. Together our Mates ransacked the techgrid infinite-memory banks to learn what we could."

Tizoc waved his hand wearily. "And my father, the late God-King Axayacatl, fancied himself a student of folklore. Wasted a lot of time interrogating elders. Truth is, Titus and I know more about my people's past than my dad ever did."

"Then you understand," I found myself saying. "You agree with Beedlewood. Forget war. Forget human sacrifice. Make the Flowery War literal."

"But I like war," Tizoc whined, "or, at least, I thought I did."

"Of course you do," Titus declared. "War is the solution to everything."

"Xochipilli is better than war. He's all about sex," Beedlewood explained. "Don't you want to be the father of your country? All the men do. Preach the way of Xochipilli. You'll be more popular than ever."

"Sex is the new war," I added. "You'll have no problem gaining recruits."

"Are you trying to end our career? Are you insane?"

I caught sight of Tlaloc holding hands with Myriad. "What's with you and this stone kid?" came his loud, booming voice. "He ain't hairy enough."

"Sure is pretty, though," she replied. Olaf and Mark nodded their heads in agreement.

"I repeat, have you gone crazy? Supporting Beedlewood? Sabotaging your role as Smiter? Whatever drove you to it? Why?"

It's the answer to our prayers… and needs.

"Tizoc, you are missing the obvious." I stared into the emperor's eyes, hoping he would mistake my desperation for conviction.

He stared back. "Be careful, Rudwulf." It was a threat.

"The Gods have revealed their wisdom. Grant the flower manifestation of the Flowery War to your own people, and the war version to the people you conquer. Peace and violence. Sex and sacrifice. The unity of the Flowery War. Do you see? Do you understand?"

Beedlewood began to protest. "No. Wait. Peace for all…"

Titus spoke up. "Beedlewood, this is why we are allies. This is the master plan we have been destined to fulfill. You teach the Azteca all about love. I will teach them all about war."

The two of them, standing on either side of Tizoc, launched into a hurried argument. The emperor listened with rapt attention. He seemed happy… and determined.

There were a few priests wandering outside. Their torches provided barely enough light for me to safely join them. I stepped out of the temple, made my way to the Chacmool and sat down on its belly. None of the priests seemed to mind.

"I'm confused. I don't know what to think."

It's those flowers. Those damned flowers. I dreamed about them. They were smothering me. Yet they made me happy. Now I know why. They are the solution.

"What are these flowers called? Do they even grow around here?"

You know how much I hate details. How ignorant I am. I came up with the basic idea. Let Titus and Beedlewood figure out the rest of it. The flowers are real. That much I know. My dream told me.

"Too much dreaming going on lately. Spreading like a disease. Something is terribly wrong."

Or terribly right. Why complain when luck goes our way? I think the techgrid is alive and well and helping us out.

My idle gaze encountered a string of lights drifting downward in the dark distance beyond Pochtlan. There had to be another resurrected pyramid out there, with people clambering over it. Searching for answers? *I doubt their luck will be as good as ours.*

"Wait till we're dead. Only then will we know what the Norns had planned for us all along."

Options. Lots of options. That's my guess.

"Heretic."

CHAPTER THIRTEEN

"You haven't taken your clothes off."
 Don't intend to, either.
 "Don't you feel out of place?"
 I glanced behind me. Hundreds of naked Aztec warriors filled the square before the great pyramid. They were staring up at Tizoc humping a woman on all fours from behind. Priests with blazing torches stood close to them, lighting the tableau for all to see in excruciating detail, if their eyes were sharp enough.
 "I remember reading an old book in the infinite-memory banks about ancient kings who regularly had sex with their wives on the roof of their palace to impress the people in the marketplace below. Eternal vigilant virility of the state or some such."
 I'd say Beedlewood must have won last night's argument. Clever of him to convince Tizoc to parade his fifty wives naked in front of his troops. Improved their morale considerably. Then browbeating Tizoc into trying out new wives in public while his soldiers introduced themselves to his harem. I call that a popular shift in government policy.
 "Titus must feel left out of it. He hasn't moved for hours. Just standing at the edge of the platform, glowering down at the soldiers. He's a one-man anti-sex league. Make war, not love."
 Don't forget, it wasn't Xochipilli lying busted on the floor of the temple, but Huitzilopochtli. I don't think Titus is anywhere near as influential as he thinks he is. Not anymore.

"His time will come. When young Tizoc's thoughts turn to plunder and rampage..."

Look! There's Beedlewood.

The self-proclaimed prophet was once more dancing close enough to the edge of the platform to be seen by those below. A roar of approval burst from the crowd. Or was it scorn?

"An amazing sight, that third arm of his waving about. Quite the mutant."

Third leg, you mean.

"His penis is a bigger role model than he is."

Once seen, never forgotten. Any politician would be envious, and jealous. Who needs public relations experts when all you have to do is strip and dance?

The heavy booming of the giant drum on the top platform of the main temple was beginning to get on my nerves. It didn't rattle the buildings or even my body, but the deep bass timbre of the beats implied that it should. Hilarious that it beat in time to Tizoc's moves.

"You're just going to stand here and do nothing?"

Like the warriors around me? They don't even have erections.

"They're young, inexperienced. Still trying to get used to the idea that sex is officially permitted."

It's too much to expect that that many men can get it up on cue. Statistically, most are virgins like me, and rightfully so. After all, it's not as if STDs have been abolished. They're right to worry.

"Not all of them. Quite a few left the square with the emperor's wives. Looking for enough space to lie down without getting trampled, I imagine."

I didn't see them go but I think Olaf and Mark left the compound even before the wives were trotted out. Looking for privacy?

"And before them, Tlaloc and Myriad. They were visible at first, then backed away. Maybe into the temples?"

I saw. She followed dutifully after him. Clearly, protecting me is no longer a priority with her. I'm a bit pissed about that.

"No, you're like Titus. Pissed that Tizoc is ignoring you."

For now. Tomorrow may be different.

I snatched a torch from a nearby stand and stalked off in the direction of the palace. Soon I'd entered the quadrangle and was walking past the latrine. Meanwhile, the sounds of the orgy faded into the background, muffled by the intervening buildings.

No one else was present. The emptiness of the place made the latrine and associated water channels even more obvious as intrusions on the original design. Like squatters' shacks filling a stadium, they didn't belong, but they were so damned useful nobody in their right mind would want to get rid of them. Except maybe a few architecture student purists, assuming any such existed.

"That would be hard to say. Building construction has been rather haphazard of late. Why are you so obsessed with these Roman toilets anyway?"

Quite a treat they are. The sponge on a stick is surprisingly soft and absorbent. Beats leaves or fingers. How do they make them that way?

"They? There is no "they." These structures are simply reconfigured nanoplastic, just like the pyramids. Probably as enduring as the famous yellow roads. They'll last forever."

What if they don't last? What if it all collapses again?

"Including the toilets? Could be awkward if you're sitting on one at the time. Hmm, I suspect Titus might have *something to do with it. If anybody knows anything about Roman sanitation around here it's him."*

Yeah, but he doesn't personally control the plastic. That's the elephant in the teacup. It's got to be the techgrid come back to life.

"Not necessarily."

You said that before. Why can't you accept the obvious?

"Because you and I are still alone. No grid. No contact. Just as dead as it was yesterday."

Or dormant? Higher functions not functioning? Everything automatic like you said explained the floodgates on the dam reacting to the volcano.

"It's hard to believe anything as sophisticated as a forty-hole Roman toilet could materialize automatically."

Unless it was pre-programmed? Waiting to be activated on a predetermined signal?

"Techgrid still dead but zombie-dead, you mean? Up and walking about? I'll have to think about this."

You do that. Meanwhile, I've got to get some sleep.

"At least Beedlewood loves you to pieces now. Nothing like acquiring useless allies."

It was the dream. Pointed me in a new direction. Unnerving. It's gotten so I'm afraid to think.

"Well, that's a blessing. Let me do the thinking from now on."

A sudden idea stopped me cold.

Could I be part of the programming? Did the techgrid plant the dream because I'm as much a part of techgrid as you are?

"What about Beedlewood and his dreams? Or Titus? Or Tizoc, for that matter?"

Them too!

"So now the techgrid is not only zombified but transformed into a super-control freak? Come on. That's nonsense."

All at once, thoughts came crowding into my brain like a panic-stricken mob, trampling one upon the other. Spinning out of control. Making me dizzy.

Buddy-bod! What if the whole world is made of nanoplastic and we're all just a bunch of temporary extrusions? Artificial constructs of yellow plastic and nothing but? What if techgrid is the one and only God? Our God? And we're just his puppets?

"Speaking of sacred testicles, were there mushrooms in your breakfast? I mean... what the Glitnir has got into you?"

I'm tired. Too tired to think straight. Too tired to sleep. I don't know what to do. Collapse, maybe.

"Why not check out the remainder of the rooms in the palace? We might learn something useful."

Why bother? I'll probably forget everything ten minutes later.

"I won't."

Fine, then. Have it your way.

The first room I entered was different from any I'd seen before. Arranged in a pattern rather like a chess board were rows of sandboxes alternating with empty spaces. Each box, about three feet square, contained fine white sand to a depth of several inches. Morose old codgers stood or squatted by the boxes, tracing patterns with large sticks. They looked terribly frustrated. Was it because they hadn't been invited to the orgy?

I wandered close to the nearest box. The sand was disturbed, with various squiggles interrupting assorted outlines, and the whole thing smeared by futile efforts to "erase" the design. An exercise in madness. Was this a therapy room?

"Anybody speak English?" I inquired.

One particularly crusty individual glanced at me, then straightened up as far as his crooked back would let him. "I speak techgrid."

"Must be one of the elite."

"What are you attempting to do?"

"Obey the emperor's command," the old man said. He looked distraught. I half expected him to shed tears. "He wants us to reinvent writing."

"What? Don't you know the techgrid alphabet? You can use that for any language."

The ancient shook his head, slowly and carefully, as if afraid it might topple from his neck.

"No, no, you don't understand. Long ago we used glyphs. Word pictures. Inscribed on monuments, on codex manuscripts. Scribes were honoured professionals. But we moderns don't know shit. Most of our heritage faded out of existence long before the big-bomb war."

Buddy-bod, can you help? Ever see anything in the memory banks?

"No, not a thing. But then, the infinite memory banks were already remarkably corrupt even before I was manufactured."

I dropped to my knees and began smoothing out the sand with my bare hands. "So what glyph are you working on? Anything in particular?"

"Something for Pochtlan. A unique glyph for Pochtlan."

"Hmm… how about this?" I traced the outline of a flat-topped pyramid, then added two small boxes representing the twin temples.

The old man frowned. "How is that different from any similar temple in other cities?"

I drew an X above the temples. "There, crossed spears. Only Pochtlan rates crossed spears."

Eyes gleaming, the oldster was perking up. "So, all cities can start with a temple sign, it just depends how it is decorated to determine which city it represents."

"You got it. Exactly what I was intending." Which wasn't true, but I didn't want him to know that.

"How would you draw the glyph for Angahuan?"

Took me a moment to remember. The port on La Bomba. Simple. I quickly outlined another flat-topped pyramid and added a wavy line underneath to represent the river.

"What distinguishes this from any other port?"

Good question. I could draw the ship upended on the broken wharf but that might be too intricate for writing purposes. Besides, I was no artist. Need something simple.

"Draw a tree on the left side of the temple. Represents the jungle."

I added the tree. The scribe's face lit up. He understood.

I heard the sound of clapping. Concerned, I turned and noticed the emperor had entered by another door and was standing close by. Was he being sarcastic? No. Merely signalling to the servants accompanying him to lay out cushions and refreshments. He sat down with a weary sigh and beckoned me over.

I sat in front of him. "Is the ceremony over? Went it well?"

The emperor took a long sip from a golden goblet. Probably something alcoholic. "No, most of my people didn't know what to do. Some got bored and drifted away. Beedlewood put on a good performance, though. Worked his way through about half the virgins by now. And your

Tlaloc and his woman, grind-bumping on the edge of the platform behind the twin temples. Spectacular. Inspiring. Rated quite a few cheers. Probably convinced any number of citizens to give it a try."

I felt a flush of anger warmed my face. I had never realized I could be so jealous, and the knowledge was infuriating. Was I so eager to lose control of myself? Willing to let my emotions betray me?

"What does it matter? She's just practicing, saving her real lust for you."

Sure. Nice try. Tlaloc is the one she wants to screw.

"Your turn will come."

Time to change the subject. "What about Titus? Did he join in?"

The emperor smiled, somewhat grimly, as if displeased. "He did not. Just stood there glowering. I sent him away to organize a war dance, just to get him out of my presence."

"He's wrong, you know. War is not the answer." Don't know why I said this, but it had to be said.

"You're doing it again! Stop it!"

"The Gods would seem to agree. The shattered War God is proof."

"The message is more subtle than that. The city flowed into collapse once. The new city could do the same. As quickly as the great temple appeared, it could be gone again in an instant."

The emperor drained his goblet. For a moment his eyes appeared glazed, as if from the drink, but then he focused them on mine, his gaze clear and intent. Fiercely intent. "And your solution is?"

"Build a new capital... away from the plastic. For that you'll need thousands of artisans and labourers. You can't waste a single man. You'll need them all. War is out of the question."

"Hmm, yes, I see." He held out his goblet for a refill. "You and Beedlewood may be right. Violence is not the answer." He gave a short, hard laugh, one that sounded weaponized. "Olaf and Mark certainly proved that."

"I don't understand."

"No sooner had Beedlewood begun to issue detailed instructions when Mark grabbed the nearest young woman and set about tearing her clothes off. Olaf got very upset, then angry. Knocked Mark down and roughed him up, then dragged him off into the shadows. I had the impression they were clinging to each other by the time they disappeared behind a building."

"Well… that's them."

"No culture, that's their problem. We Aztecs are cultured. You're going to help me prove it."

"I am? How?"

"You and I are going to get gloriously drunk and write equally glorious poetry. Have some pulque."

I was handed a goblet full of semen. At least, that was what it looked like. Hesitantly, I took a sip. It had hardly any taste and was a bit slimy in texture, but it went down warm and musty and seemed to have a kick to it. Ah, what the Gnipahellir. You don't get drunk with an emperor every day. Might as well go along. It was an imperial command, after all.

"Just don't get too drunk."

Is there such a thing?

"Trouble is," the young emperor said, "I've been pushing Aztec culture every time I make a speech. Especially poetry. Proof of a higher culture, right? A lot of it survived the conquest, but not to the present day. Most annoying."

"Nothing? Nothing at all?"

"Just one poem. I keep it close to my heart." The emperor closed his eyes, raised his face to the Gods above, and began to sing:

"Nic quetza tohuehueuh niquin nechicohua—tocnihuan on in melelquiza niquin cuicatia. Tiyazque ye yuhcan xi quilnamiquican xi ya mocuiltonocan—in tocnihuan."

All the servants and sages present applauded. They were deeply moved.

I, on the other hand, felt awkward. Time to be diplomatic.

"Your majesty, forgive me. I am but a humble citizen of the city state of Vancouver. I speak only Eng—techgrid."

The emperor's eyes blinked open. "Ah, yes. I forgot."

"What wondrous concepts do the words convey? What beauty and wisdom?"

"Don't suck too hard. You don't want to seem condescending. Might anger him. A drunken, angry emperor is a bad drinking companion."

He's not that drunk—yet.

"It is essentially a sad song of celebration, something like… 'I place my drum. I call my friends. With me they find joy. Together we sing. Soon we go beyond. Keep that in mind. Till then we are happy. Oh, my friends!'… My translation is inaccurate but close enough. Titus would probably declare it equivalent to the ancient Roman saying 'Eat, drink, and be merry, for tomorrow we die.'"

"The Romans knew how to live."

"And so do we, or at least we did. That's the legacy I want to leave my people. The joy of life."

"Which is why keeping them alive in peace is preferable to sending them off to die in war."

"And sacrificing flowers is better than sacrificing people."

"Exactly," Tizoc said, nodding his head.

"Stop killing our employment prospects."
Stop criticizing my strategy. I know what I'm doing. I don't know why I'm doing it, but I know what I'm talking about.

"In the ancient of days, we used to love flowers," the emperor declared, throwing up his arms in a sudden burst of frustration. Pulque spilled from the goblet in his right hand. He didn't notice. "All the houses in the capital were flat-roofed, each with its own rooftop garden. What did we grow? Flowers! Beautiful ephemera. Botanical Mayflies. Transient paradise. Inspiring."

"Seems to me you just composed a poem. Translate it into Nahuatl and your people will love you all the more."

"Hmm, good idea. They say the best Emperors of the Azteca were also the best poets of the land. I would be following in their footsteps."

The emperor's goblet was refilled. So was mine. I was beginning to enjoy myself.

"So, tell me, what would you compose?" the emperor asked, leaning toward me with eager eyes. "What does your heart wish to sing? I'll memorize your words and translate them when I'm sober."

I felt a bit nonplussed. Poetry was hardly my area of expertise. But inspiration comes in all forms. In my case, memories from my crèchehood. I improvised.

"Ha, ha, dark priest,
How went your cull?
Many, many heads,
Three bags full."

Tizoc pursed his lips. I sensed disapproval. "Morale booster for acolytes maybe, but no popular appeal."

"Don't make him angry. You can do better."

"One, two, three, four, five,
Once I caught a king alive,

Six, seven, eight, nine, ten,
Time to torture him again."

"But that's one of *my* sacred duties," the emperor complained. "You seem to be making light of it. I don't want my subjects laughing at me."

"Little miss servant girl
Sat on a blackened skull,
Along came the Bat God,
Who flew down beside her—"

"No! No!" Tizoc cried. "Far too generic. The language has to be precise. Vivid. And easily translatable into Nahuatl."

"By Odin's cock-ring, don't get our head cut off!"

"Let's be logical," I said, glancing about in desperation, seeking inspiration. Aha! It was all around me. "Like these old guys creating glyphs. We need basic building blocks, words that are suitable, that convey Aztec sensibilities."

"Flowers!" the emperor shouted happily.

"I can think of a whole bunch: jade, heart, eagle, flint, fire, knife, water, temple, feather, cloak, serpent, jaguar, song, pulque, more pulque…"

"Those are just words. As you say, a bunch of words. Meaningless." The emperor looked disappointed, his enthusiasm visibly draining away.

"Ahh, but it is how you use them. Consider this… 'Jade heart of my father, Lord of the fire of memory, hear my prayer. Beat the drum. Sound the conch. Call the cloak of flint, the feathered serpent. Bring the waters of the night. Dance like the jaguar before the altar, the beating heart of the temple. Forget the flowery war. Praise the flowery peace, the newborn Sun.'"

"That's terrible."

The emperor burst out laughing. "Not bad for someone who knows absolutely nothing about our culture, or about poetry in general. Serves me right for asking an ignorant non-believer to appeal to our faith and custom. 'Cloak of flint'... what in the name of the fleshless dead does that mean? Who or what are you talking about?"

Sometimes it is safest to appear nonchalant. I shrugged. "I don't know. I was hoping you could tell me."

The emperor sat back, looking thoughtful. "Reminds me of the look in Titus's eyes when he rants at me. He says I can promote life and sex all I want, but I must always be prepared to kill, for every nation has enemies. More than are known. Do you believe that?"

I didn't know what to say. I kept silent.

"Last night atop the pyramid. Did you see the temple in the distance, or at least the torches of people crawling over its surface?"

"Something like that. I wasn't sure what I was looking at."

"An unknown temple," the emperor mused, staring morosely at the pulque in the bottom of his goblet. "Evidently reared up same time as ours, but in a region where none existed before. Down the slope in the lowlands toward the eastern sea. About a day's distance. An intruder. Perhaps an unknown God, a hostile God. An emperor needs to safeguard his people. Don't you agree?"

"Yes," I stated firmly. "Anything else would be dangerous."

"I sent an armed scouting expedition. They should report back to me late tomorrow. Can't afford to risk strangers discovering my sacred mounds."

"You have more than one?"

"Why do you ask?" Tizoc not just serious, but suspicious, to judge by the lowering of his tone of voice.

"You're more blessed by the Gods than the Caique of Tzintzuntzan. He's only got one."

"Quick thinking. I'm impressed."

"Point is," I continued, "safeguarding wealth is excellent strategy. Now, about this poetry…"

The emperor chuckled. Pulque apparently sent his mood swinging like an arrhythmic pendulum. "This business of dancing like a jaguar. How does one do that?"

"Stiff-legged? With much growling and roaring?"

"No, no. That's wrong. Too comic. Better to leap and caper, sword and shield in hand, wearing a jaguar pelt and the helmet of a jaguar knight. That, my friend, is dignity personified. And do you know what it takes to describe that?"

"Blind luck?"

I shrugged." No idea."

"Pulque! We need more pulque!"

It's going to be a long night.

"And an even longer morning."

CHAPTER FOURTEEN

I don't know how long we were up drinking. Seemed like forever. We got better and better, the emperor and me. We were more than poets. We became the Gods of poets.

"In your own mind."

Don't forget, I composed an epic poem, as grand as the Iliad, as wonderful as the Odyssey.

"Which you can't remember now. Not that it matters. Only snippets of those epics remain. Only snippets did you compose."

You were as drunk as I was. You must remember something.

"Yes, something about the US Seventh Cavalry beating a retreat. As I recall, it confused the emperor."

It was genius, I tell you. We were transformed, exalted by the Gods. Our minds soared.

"I also remember you were lucky to be able to reach the latrine. You came close to pissing yourself. Frequently."

Say what you will. Aztec culture took a step forward last night.

"Sure, which is why you sacrifice to the Gods of the hangover today."

I'm recovering, all right? Lounging on comfy cushions outdoors in the palace quadrangle was pleasant. I had numerous pitchers of water at hand. The air was clean and fresh, the light diffused by the cloud cover brighter than I remembered. Green things were growing out of the cracks between the flagstones of the pavement. I felt reborn, a trifle weak perhaps, but otherwise a veritable risen phoenix. *Perhaps getting drunk was cathartic.*

"*In your case, more like a purge.*"

Could be worse, I could be as bad off as they are.

I pointed at Mark and Olaf. They were supposed to be standing guard at the main door of the palace, one on either side, standing smartly at attention. Instead, they teetered in the centre, partially blocking the doorway as they propped themselves up by leaning against each other. Their eyes were closed, their foreheads wrinkled in pain.

"*I bet they think they're earning their gold back with a vengeance.*"

Suffering for it anyway. You know, it occurs to me, the city is quiet when the entire population is hung over. It was quite the party.

Someone kicked me in the back. I resisted the urge to sprawl forward. It wasn't that hard a kick. Meant to be playful? I squirmed about to look.

"Feeling good this morning?" Myriad inquired. Her face was buoyant, positively cherubic. And what a beautifully embroidered tunic she was wearing! I pointed wordlessly at it.

"This?" she said, grasping the edges to fully display the colourful frontal design. "Don't you recognise her? A full-length portrait of Xochiquetzal. The emperor gave it to me. Said it suits me."

I grabbed the nearest pitcher of water. My forehead felt thirsty again. Only way I can describe it. "No doubt a reward for your display yesterday."

She dropped to her knees beside me. "Feeling jealous?"

I refused to look her in the face. "You wouldn't make love to me in front of the passengers on the airplane, but screwing Tlaloc before thousands of onlookers was perfectly fine?"

"I was just following protocol. When in Pochtlan, etc."

"I don't like it. Don't you feel anything for me? Anything at all?"

"Of course I do, but…" Her face clouded over. All hint of levity was gone. Damn it, she was getting serious. "You know I don't like fooling around with virgins. Something shameful in that. I prefer virile, experienced men."

"And here I am," Tlaloc thundered, suddenly looming over us. He literally thumped his chest. Who does that? "Everybody happy? I feel great," he said, his grin broad enough to bridge a river. He hauled Myriad to her feet and kissed her.

"I would ignore their sex life if I were you. Self-pity is a bottomless pit. You don't need a handicap that big."

I'm human, aren't I? I have emotions.

"Useless things, emotions. Weren't you planning on retiring before you took up sex? Business first, then pleasure?"

When did I ever say that? You're making it up.

"Just one of the many rationalizations you've come up with to avoid sex. You have so many you've lost track."

A movement atop the quadrangle gate caught my eye. I was glad of the distraction. It was Beedlewood, beckoning to us. I didn't feel like indulging him, but I'd seen him climb the stairs earlier in company with the emperor, so there was a good chance this was an imperial summons. Best not to refuse.

"We're wanted," I stated flatly, lurching to my feet. I marched toward the stairs that rose outside the gate. Granted, I had a hard time walking in a straight line, but by the Gods I was resolute in my purpose!

The stairs were especially challenging. I would have liked to cling to the railing, but there wasn't any. I made do by leaning against the building as I took the steps one at a time with all the enthusiasm of a child consuming spoon after spoon of bad-tasting medicine. My reaching the level of the roof was a triumph of determination over nausea.

The emperor was sitting cross-legged on a mat at the outer edge of the roof, looking down into the pyramid square below. He appeared serene, even relaxed, but then he was five years younger than I was. Not as prone to human frailty as I. Beedlewood sat to his left, I chose to kneel on a cushion to his right. Myriad and Tlaloc elected to sit on the edge to my right, their legs dangling down, swinging back and forth, as they kicked their heels against the wall beneath them. Carefree, yes, but disrespectful. Mark and Olaf we didn't ask to join us. They wouldn't have survived the ascent.

"A lot of nonsense," Beedlewood sputtered. "He's out of his mind."

He was referring to Titus, who stood on a wooden reviewing stand backed against the twin-temple pyramid. He was flanked by drummers clustered around two large drums of the type normally found atop the pyramid platforms. In front of him, in a semblance of a coherent formation, were ranks of hungover soldiers dressed in peculiar costumes. They wore tunics covered in pine needles, and on their backs bore frameworks of wood to which large sprays of pine branches were fixed, fanning out evenly in imitation of a peacock's splayed tail feathers, but with infinitely less aesthetic effect.

"Weird. That's very weird."

"What am I looking at?" I muttered. The emperor heard me.

"Titus remembered something he read long ago," he explained without turning his head toward me. "The greatest warriors danced in unison before the emperor once a year. Thousands upon thousands of them. I see Titus has managed to round up a couple of hundred. They don't look enthusiastic."

"But dressed as pine trees?" Beedlewood protested. "What's the point of that?"

"Shush!" the emperor hushed him. "They're supposed to be sporting arrays of feathers, but since we don't have trade relations with the hot lands of the South, pine branches are the best Titus could come up with. An approximation. Imagine brilliant colours. Imagine lightness and grace. This is one of our finest traditions come to life!"

"Seems you're not the only one given to wishful thinking."

Titus raised both arms, then dropped them. Both drums boomed loudly in response. I half expected to see the heads of the assembled soldiers jerk backward as the noise crashed into their faces. Instead, they lifted their right feet in unison and stamped the ground hard with a resounding thump. Titus raised his left arm. Again, the drums were struck. Left feet crashed to ground. I was already bored. It looked to be an exercise in monotony.

Then a miracle happened. The drummers ignored Titus. The dancers ignored Titus. No matter how much he pranced and waved his arms, no matter what instructions he shouted, the drummers paid no attention. They developed a steady, repetitive beat but with undertones of occasional improvisation. Meanwhile, the dancers turned and swayed as one, arms and pine branches outstretched, their back-rack fans framing each individual and lending solemnity to the performance.

Faster and faster the drums beat. Faster and faster the dancers twirled and stamped and leaped, never shifting out of place but always moving, swaying, dancing. Though no feathers were present, pine boughs a poor substitute, the soldiers resembled a flock of birds prancing before potential mates in vivid display. It was an astonishing sight.

"This can't be the work of Titus. He's not that creative."

Nature. The power of nature. Of men gripped by nature. That was what we were witnessing. Men inspired by the power of creation, by the manifest will of the Gods, men who were possessed by the Gods themselves. If these were meant to be birds, they were eagles, raptors, birds of prey. This was a warrior's dance, no question about it. I found myself beating time with my fists on my knees.

Poor Titus collapsed on the reviewing stand. Fainted. He was ill-equipped to dance, and even less suited to endure physical exertion under a cloud of frustration and anger. It was all too much for him. No one cared. No one moved to help him. Let him sleep to the rhythm of the drums and dancers. He was irrelevant to the purpose of the ceremony, an outpouring of militant passion even greater than the orgy of the night before. We were all about to take wing, to fly up into the clouds. I could feel it in my bones. We were about to soar.

The emperor shot his right hand into the air as far as he could reach. The drummers must have been keeping an eye on him because they ceased drumming immediately. The soldiers, taken by surprise, slowly shuffled to a halt, lowering their arms, letting the pine branches droop. The overpowering atmosphere of ecstasy and exaltation faded rapidly away, to be replaced by dull fatigue.

Tizoc waved his arm impatiently, dismissing his soldiers. They began to disperse, though not before taking off their back racks and piling them in the centre of the square along with the branches they'd waved and thrust during the dance. All this flammable stuff would make a fine bonfire once the evening arrived.

"Tlaloc, go down and drag Titus inside the palace," the emperor commanded. "If he's still alive, revive him. Comfort him. Tell him I approve of the dance and will speak to him when he's recovered."

Tlaloc scrambled back from the edge of the roof. "At once, your Majesty. I obey."

"I'll help" Myriad chirped brightly, and together they headed for the stairs, putting a sour taste in my mouth.

"Get your mind off them."

I'm trying. They're not making it easy.

"You approve? How can you approve?" Beedlewood complained. "It was a shameless display of war mania. It was disgusting."

Tizoc laughed. It occurred to me that he laughed rather often for an emperor. Maybe it was just something he liked to do. "No, it was beautiful. Something I want to encourage."

I spoke up. "I don't understand. It was as if your soldiers already knew the dance. How could Titus train them on short notice for a dance as complex as what they just effortlessly performed? Doesn't make sense."

"Both of you have it wrong," the emperor replied, still chuckling. "It's a traditional village dance hundreds of years old, going back before the war, maybe even before the conquest. Normally countered and complimented by an equal number of women facing the men. It's a harvest festival dance. A dance of celebration."

Beedlewood looked puzzled. "Did Titus know that?"

"I doubt it. Both the drummers and the dancers had sense enough to ignore whatever nonsense he'd come up with and simply go with the familiar. I'm proud of them. They put on an impressive performance."

"If you like pine needles."

"So, Titus failed," Beedlewood said, smiling. "I'm glad."

"No, he succeeded. It was celebratory to the point of euphoria. Far better for soldiers' morale than mere marching practice. Once I've got enough damn feathers imported, I'm going to restore the war dances of old to their full glory. Granted, nobody knows the steps, but I'll just co-opt the surviving dance traditions. After a generation or two people will take the war-dances for authentic tradition. Newly invented traditions are the best ones. People cling to them with the fervour of fresh converts."

"But... but..." Beedlewood was beginning to frown.

"Oh, don't worry," Tizoc said. "I'm not grooming my soldiers for war. I'm just grooming them to be better soldiers."

Beedlewood's eyes seemed to go out of focus, as if they were searching the distance for meaning. But what the emperor was getting at was perfectly clear to me.

"I'm sure you think so."

"Worthy of a poem, maybe?" I suggested.

"Hah, not by you," the emperor retorted. "Besides, we're out of pulque. First time we ever ran out. Fortunately, we've plenty of aguave leaves. Only takes twenty hours or so to ferment a fresh batch. And then it has to be drunk before it goes sour. Closest thing to a perpetual motion machine we Aztecs ever invented, hey? If only we could harness the energy."

Beedlewood tried to smile in response to the emperor's humour, but it was a crooked smile, devoid of genuine emotion. Normally he looked like a lecherous satyr when he smiled, but at the moment he resembled a senile one on the verge of absent-minded drooling. His brain not quite in gear.

"Hmm," Tizoc mused, "We were out of pulque by sunrise, but maybe there were new batches already underway. Let's go back to the throne room and find out." He rose to his feet and headed to the stairs. Beedlewood and I reluctantly followed. *More pulque is not exactly our priority.*

"It might kill you."

Tizoc took up our conversation when we reached the bottom of the stairs. "Rudwulf, I noticed you didn't attempt to participate in the orgy. I assume it means you're a normal man? Still a virgin like I was till last night?"

"Like you? What about your fifty wives?"

"All political matches. All daughters of assorted men of power. Oh, I like to fool around," he added. "Tickle and giggle. It's very relaxing. But I can't afford children. Can't afford palace intrigue. I haven't killed all my internal enemies yet. It certainly wouldn't do to spawn any more."

"I wonder if he's heard of Machiavelli?"

Who?

"Old time master of etiquette. Never mind."

"In answer to your question, Majesty, yes, I'm normal. How does this help you?"

"I imagine it leaves your mind wonderfully free to concentrate. No doubt accounts for your success as a Smiter."

"I believe so, yes. That and my diligence and dedication."

"And blind luck. Mostly luck."

"But your majesty..." I said softly. "What if a woman you banged last night gets pregnant?"

Tizoc giggled. First time I ever heard an emperor giggle. "There was just the one," he replied. "Wife of my chief scribe. She has incredible stamina. Even better, proven infertile. I'm no fool."

"Except for the possibility the scribe is now an even greater enemy than before."

The emperor started. His black eyes flashed past me at the gate behind us. "My troops. They're back ahead of schedule."

For the briefest of moments, I anticipated dancers entering. Then I remembered about Tizoc's scouting party. Armed men were coming through the quadrangle gate at a slow trot. Most were Aztec, the rest obviously not. They were darker-skinned for one thing, wearing knee-length kilts and armoured shirts, and strange, pointed helmets. The long spears and rectangular shields they carried swayed in rhythm as they jogged.

"Not captives," Tizoc observed. "Foreign soldiers still carrying their weapons. They are being escorted rather than led. Interesting."

A soldier raced ahead to debrief the emperor. There was a quick, whispered conversation.

"Assyrians," Tizoc said, his gaze riveted on the approaching rabble. "My scouts met them halfway to the unknown pyramid. They had arrived at the valley pyramid early last night and immediately set out to come here rather than rest. You'd think they'd be tired. It's a long walk from Nineveh to Pochtlan."

"That's insane. Even before the techgrid went down it would have been a long flight. Since the collapse, I doubt there are any sailing vessels handy for crossing the Atlantic. The automated freighters used to carry travellers, remember? They'd be inactive now. How can an Assyrian unit make it this far? Doesn't make sense."

You're speaking gibberish. They're here, aren't they? Proves they've got tech-transport of some kind. Maybe we can make use of it. And aren't they cute? Quite the effort.

I was referring to Mark and Olaf. Having become aware of the approaching foreigners they had staggered forward to stand fairly smartly on either side of the emperor, once again pretending to earn back their gold. I could tell they were attempting to intimidate. In truth most people would keep their distance from these two, but only because they looked seconds away from projectile vomiting. Would that deter an assassin? No idea.

The Aztec scouts who first entered the quadrangle formed up and turned to face the Assyrians as they came in. The latter were definitely tired. Their column lost all cohesion as they dropped to the pavement to sit or squat or even stretch out full-length. Didn't seem to give a damn about the person they were escorting. Tizoc smiled. He was amused.

A solidly built wagon with four man-high wooden wheels came through the gate, dragged by a pair of oxen. They were led by a short man wearing only a grimace etched onto his face as he plodded toward us, the reigns wrapped around the wooden staff he used as a walking stick. He seemed less than enthusiastic.

"No surprise there."

I leaned forward and whispered into Tizoc's ear. "That's Vasco de Pátzcuaro, the Caique of Tzintzuntzan."

"You don't say? How strange. What's he doing with Assyrians?"

"Good question."

At once, he had his answer. A hundred Egyptian sailors poured through the gate and followed the cart toward the emperor. Each of the Egyptians was carrying one or more modern weapons. Tizoc's face fell. He was clearly not pleased.

I noticed the body of the wagon was cloaked by gauze curtains. Someone or something was hidden behind them. The Caique didn't seem to care. Once the procession had stopped, he dropped the reins and leaned on his staff, keeping his eyes downcast. This was obviously a defeated man. He didn't even glance at the emperor.

"Quite the transformation. Seneferu must be more ruthless than we thought."

"Gods damn me to the underworld," came a loud voice. The person in the cart started battling with the curtain, clutching it, pulling it back and forth violently, finally ripping it from its rail supports and throwing it to the ground. His sweating face appeared, glaring at one and all. Then, catching sight of me, he smiled. Suddenly he was happy.

I was stunned. Wolfgang Seneferu was the last person I'd expected to meet in Pochtlan.

"Well, I'll be buggered. More ruthless, and more resourceful, too?"

"Your Majesty," Seneferu said, beaming. "Good of you to send your men to guide me in. The Great King Ashurbanipal will be thrilled when he learns of your beneficence."

"No doubt,' Tizoc commented drily. "Brought me any gifts?"

"Toys to amuse? I'm afraid not. My mission is strictly diplomatic. Which reminds me, is Titus here?"

"He is resting, or possibly dying. No matter."

"Excellent. Is there some place I can rest? And eat?" Seneferu's face darkened. "But first I need to get out of this damn cart." So saying, he began pulling at the stakes that made up the body of the wagon. "I hate these new-fangled contraptions. Give me Buzz-cars any day."

Wordlessly, Pátzcuaro shuffled over to the side of the cart. Working his staff like a crowbar, he quickly levered out a dozen stakes, creating just enough room for Seneferu to squirm through and drop to the pavement.

"The Caique is more fit than he looks."

Yes. There's still muscle in him somewhere.

Olaf stood strangely staring at Seneferu. Something was obviously bothering him. Making him uncharacteristically somber. Quite a change. "Lord Heir," he cried, his voice unusually demanding. "How did the Assyrians get here? I know the oceans. It's not possible. Tlaloc will confirm."

"What, the God? Or the captain?" Seneferu was dressed in an outlandish kilt of fluffed white wool. (It added considerably to his non-existent girth.) Over it, he wore the usual absurdly ample tunic, this one equipped with large pockets. He dug his hand into one of them, brought something out in his fist, then unfurled his fingers to display what he'd found. "What do you think this is?"

I leaned forward, hoping that would improve my vision. I could see a thin slab of milky crystal two-inches square resting on his palm. Not gem quality as far as I could tell.

"It's real," Olaf declared with firm conviction. "My ancestors used them. I've used them. It's a Viking sunstone. Can detect the sun even when it's below the horizon. Or in cloudy weather. Yours looks to be high quality. Made of Iceland Spar?"

"Correct."

"Fine. Perfect for navigation in the post-techgrid age. But what ship? Not a Viking longship. Nobody makes those anymore."

"Ah, but this starstone's special," Seneferu said. "You can do much more with it. For example…" He raised it to his eyes and began turning slowly in place. "Who knows what I will see."

When he had turned far enough to face the twin temple pyramid, he stopped. Something had focused his attention. For a long, long moment he gazed through the sunstone. "Huh," he commented. "Unexpected."

Then Seneferu tucked his prize back in his pocket, quickly and efficiently. Almost as if he no longer imagined his immense size strained the fabric of his clothing, making pockets unusable. I began to wonder if he thought he had lost weight.

"I doubt it."

"Anyway, the point is, it didn't come on a ship. There was no need for that," he added. "This type of sunstone is more powerful than you imagine. They're the key to conquering the world. I kept one and gave Ashurbanipal the rest. He is very fond of them. Already, he's thinking of invading Iceland to reopen the Helgustadir quarry where the best Iceland Spar comes from."

Olaf looked stunned, as if he'd just been face-slapped. Meanwhile, the emperor was staring thoughtfully at Seneferu, as though deciding which of his many questions to ask first.

I had questions too.

"Enough chitchat," Seneferu said. "I'm hungry, and I'm thirsty. Where do I go?"

"Follow me," Tizoc replied in a pleasant, welcoming voice. "I'll see to it that your every need is catered for. Till it's my turn."

CHAPTER FIFTEEN

Seneferu proved to be difficult to handle. While I held his right arm and Beedlewood his left, he waddled slowly, so very slowly, as if he actually did weigh hundreds of pounds.
"He must be genuinely tired."
"The throne, seat me at the throne," Wolfgang whispered.
"I don't think that's a good idea," I whispered back. "Tizoc won't be pleased."
"I have as much right... more." Pause. "Besides, I need its stiff wicker back to hold me upright. Lean me against it so I don't collapse."
When we reached the throne, we carried on with our by-now-accustomed pretence of struggling to lower his "swollen" frame to the level of the platform. With his back fully supported, he sat comfortably upright, his legs jutting straight forward and his arms hanging limply to either side. The only energy emanating from his body shone from his eyes. They glittered with malice for all.
"Thank you, Rudwulf. Knew I could count on you."
"To stand still as a target? Don't forgot he wants us dead."
Along with many others. We may not be a priority anymore.
Servants came and placed cushions in front of Seneferu. I sat down on one of them. Might as well be comfortable.
"Do you notice how being enthroned enables him to dominate the room? He's a clever boy."

He's more than that. Last time we saw him he was working for his father, remember?

"Might still be."

"Wolfgang, correct me if I'm wrong," I began slowly, hesitantly, as if in deference to him. "The last time we met I signed a contract with your majestic father, Pharaoh Horemheb. You represented him. You were an instrument of his will."

"Good point."

Seneferu briefly abandoned his wall of comfort and leaned forward, his so intense that it felt as though his eyes were trying to drill through my face to the back of my skull. I braced myself to hear a threat.

I wasn't wrong. In a vehement whisper he warned me, "Don't forget whom you work for. My father is your Lord and Master. He owns you."

"Does that make *you* my enemy?"

"Ah, the light dawns," Seneferu said. He settled back against the wicker, looking smug. "Maybe, maybe not. I'll do anything, as long as it serves my father's interests."

"The lying bastard. There's no doubt the missile came from The Wrath of Ra."

I know, but why would Horemheb sacrifice his own interests?

"Order given in his name by Seneferu?"

At least we can be sure it wasn't Beedlewood's fault.

"Ahh! Now I see your clever plan. You sucked up to Beedlewood to get him on our side, then sucked up to Tizoc, all in order to thwart Titus and ultimately earn a bonus from Horemheb."

Did I?

"It's brilliant. Always amazes me how you manage to keep your innermost thoughts from me until the last moment. Proof you're still thinking like a Smiter. Congratulations."

Actually, I'm just making it up as I go along. Haven't a clue what to do next.

"Don't be modest. You boast to others. Why not to yourself?"

I couldn't help but notice out of the corner of my eye Beedlewood sidling up silently to sit within earshot of us. Abruptly recalling that we weren't alone, I observed the Aztecs who had accompanied us into the chamber, men I took to be Tizoc's advisors and officials. Now, they were pulling away from the three of us and spreading themselves around the room. Only the servants bearing trays of food dared to approach us.

I had a bad feeling. Either the welcoming dinner was turning into an international conference, or everyone knew what to expect when Tizoc arrived and saw the interloper sitting on his throne.

"Something else I wish to ask," I said. "How did you take over from Pátzcuaro? He struck me as a born ruler."

Seneferu chuckled. "I took you for a role model and slaughtered a couple of hundred citizens. Besides, my automatic weapons greatly outnumbered his pitiful arsenal. Let's just say I used your methods to convince everybody to obey me. Nice and simple, the way you like it."

"Great. Now all the survivors in yet another city hate your guts."

I don't think so. I doubt he gave me credit. That would weaken the impact of his actions.

"There's Tizoc," Seneferu noted. "Disrespectful of him to keep me waiting."

The emperor had finally entered the palace, but there was till no sign of Mark and Olaf. What had they been doing outside? What were they doing now?

I flinched as Tizoc jumped up and landed on the cushions next to me. To my surprise, however, he appeared playful, albeit with a petulant pout on his lips. Put out at being left out of the conversation, perhaps? Or suddenly remembering the not-too-distant past when his advisors ignored him while discussing affairs of state because of his youth? At any rate he seemed vaguely annoyed.

"No wonder. Away from his throne he's just another face in the crowd listening to Seneferu pontificate."

I don't think any of the Aztecs are going to forget their place. They're not stupid.

"So, Wolfgang, if I can call you that," the emperor began, "do tell how you 'walked' into my Empire."

"Be happy to, Tizoc, if I can call you that," said Seneferu. "But first, where is Titus? We need him to join our conversation."

Tizoc snapped his fingers, and an attentive servant nearby ran from the room, no doubt to make inquiries.

"I see what you mean. Tizoc knows how to rule. His people understand that."

Olaf and Mark were still missing. Perhaps they were stretched out on the naked stone of the courtyard pavement, not a cushion between them, fast asleep. They might have decided to slumber through their hangover and wake up fresh and energetic in the morning. Or maybe they just wished for death and thought being unconscious would make the experience easier to endure. Nonetheless, I was impressed by Olaf's momentary snap into focus earlier. Something about the sunstones touched him deeply. *Me, I've never heard of them.*

"And you call yourself a Viking."

No, I don't. I just get my kicks from Odin. Never claimed to be an expert.

"Wolfgang!"

It was Titus. For an old man he looked the picture of health, bursting with energy. He strode rapidly and steadily toward Seneferu, as Myriad and Tlaloc bustled to keep up. What miracle had they accomplished?

Titus knelt before Seneferu and attempted to embrace him. "Wolfgang, my dear, dear friend," he declared.

Seneferu briefly clasped Titus, but lightly, so as not to imply too much. "Titus, my dear. dear friend," he proclaimed with equal insincerity.

Myriad and Tlaloc sat down close behind me. I leaned back and whispered, "What did you do to him?"

Myriad replied softly, "He woke up as if having an orgasm. He was shaking all over with excitement. His Mate was dreaming to him again. That's why he is so happy."

"How do you know?"

"He flat out told us. He was so proud."

Hmm, if he can commune with Fuzz Bucket again, does this mean he can contact Mussolini?

"He'd need the techgrid for that. It's still down, as far as I can tell."

And yet it appears something is waking up.

"Don't worry, I've given a lot of thought to what we should do if the techgrid regains consciousness."

You have no idea how uncomforting that sounds.

Titus pulled away from Seneferu, only to roll to one side and sit down beside him, leaning against him, practically nuzzling him. You'd think they were lovers. I noticed Beedlewood staring at them both with undisguised hatred. He was biting his nails. I'd never seen him do that before.

"I take it the two of you are in accord," the emperor atated. "About what, exactly?"

"Need you ask?" replied Titus. "The triple alliance. The Roman Empire, the Assyrian Empire, and the Azteca Empire, as one against the Egyptian Empire."

"Positively Imperial!" Seneferu said, laughing. Hard to tell if he meant it.

"Yes, Titus, I know what I stand to gain from it," Tizoc replied. "On your many visits you talked my ears off with your blunt explanations. But the plan called for my army, once trained, to be transported to North Africa by aircraft and ship. Can't do that now. So, what's the point of the alliance?"

For a moment Beedlewood began to relax, and Titus to tense up.

"No problem," Seneferu said. "The Gods truly favour us. First, they revealed the presence of the sacred caches. Then they caused the cities to rebuild themselves. And now, most marvellous of all, they opened new Gogetters."

I wanted to ask, "Where?" but somehow felt that would be demeaning. I kept quiet. So did everyone else.

A brief expression of annoyance, or possibly disappointment, flashed across Seneferu's face. His composure quickly returned. He wasn't a monomaniac for nothing.

"My Mate awakened, at least enough to be in a dream state," he continued. "Fed me a dream, which led me to a small cache of sunstones in the sacred mound at Tzintzuntzan. They are unique. When you look through them, the presence of a functioning Gogetter is revealed by a flickering brilliance, like an immortal blue flame sent by the Gods. Otherwise, it's invisible."

The techgrid is alive and spreading dream-inspiration everywhere!

"To cross-purposes? It's not normal for the techgrid to compete against itself. Too weird."

"So, my army can go anywhere?" Tizoc asked with a grim smile.

"As long as I am with them," Seneferu answered.

"Great! Let's celebrate." The emperor clapped his hands.

An indescribable tumult of sound flooded into the palace, worse than the earlier dance or the orgy the night before. Multiple drums beating close to the palace doors. What sounded like dozens of conch shells being blown by enthusiastic priests with gigantic lungs. An ocean of shouting assaulting our ears. Nothing musical about it. This was, quite simply, an agonizing attack of noise, worse than hundreds of hammers beating on anvils. Even Tizoc was forced to press his hands over his ears in pain.

"I'm not sure, but I think I hear screaming. High-pitched screaming."

Women? Or men under extreme duress?

"Can't tell. It's gone now."

Gone? Hardly. The racket seemed to go on forever. Curious concept for a celebration, I thought. And annoying beyond measure.

And then it was over. Profound silence reigned. No one dared make a move.

Olaf and Mark came into the throne room with their arms linked, carrying Pátzcuaro the way they had previously carried Seneferu. What a transformation! The Caique wore a brilliant white tunic, and Tizoc's turquoise cape had been draped over his shoulders. Although a little dazed, he appeared relaxed and unafraid. Perhaps he was on his way to becoming his old self? Was that Tizoc's intent?

The emperor instructed Olaf and Mark to gently place the Caique nearby and attend to his needs. They promptly offered him fresh pulque. Then they gathered several mugs' worth for themselves.

I sensed Seneferu wanted to say something, but all eyes including his were fixed on the main entrance. His Assyrians were entering one by one, their slow measured pace dictated by that of the Azteca spearmen escorting them. Each Assyrian carried a tray bearing the freshly severed head of an Egyptian sailor. The Assyrians placed the trays close together on the floor and quietly withdrew. Even more disconcerting, they kept returning with additional trays and additional heads. It soon became evident that the entire Egyptian contingent was going on display.

"Thus, the first blow against Egypt is delivered by Azteca might," Tizoc announced. "Besides, I've always wanted to construct a skull rack as per our tradition. Now I can begin. You don't mind, do you?"

Seneferu appeared taken aback. "How did you... my men were well armed..."

"Being served pulque by naked women wanting to caress them lowered their guard. They didn't notice the priests behind them, wielding obsidian knives... well, they may have been distracted by pain for a second or two as the knives were plunged into their backs, but I'm sure none of them felt their heads being sawn off. The purpose of death isn't suffering. Don't you agree?"

Seneferu looked thoughtful. "Well, yes. I *am* estranged from my father. He set me up with Ashurbanipal, but the Great King offered me a better deal."

"Fine. Now answer some questions," demanded Tizoc. "What in the name of Xolotl's Mictlan is an Assyrian temple doing in my territory?"

"Oh, I don't know," Seneferu said distractedly. "You'll have to ask the Gods. They can be beyond annoying. My men didn't have any problem driving my cart to the Gogetter atop the Temple of Nergal in Nineveh, but your local temple was much steeper, more precipitous. They had immense difficulty lowering the oxen, the cart and, of course, myself. Very embarrassing."

I was curious. "To what deity is this new Assyrian temple dedicated?"

Seneferu waved one pudgy hand as if shooing away a fly. "Couldn't be bothered to notice. I was too busy trying to figure out how to get down."

"Maybe that was a mistake? An insult? And the God decided to punish you by making the steps steeper?"

Seneferu glared at me as if he thought that was the most idiotic suggestion he had ever heard.

"Never mind that," Tizoc said. "I've got plenty of soldiers. They can always haul you up to the platform in a sling when you decide to go back. But why are you here now? I still need time to prepare my army."

"There's no need for any need," Beedlewood muttered.

Tizoc raised his hand. Beedlewood took the hint and confined his next utterances to indecipherable mumblings.

Seneferu stole longing glances at the mountains of food being placed before him. He was getting impatient. "Consultation," he said. "The Great King wants to meet with you personally. He summons you to Nineveh."

Silence. That didn't go over well.

"Let him come to me," Tizoc said, with visible effort keeping his voice even.

Seneferu looked him in the face, his own expression a portrait of utter impotence. "But Il Duce will be there. It will be a three-way conference among equals."

"Musso will be present? Of course he'll want me to attend. I've got to go," Titus said. "And you too, emperor," he added. "It'll be a thrill! A privilege!"

"For some," Tizoc said. "Not for me. I must remain here. There's work to do."

"There's no cause to be afraid of the Gogetters," Seneferu said. "They're quite safe. I know how to operate them. I'm one of the chosen ones. The Gods smile upon me."

This went over even less well.

"As do I," Tizoc replied, though his smile seemed more like a jaguar baring its teeth. "Perhaps in anticipation of sacrifice."

Seneferu thought for a moment.

"Very well. I need to report back that you are not ready. Let Titus come with me. Il Duce will trust his word more than mine."

Now it was Tizoc's turn to think. He contemplated, not Seneferu but Beedlewood, who looked fit to burst, so strong was his frustration over being forbidden to speak. Poor fellow appeared agitated to the point of apoplexy. Apparently, Tizoc found this amusing. So did I.

"Take the prophet with you," the emperor said. "Beedlewood can explain the kinder, gentler Azteca Empire and why we withdraw from the alliance. Such is my decision."

Beedlewood's face lit up with glee. His eyes fairly shone with triumph. Seneferu and Titus, on the other hand, looked stricken. They went pale as stone statues covered in frost.

"Majesty! I can't tell Musso that," Titus cried. "It will make him angry. He will add you to his list of enemies."

"Remind him Gogetters work both ways. I'm perfectly prepared to use my army to defend my empire. Basically, I just want to be left alone, with Pátzcuaro as my one true vassal. Make that clear."

"Are you certain you don't want to tell this to your former allies face to face?" Seneferu inquired, his eyes narrowing to slits with just a hint of betrayal glittering through them.

"Reasonably certain. I'll rely on you to get the word across."

"In that case, no need for Beedlewood to accompany us."

"I disagree. I insist you take him. He is my gift to your Great King."

Beedlewood laughed. "He will reject me, but I will persevere. In the end, I will convert him. But my path will be greatly eased if you send Rudwulf with me."

"Oh, great."

Might be. Use your imagination.

"The Smiter?" Tizoc replied. "I have no use for him. Take him."

"He's bound by contract to my father," Seneferu stated. "That makes him… inconvenient."

"No more than Beedlewood. Besides, I'm sure Rudwulf would be open to some freelance work. But more to the point, they will be my emissaries. I won't like it if anything happens to them."

Seneferu closed his eyes and recomposed his features, the better to conceal his treachery, no doubt. But some things are harder to hide. In the end, he still looked glum. His hand strayed to a bowl of scorpions simmered in tomato sauce. Absently, he plucked one out and began to munch. I had the sense he was cycling through a myriad of possibilities, in search of the one that would benefit him the most.

"A good habit to maintain if you can manage it."

I felt Myriad breathing into my ear. "Of course, Tlaloc, Fucky Loo, and I, will come with you," she announced. "Someone has to keep your bottom dry."

I heard a muffled snort from Tlaloc. A protest? Against the inevitable. Merely a recognition of defeat. We're all victims of fate. Being Myriad's lover a better fate than most, curse him.

"Tlaloc too? Hmm, I'm not sure…" Tizoc said, frowning slightly. "I really like those proposals you made, those wonderful bas reliefs you had in mind…" Then his face shifted. It appeared more youthful, his expression free of worry.

"So be the will of the gods. It seems I am to be rid of the lot of you. Which reminds me…" He gestured toward the end of the hall. "Take Mark and Olaf. Tell them to protect Tlaloc. I want him back alive and eager to carve. Only then will I return their gold to them."

"What about Rudwulf?" Myriad asked.

"He can protect Beedlewood."

"No, I mean, shouldn't they protect Rudwulf?"

"What for? You're his bodyguard. Perfectly adequate, in my opinion. More than he deserves."

This was getting ridiculous, and way too complicated. I offered a solution. "How about everybody in our mission protect everybody, and in particular, the mission itself? Leave it at that?"

I caught sight of a momentary expression on Titus's face. A brief flicker of contempt, as if silently labelling us amateurs.

"Well, you do insist on making it up as you go along. Isn't that the definition of amateur?"

Definition of adaptability and flexibility, otherwise known as survivability.

"And what, precisely, is your mission?" Titus inquired, looking at me. "Do you even know?"

"To tell Mussolini and Ashurbanipal to piss off," I replied, smiling.

"And I will take advantage of their despair and anguish to lead them into a paradise of peace and love," Beedlewood said, without a trace of sarcasm as far as I could tell. He paused, then added hesitantly. "They do like sex do they not? That's key to the conversion."

"Not with each other, no," Seneferu mumbled. "But in general, yes."

"Then it's settled," Beedlewood said. He seemed content.

"Yes, it's settled," Seneferu declared, his eyes now wide open. "Nothing more to talk about. Let's eat." He leaned forward and pulled towards him as many of the food-laden dishes as he could reach. Not so much a gourmet as a glutton, this one. Was his obsession getting out of hand?

"Excuse me mighty Lords, while I draw Rudwulf aside," Tizoc said. "My instructions to him are best kept from your ears."

Titus looked alarmed, then insulted. A creature of instinct and impulse, he could be mercurial at times. Seneferu merely waved an unconcerned hand. Possibly he recognized bluff when confronted with it. Then again, maybe food was a higher priority for him than diplomacy.

Walking with Tizoc out into the quadrangle, I was amazed to see no sign of bodies, no dried blood. Already, a layer of dry sand covered in fragrant flower petals had been spread over the pavement. *You'd never know a massacre had taken place.*

"Damn, but the Azteca are efficient! Maybe they deserve to rule the world."

Tizoc put his arm around my shoulder. "I like you, Rudwulf. You're as selfish as I am. You deserve a kingdom of your own."

"Got one to spare?"

"Not yet. But I've been thinking about your words. About the nanotech collapsing again."

"Could happen."

"Will of the Gods?" he mused. "Or of the techgrid?"

"Might they not be one and the same?"

Tizoc stopped and turned to face me, keeping a hand on my shoulder. His gaze was disconcerting.

"To my people, yes. Trouble is, they have a tradition of self-sacrifice. If I build a new capital, they may feel I am abandoning the divine, abandoning them. Then they will abandon me."

I stared back at him. Coward that I am, I couldn't meet his eyes, so I focused on the space above his eyelids, hoping he wouldn't notice the difference.

"Tell them the truth," I said. "Keep them servicing the temples even when the new city is ready. They'll appreciate the risk. It will add a frisson to their daily lives, an extra aura of excitement. It will bond them to you."

"The truth? Hah! I hadn't thought of that. What a brilliant idea!" Emperor Tizoc declared, smiling delightedly. "You've solved my most pressing problem. Excellent. If you ever make it back alive, I will reward you handsomely. Now let's return to the feast." He scampered back across the threshold like a young boy about to receive presents.

"Always wise to please an Emperor. I'm proud of you."

I'm proud of me, too. I just wish I knew where I get my ideas. I feel a sudden surge of confidence and I blurt things out. Then I'm back to wondering what the hell happened.

"Simple. Your subconscious is smarter than you are. That's a blessing. Don't question it."

CHAPTER SIXTEEN

Another morning, another muddle. For one thing, it was a muggy day. I sat on the edge of the platform of Pochtlan's great pyramid, hoping to catch a breeze from the ocean out of sight beyond the lowlands. Disappointingly, the extra height made no difference. The air was just as close and still there as it was on the ground. *If it becomes too hot to perspire, we'll die.*

"Oh, I don't think it ever gets that warm here, or anywhere. The ubiquitous cloud cover protects us from much of the sun's heat. One of the advantages of global warming."

I heard it was the glittering shards of space debris in orbit that protect us.

"Urban myth, maybe. The sun does shine in England occasionally. People die then."

I don't know. Never been there. Another myth?

I stared between my feet at the struggling figures below. One thing was absolutely certain, those Azteca guys weren't even breaking a sweat.

It was true. The palanquin sled that had been rigged up for Seneferu—and didn't he look scared? I could make out the whites of his eyes even though he was still a hundred feet below me—was sturdy enough to hold his alleged bulk securely, yet light enough for a mere forty men climbing the steps to haul him up one step at a time. But how strong were the ropes they were using?

"It's quite the slope. I'm still amazed they got the cart up."

The cart, but not the oxen. It was smart of Tizoc to order them left behind. The locals are in awe of them. I think he plans some sort of sacrifice and feast after we're gone.

"Something to do with restoring Pátzcuaro to power, no doubt. I imagine the old boy will be eternally grateful."

I became aware of someone coming up from behind and sitting down beside me. It was Tizoc. I was also conscious of the fact that his feet looked better than mine. For one thing, his sandals were better made. For another, his toenails were manicured. Put mine to shame.

"They'll be at it a while yet, I suppose," he mused.

"Wouldn't it have been easier to install a capstan or two here on the platform? Or a pulley system of some sort, perhaps anchored on the temples?"

"My people thought of that, but this building is made of adamantine nanoplastic after all, not the stone and plaster it resembles."

"So are the latrine sponge-sticks," I pointed out. "They're nice and soft. Surely this structure's outer layer is soft enough to answer to hammer and chisel?"

The emperor shook his head. "You'd think it would be designed that way, but no. Even the movable items, like the Chacmool and the balustrade braziers, even the fragments of broken gods, are of a piece with the building and cannot be moved. This colossal heap of plastic is as hard as diamond. Can't carve my name on it even if I ordered Tlaloc to do it."

"That's nanotech for you. Damn near perfect—when it works."

"I could try painting slogans or images on the sloping panels, but I don't know if any paint will stick."

I couldn't come up with anything to say, so thought it best to let the emperor ramble on.

"I followed your suggestion. Told my court the city could melt at any time. Now their lives have a sense of urgency. They're really excited, inspired even. Suddenly the future is dynamic. No more fear of the dull same old same old. They're eager to look to me for guidance."

"Exactly as I predicted." *More or less.*

"Emphasis on less."

The emperor chuckled. "But it's all a lie."

I was astonished. "Really? How do you know?"

"The founder, Quauhcoatl, he who predicted the eagle on the cactus, came to me in a dream."

"Dreams again?"

"He said many things," Tizoc went on, "much of which I didn't understand. But one thing he made clear. The new buildings are forever. They will last longer than humanity itself. The nano-bodies composing them are dead and permanently locked in place."

It was my turn to chuckle. "A kumquat could last longer than humanity itself, the way things are going. Sounds to me like a communication from the techgrid."

Again, the emperor shook his head, this time with more vigour. "Frankly, I think my gut feelings came forth as a night-time vision. I trust my gut."

I refrained from saying that an emperor had to trust someone so why not his internal organs? I never trusted mine. Always had the sense they were ready to betray me at a moment's notice. Especially after I had eaten.

"I think he depends on his subconscious mind much as you do yours, only his is more in tune with reality."

Is it possible for the techgrid to implant dreams without any indication it is responsible? I'm beginning to wonder.

"No more than to pick strawberries from a barren, empty field."

Are you sure? Do you know enough about the techgrid to be certain it's no longer with us?

"Only what I remember, which isn't much. But if it were alive I'd still be connected and would be able to answer your question. The fact that I can't proves it's dead, or at least inactive and dormant, which is as good as dead. And yet... it must be behind the dreams. That implies purpose. Strategy. Can a zombie think?"

In other words, you are operating on a basis of ignorance, just like me. No wonder we make such a great team.

"I think we'd better get out of the way," Tizoc said, rising to his feet. "They're getting close."

Indeed, the leading rope-men were within twenty feet of the summit. I could even hear them fraudulently gasping and grunting. They were having a great time making fun of Seneferu. Impressively, the noises they made were in unison. Such a unified effort indicated either intense discipline or desperation.

"I hope Seneferu appreciates it."

I doubt it. He still looks to be in the grip of abject terror.

I hustled away from the edge of the platform and approached the oxcart now resting between the Chacmool and the twin temples. The dozen Assyrian soldiers who had arrived with Seneferu the previous day didn't look at all thrilled to be going back so soon. For one thing, with the oxen no longer available, they'd be the ones pulling the cart. Hence, their concern watching Mark and Olaf load the cart with our baggage.

"Leave room for Seneferu," I called out.

Myriad, who was overseeing the loading, turned to me with a grin. "Don't worry, we're going to rely on his imaginary weight to hold everything in place."

Titus was sitting on the Chacmool with his arms folded. "I don't see why you don't make a place for me," he complained.

"Don't be silly," Myriad said. "We're going to need you to help push."

I walked up to Mark and Olaf and saw them taking a break among the bundles. Under the circumstances, they seemed unusually content, I thought. Glancing about for Tizoc, I caught a glimpse of him entering the temple to the lovely Xochiquetzal. So he was out of earshot. Good.

"Pity about your gold," I said.

Olaf stroked his beard. "Oh, I don't know," he said, speaking slowly as if trying to consider all possible futures. "If we ever make it back, Tizoc will probably return it to us as promised. Doesn't matter, though. We can always get more. Assyrians like to plunder. Ashurbanipal must have acquired some by now, or he will once he ransacks the caches. We'll get gold either as pay for bashing heads or by stealing it. Credits are useless now. Gold is the thing."

Mark smiled. "You said your mission is to piss off Ashurbanipal. In a way, that's our mission too."

"We have to ride herd on these guys. Could get us killed."

I looked back at Titus. He was staring intently at the first of the rope-haulers appearing above the edge of the platform. Not paying attention to us. I still had time to change the subject.

"Olaf, what is your honest opinion of the sunstones?"

He shrugged. "They're good at finding the sun, but as for what Seneferu says it can do? Either it will or it won't." His voice dropped to a whisper. "Wherever we wind up, we might need to leave in a hurry. That sunstone could come in handy."

"He wants to rob Seneferu? Risky."

We don't have to. We're being taken where we want to go.

"We don't know how to activate these new Gogetters."

Simple. *We watch carefully when Seneferu triggers one.*

Myriad clapped her hands. "Back to work, boys. We'll be leaving soon." As Mark and Olaf reached down to finish their task, Myriad strode forward to help. I walked back to stand beside Titus.

"You wouldn't happen to have a sunstone of your own?" I asked.

"What?" Evidently, I had distracted him. He looked peeved. "Of course not. They're very rare."

"Seneferu got his from the cache in Tzintzuntzan. Maybe in other caches elsewhere..."

"Don't know. I'm sure Musso has opened his. Horemheb, too, though I doubt it. He'd be reluctant. No matter. So far, only Wolfgang and Ashurbanipal have the ability to find Gogetters. But once they're discovered, anybody can operate them... in theory."

"What about his grandiose announcement that he was switching allegiance?"

Titus snickered. "It's no surprise to me. I helped him plan it. Truth is, we've been working together for ages."

"Didn't seem that way in Tzintzuntzan."

"Diplomacy, dear chap. Diplomacy, art of. When in doubt, lie."

All the men dragging Seneferu were atop the platform now and straggling past the Chacmool, leaning forward to add their weight to the ropes. I could see the runners of the palanquin poking up above the top step. At some point, several haulers were going to have to untie themselves and grab the runners to tip the contraption securely onto the platform.

"Wouldn't be at all surprised if they disentangled themselves and let go of the ropes. I would."

They won't. But I bet Titus would like that to happen. I'd describe his current attitude as morbid fascination.

"Comes easily to diplomats."

"Finished!" Myriad announced.

Beedlewood emerged from the temple of Xochipilli. He stood framed in its wide doorway, arms raised in the style of a prophet of old. "Titus will fail! The God has spoken!"

"He said no such thing," Titus yelled back. "He doesn't talk to cranks!"

Just then, Tizoc came out of the temple of Xochiquetzal, followed by Tlaloc. "Both of you shut up," the emperor said forcefully. "Remember, I want you to present a united front to the Great King. You are to act in my interests."

"Not much chance of that."

Titus could be seen to suppress a smile.

With a loud crash, the palanquin plunged forward onto the platform and was dragged to a secure position away from the edge. Pretending to be exhausted, the haulers dropped to their knees and lay down without bothering to disengage from the ropes. The Assyrians seated near the cart applauded politely, if briefly.

"Magnificent scene," Tlaloc commented as Myriad came over and slid her arm around his waist. "You must let me carve my version of this tableau someday, depicting everyone in place as we are now. I would need only a few tons of stone hauled up here for my purpose. Having examined the statue of Xochiquetzal closely, I feel inspired."

A tentative smile played on Tizoc's face. "And why should I let you do this?"

"This mission will become legend. Let the Azteca celebrate the legend for centuries to come. Every time they gaze upon my carvings the tale will spring to life in their hearts."

"They won't see your work. Once you're gone, only priests will be permitted to ascend to the heavenly twins, or an army or two."

Tlaloc shrugged. "It will be enough to sell ceramic figurines duplicating my sculpture to pilgrims and tourists. The myth will endure."

Tizoc's smile became genuine. "I'm tempted. You think of everything. I'm beginning to be reluctant to let you go. Any idea how long it would take you to create your masterpiece?"

I decided to interrupt their conversation. "Great Speaker! You won't be able to control access to this space. What about other ambassadors coming through the Gogetter? Or the vanguard of an invading army? Hordes of armed men could materialize at any moment. Wouldn't it be better to fortify the platform so that intruders would find themselves in a killing zone, hemmed in by stout walls manned by your most ferocious guards?"

"What prompted you to spew such nonsense?"

The smile vanished from Tizoc's face. "You are being practical again. Hmm. There is something in what you say."

Titus staggered to his feet. "I protest. Such measures would offend all decent embassies arriving in good faith. It would be seen as an act of aggression."

Beedlewood waved his arms to attract attention. "I agree with Titus. Defensive fortifications are the very opposite of peace and love. Putting a chastity belt around the platform would offend the sexy twins!"

"Majesty, who knows the erratic minds of the Gods?" I said, speaking rapidly to get my point across as quickly as possible. "Remember that the Emperor Norton once proclaimed, 'The Gods help those who help themselves.' Look to the security of your people."

Tizoc's countenance began to cloud over. "Again, you give me much to think about. You are becoming annoying, yet relevant, always relevant. Once I've had more pulque to drink, my mind will be cleared by alcohol, and I'll be able to decide. Tonight, perhaps."

"Get me out of this damned thing!" Seneferu screamed. We all turned to look at him. He had recovered from his fear and was now exhibiting anger. Fortunately, we were clever enough to hide our smiles. No point in provoking him. He was a sorry sight, baleful eyes gleaming from above his sweat-damp, tent-like tunic, his hands still fiercely clutching the railings on either side of the narrow palanquin. A less impressive emissary would be impossible to imagine.

The Assyrians remembered who they were working for. They rushed forward to swarm around Seneferu, undoing all the safety straps, dismantling the railings and tugging at his limbs. In seconds, they had tumbled him out of the palanquin and onto the platform. He was free, in a sense, though he fanatically believed gravity still held him in its grip. He lay in a heap, as if unconscious.

Tizoc stood, hands on hips, staring down at him. "Is this how you intend to materialize in front of Ashurbanipal? Seems undignified."

A sigh escaped from Seneferu. Then, after a pause, he stated, "It is not uncommon to abase oneself before the Great King." He heaved his allegedly corpulent self upright, sat awkwardly sprawled for a moment, then (astoundingly, given his self-image) gathered his legs beneath him and stood up. The Assyrians started to applaud, then thought better of it. He pulled the sunstone out of his tunic pocket, held it before his eyes, and began slowly rotating in place.

"The light is flickering rapidly," he said. "Bad sign. Might be about to shut down temporarily."

"For how long?" inquired the emperor.

"A day. A month. Maybe a year. Idiot Gogetters are unreliable. Best get moving." He began waddling toward the cart. "Wherever I'm headed, I'm damned if I'm going to walk there. Bad enough the sunstone didn't inform me of this Gogetter's presence till after I arrived. Waste of time showing up at the valley temple. Ashurbanipal owes me one."

He stopped at the side of the cart and stared upwards. His seat atop the baggage loomed a good ten feet above the pavement. "How do I get in?"

Tizoc spoke rapidly in Nahuatl. All the soldiers who had hauled Seneferu up the steps of the great pyramid instantly leaped to their feet. Many clustered together to form a human ramp. The rest grabbed hold of his limbs and began pushing and pulling him upward. Eventually, they got him to the summit, where he flopped into position, riding the topmost bundles. Somehow, he managed to keep hold of the sunstone. Myriad had been right. His weight, slight as it was, settled the baggage nicely and presented him with a secure perch. He looked down at the Assyrians and barked a command in their language.

The Assyrian soldiers shuffled slowly into place at the front of the cart and picked up the traces. They looked less than enthusiastic.

"They're leaving us to do any pushing that's required," Myriad noted.

"We can push hard enough, if need be," Olaf said.

"Or force them to pull harder," Mark added.

An expression of alarm passed over Seneferu's face. "Where are my spears?" he cried. "My spearmen have no spears!"

Tizoc shrugged. "I noticed their flint blades were knapped differently than ours. Bound differently too. So, I had their spears collected and given to my armourers for examination."

"You had no right to do that!"

"I'm the emperor. Of course I have the right, every right, my right." Tizoc smiled. "Besides, it would hardly do for your troops to appear before their great and mighty king in a threatening and dangerous manner."

Olaf turned to show us what he was wearing on his back. "I still have my macuahuitll."

Mark turned his back to us as well. "And I my pair of stone axes."

"Great. Wonderful," Beedlewood commented. "We can watch you smiting a foe or two while the rest of our enemies tear us to pieces."

Titus clapped his hands to demand our attention. The report his cupped hands made was sharp and resoundingly loud. Evidently, the man had hidden strengths. "You're a bunch of hysterical mental consumptives," he said. "I represent Musso, the World-Emperor. Seneferu represents the Great King himself. In no way is Ashurbanipal going to mistreat his own embassy returning. We are all perfectly safe."

"I hate it when professional diplomats say things like that. Normally they lie to others. Here he is lying to himself."

It strikes me we're not much of an embassy. More like a gaggle of carpetbaggers and mountebanks.

"The very definition of an embassy. You know that."

The emperor clapped his hands, even more loudly than Seneferu had done. "His embassy, yes, but also *my* embassy. Remember?"

Seneferu shook his head in annoyance. "Yes, yes, Beedlewood's role, and Rudwulf's. I know very well the triple alliance demands that all partners' needs are met. We're not out to screw each other. Our goal is to work together to screw Horemheb."

"Nicely put. You're a born diplomat."

Seneferu nodded his head in agreement. "But, unless you want to accompany us, you'd better clear off the platform now. Get your soldiers off. And any priests lurking about."

"I sent the priests down before you arrived."

Again, firm words from the Emperor in Nahuatl. Clearly eager to leave, the Aztec soldiers raced to the edge of the platform and disappeared as they cascaded down the steps.

Tizoc raised his right arm in farewell. "Beedlewood, fulfill my commands. The rest of you, good luck. If any of you survive, I will reward you." He dropped his arm. "Provided you successfully return, of course." And with a twinkle in his eye, he turned away and calmly left the platform. Emperors know how to be dignified when the occasion demands.

"Of course he's dignified. He doesn't have to fear coming with us."

Crafty bastard. Sending us to do his dirty work.

"Sending Beedlewood to do his dirty work. Your mission is to offer to do Ashurbanipal's dirty work. Don't forget that."

Myriad called out to Seneferu. "Where should we stand? Anywhere in particular?"

Seneferu pressed the sunstone to his forehead. "Anywhere within a hundred feet of me will do. Now leave me alone. I have to concentrate. Don't distract me. That could be fatal to us all. So, everyone shut up and keep quiet."

He closed his eyes and leaned forward, as if bowing to Nergal. Then he began muttering, speaking faster and faster but in low tones impossible to hear.

"So much for your theory that all we have to do is listen to what he says."

I stepped quietly forward and leaned against the side of the cart. Even standing on tiptoes I couldn't make out what Wolfgang was saying.

"We may be reduced to getting him drunk at some point in the future and simply asking him what the magic words are. Doubt he'll answer, though."

Wait. Wait. I think he's getting louder.

Indeed. His muttering had become rapid mumbling. It was the same word repeated over and over in a continuous stream. "Nergal," he was saying. "Nergal, Nergal, Nergal, Nergal!"

"Is that all? That's what triggers this high-tech contraption?"

I confess I'm disappointed.

"NergalNinevehNergalNineveh—"

All at once, a blinding flash of brilliant blue light washed all of reality out of existence.

"Gods damn it, that's bright!"

CHAPTER SEVENTEEN

I felt no physical sensation, not even of motion, as we travelled through the Gogetter. One second, I was staring at Seneferu, the next I was rubbing my eyes in an effort to restore my sight. The pounding of my own heart was loud in my ears, and there was an overwhelming solitude, as if I alone constituted the universe and nothing else existed. Fortunately, it was but a momentary impression.

As the blue light faded, I found myself in a shadowed hall, staring at a bald man wearing a white kilt. He'd been frozen in the act of using a mop and bucket to whitewash a stone pillar. Open-mouthed, he stared back in utter astonishment. His Adam's apple bobbed, a strangled gasp issued from his mouth, and suddenly he was in a flurry of motion, dropping the mop and scrambling toward a distant monumental doorway. There were other men, identical in appearance, fleeing as fast as possible. To say we had taken them by surprise would be an understatement.

"I don't think we made it to Assyria."

I turned away from the pillar. There were dozens more of them, each about ten feet in diameter, supporting a lofty coffered ceiling a good fifty feet overhead. A row of narrow clerestory windows on either side of the roof let in a pale, diffuse illumination. The pillars bore bas relief carvings depicting odd combinations of figures and symbols, their painted colours muted in the gloomy half-light. It was all curiously sombre and depressing, as if the decorations were not meant for human eyes.

"Looks Egyptian to me."

Could it be an Egyptian temple erupting out of Assyrian soil like the Nergal temple outside Pochtlan? A whim of the techgrid? I mean, all is not lost? We might still be safe?

"I doubt it. Look at Seneferu."

I looked. He'd buried his face in his hands and appeared to be sobbing. Not a good sign.

"Wolfgang!" I shouted. "Can't you just repeat the procedure? Get us to where we want to go before the baldies come back with whatever spear-bearing buddies they can round up?"

His hands dropped listlessly, coming to rest on protruding bits of baggage as he raised his head to look at me. "You don't understand. We're in Egypt. My father is going to kill me, and you."

"Why did you bring us to Egypt?"

"I didn't," Seneferu said, his voice rising to a wail. "The techgrid is toying with us. We were supposed to go before Ashurbanipal, then come with him and his army here." His eyes grew wide. "The Great King is noted for his impatience. He won't wait for long. Then he'll start the conquest without us. His assault troops could arrive at any moment!"

"Didn't you say these Gogetters take a while to recharge? That should buy us some time."

He liked the straw I was offering. He clung to it with a passion. "Yes, yes, time to think!"

This was frustrating. I was beginning to suspect Seneferu knew bugger-all about Gogetters. "How do these damn things work nowadays, anyway? You never told us."

"Your Mate sets it up, via dreamthought. Just do what it says."

"You're saying the techgrid is back online?"

"No, something better. Dreams. Beautiful dreams."

The voice of Titus boomed unexpectedly among the pillars. "Will you two shut up? You're missing the essential. We are still an embassy, albeit to Horemheb on behalf of the Triple Alliance. Your father won't dare harm any of us. We're diplomats! So quit your worrying."

"He's got a point. A very good point. Worth a try."

"But Titus, what do we propose to Big Daddy of the two kingdoms?" I asked. "What do we say to him? What do we offer him?"

"I'll think of something," Titus replied. He raised one finger to point at me. "Besides, he's got you under contract. He'll probably be deliriously happy to see you. Just praise us and get him to shine his Ra-like benevolence upon us. I'll do the rest."

"But don't ask me to be polite to him," Tlaloc said. He was standing close to a pillar, running his fingers over the bas reliefs. "He must be a barbarian. Imagine! Getting his minions to cover up this lovely art with whitewash. What sort of moron is he?"

"A vengeful, murderous, bloodthirsty moron," Seneferu said, beginning to throw assorted baggage from the cart. "Fortunately, he loves flattery, but not from me."

"Rather clever, that. He's lowering the height of the baggage so he can get down safely. Thinks on his feet."

Nah. Just giving himself something to do to avoid contemplating the prospect of his impending family reunion.

Myriad strolled up to Tlaloc and put her arm around his waist. "Seneferu, does the Pharaoh like tits? Is he sex-mad? Could I possibly soothe his outrage?"

"Absolutely not. He loves only power."

"Okay... then how about I sidle up to him as seductively as possible, and while he is glorying in his self-satisfied immunity to my charms, as soon as I'm close enough I'll break his neck and then you get to be Pharaoh. That would solve everything, wouldn't it?"

"Now, wait just a moment," Titus said. "Not necessarily. We need a pact before I allow that to happen. Musso and Ashurbanipal will need guarantees."

"From the look on Seneferu's face, I'd say he is giving Myriad's proposal serious thought."

Not for long. Unless Horemheb is a complete idiot, I doubt he lets strangers get past his bodyguards.

"Tizoc was nice and informal. So was the Caique."

Yeah, but I suspect a Pharaoh is a stickler for protocol. Weren't they supposed to be Gods?

"In the case of Seneferu that would require enormous suspension of disbelief."

I have the feeling Horemheb is quite different.

"No point in debating. We won't know till we meet him."

Having reduced his distance from the floor, Seneferu slid over the end of the cart and landed on his feet. I'd expected him to crumple on impact, but once again he proved me wrong.

He issued instructions to the Assyrians. Evidently displeased, they immediately sat down as if in protest.

"Never mind them," Seneferu said. "I'm leaving them behind to greet Ashurbanipal. Best to keep the Assyrians out of my father's sight. That way we might stay alive long enough to be rescued." He waddled toward the open exit, though at a speed more reflective of his actual weight. A demi-god in a hurry.

Compared to the dim lighting of the hall, the scene beyond the gateway was a blaze of light. This struck me as odd.

Buddy-bod, we're halfway around the world... shouldn't it be dark outside? Nighttime?

"Uhmm… no. It was early morning when we left Pochtlan, so probably late afternoon here."

Don't you know?

"I'm just like you. No calculator in my brain. I'd need to consult the techgrid. Can't, of course."

I'm less than impressed.

"Just keep your wits about you and keep us alive. That's all I ask."

"Wait for me! Wait for me!" It was Beedlewood. We turned and saw him rushing toward us from the opposite end of the hall. Where had he been? What had he been up to?

"Probably masturbating behind a pillar. Getting rid of his excess enthusiasm."

Be nice.

Beedlewood caught up to us. "You'd have to see it to believe it," he spluttered, puffing to regain his breath. "Chamber at the other end. Taller than this room. Giant statue of a Pharoah, or a God, or a God-Pharoah. Whatever. Big boy!"

"Which one?" Tlaloc asked.

"Can't say. He's covered in gobs of white plaster, and whitewash on top of that."

Tlaloc struck the palm of his hand with his fist. "Damn these barbarians!"

Myriad's eyes shone with concern and pity. "You shouldn't be offended when the Gods are insulted. It really is a waste of time, you know. Calm yourself."

"I don't care about that. It's the art. Great art should be worshipped, not treated like garbage."

Titus chuckled. "I'm afraid you don't understand the purpose of art."

"Of course not. What do I know? I'm just an artist." Visibly upset, Tlaloc appeared poised to deliver a prolonged rant.

"Since our lives may depend on any and every word we say," Seneferu said, "I suggest you keep your high standards to yourself."

Stepping over the threshold stone was impossible. It was several paces deep and had to be crossed. As well, the enormous lintel hanging twenty feet overhead must have weighed forty tons or more. Passing underneath it made me shiver in apprehension. This was not a good place to be during an earthquake.

"Idiot. These nanotech plastic structures are all of a piece. The "individual" building stones are just an illusion, a decorative façade."

Yes, yes, I know, but it's a powerful illusion. Damned real to look at.

"So, don't look."

But I did, and noted the massive wooden doors folded back to either side. They hung on large, well-oiled metal hinges. And they looked movable. "Wolfgang, if we secure these doors shut, we can keep the Assyrians hidden from casual observation."

"Good idea. I wouldn't be surprised if the priests we saw fleeing were too terrified to note who and what we are. All the same, shut the Assyrians in, will you?"

Tlaloc and Myriad ran to the doors. They swung easily. Even better, a sturdy bar took but a moment to pull down and lock the temple doors firmly closed.

The immense open court beyond the gate lacked the colonnade I anticipated. Its perimeter consisted of high stone walls covered in bas reliefs. Predominantly, they depicted pharaohs striding forward with maces held high to smash in the skulls of writhing foes half their size. Dead bodies lay everywhere beneath the feet of the pharaohs. Here and there, cross-legged scribes were shown jotting

225

down statistics regarding assorted piles of ears, noses and other members cut from the dead.

Quite the ego tantrum.

"You think? I notice these haven't been whitewashed. Evidently, this is a message worth preserving."

At the far end of the court sat a portal framed by two massive pylons. To us, it was just an exit. From the outside, however, it would appear monumental, making anyone seeking entry feel small and insignificant. *A pretentious exercise in intimidation, seems to me.*

"There's nothing subtle about Pharaohs."

"Well, here comes a delegation," said Seneferu. "Once we get this over with, we'll have a better idea of our status."

A trio of baldies were approaching between the pylons. As they got closer, I noted that all three were wearing identical gold chains around their necks and holding identical wooden staffs in their hands. However, the gold knob atop the staff belonging to the lead baldie appeared larger than the others, being crowned by a spray of feathers. A sign of authority, perhaps.

"They're bald because Egyptian priests shave their heads. Their entire bodies in fact. Don't disrespect them. Next to the Pharoah's ministers, these are the real power in the land. If modern Pharaonic Egypt is anything like the ancient kingdom, that is."

What have they got against hair? A fetish for naked skin?

"Just being practical. Priests are supposed to be pure and spiritual. That's hard to achieve if you're covered in lice and mites. By the way, remember not to touch them. They shy away from hairy people."

They're really going to be creeped out once they get a good look at Tlaloc.

"Hmm, potentially useful, that."

The three priests halted before Seneferu. He gave no sign of acknowledgement, other than to stare stonily as if expecting them to fling themselves at his feet.

I was astonished to see that the "feathers" radiating from the top of the lead priest's staff was nothing more than a sponge-on-a-stick tied on with string. Rather took away from his aura of authority. What was equally astonishing, Seneferu was maintaining his fixed, remorseless expression, showing not so much as a twitch of his lips. But then, I wasn't chuckling either.

"Never laugh at underlings who may have the final word on whether you're allowed to meet a glorious leader. It's often the last mistake a diplomat ever makes."

Has your brain slipped into automatic mode? Of course I know that. I'm no fool.

"Just checking. You have a tendency to be distracted by your own thoughts."

Distracted by you, you mean. Stop it.

The lead priest, or whatever he was, dropped his staff and fell to his knees, head bowed, arms widespread in submission. His assistants did the same. Seneferu smiled, rather smugly I thought.

All at once, with unexpected speed and agility, the priest leaped to his feet, took two steps forward, and slapped Seneferu across his face, wiping away his smile. Then the priest stepped back two paces and dropped to his knees again. Twice more this happened, leaving Seneferu scowling indignantly. He'd evidently been caught off guard.

Now the three priests resumed standing in front of Seneferu with calm, neutral expressions as if patiently waiting for his command. Not even a hint of satisfaction in the visage of the one who'd done all the slapping. It had been a duty performed, nothing more.

"Not the usual protocol, I take it?" I whispered. Didn't know why. The priests probably didn't know techgrid English, so no need to worry about being overheard.

Seneferu sighed. "Showing respect for me as the Pharoah's son. Showing disrespect because my father considers me a traitor. At least their attitude is balanced. Annoying, though."

"Let's hope your father's response to your arrival is equally balanced," Titus commented.

The priest said something in a local language and marched off toward the exit gateway, accompanied by his sidekicks.

"They want us to follow them," Seneferu explained.

The three priests turned to the right and disappeared single file through an ordinary-sized doorway lost in the vast expanse of the wall defining the courtyard.

"Just realized something."

Another surprise epiphany? Terrific.

"What Seneferu revealed. These new Gogetters don't function like the open gateways of old. More like ambush predators that grab whatever's near by and shove it through, then shut down."

So?

"So, your vision of armies pouring through to invade is impossible. Your warning to Tizoc was nonsense."

I was reluctant to give in to this logic. Maybe there's a way to prop a Gogetter open, and Seneferu just hasn't discovered how yet?

"Mmm... it's peculiar. The techgrid knew it would go down, knew that transportation would plunge back to stone age levels. So why the last gasp effort to create new Gogetters? To keep long-distance communication open, at least in terms of couriers and embassies? Maybe a limited trade in luxury goods?"

So? Whatever works. Proves they had our welfare at heart.

"Heart? What heart? It's a machine mind. Dead even when it was alive."

Semantics again?

"And those caches. They set them up a century ago."

You're stating the obvious, as usual. Don't you ever get tired of doing that?

"This long-term planning... what's the ultimate goal? What have they got planned next?"

Maybe nothing. Automatic programming could be their ghost, and we could see less and less of that as time passes, bringing decay and entropy. Maybe they died sooner than they expected. Maybe their master plan was cut off at the knees. Maybe I'm beginning to get bored.

Seneferu beckoned to me from the doorway. "Rudwulf! Stop wool-gathering. You look like you're arguing with yourself. And the expression that comes over your face your face when you are doing it makes you appear constipated. Are you aware of that?"

I stood tall and strove to look dignified. "I never argue with myself when facing a mirror, so how would I know?"

"My Point is, you're wasting your time just standing there. Aren't you hungry? They probably have food on this side of the wall. Maybe something to drink. Come on. I'm the son of the Pharaoh. They owe me something. Like feeding me and keeping me alive. You can have my crumbs." And with that, he turned and waddled out of sight.

"But we ate less than an hour before climbing the pyramid to get to the portal," I muttered to myself. How could he be hungry already?

Myriad tapped me on the shoulder. "As your bodyguard, I advise you to follow. It's a bad idea to stay put pretending to be a statue. Even worse to separate before we know what we're up against."

"*She's right.*"

"Well, I'm thirsty," declared Beedlewood, pushing past. "I need to get drunk and relax."

Myriad gave me a not-so-gentle shove.

Fine. I'll move.

The doorway led us into a seemingly endless series of interconnected courtyards lined with mean mudbrick cells, hastily assembled. The walls weren't even plumb. I couldn't tell whether they were part of the plastic temple or recent construction. If they were fake, the bits of straw poking out of the bricks were a nice touch of authenticity.

"*Does have a temporary feel to it. Storage, or quarters for the maintenance crew, or both.*"

What maintenance? They can't replace or change a thing. This monolithic behemoth is as inert as the ones in Pochtlan.

"*Except for the doors. They moved just fine.*"

We entered a courtyard lined with mudbrick bins. Titus was already tearing though them looking for anything edible, and Beedlewood hurried to lend his assistance. Meanwhile, Seneferu sat on a sturdy wooden bench conferring with the three baldies. Mark and Olaf leaned against a wall, keeping their eyes on Beedlewood. I wondered about their motives. Myriad and Tlaloc passed by to explore the next courtyard.

Leaving me alone? So, all of a sudden, she thinks I'm safe?

"*Probably checking to make sure there aren't any armed men in there waiting to spring an ambush.*"

A dozen baldies emerged from the doorway Myriad had just gone through. Fortunately, they were not armed. Each carried a mop and bucket filled with whitewash. It slopped back and forth as they walked. They really seemed determined to make Tlaloc feel miserable.

"Don't worry about it," Seneferu called out, and I turned to listen. "The priests tell me Horemheb doesn't like any art portraying other Pharaohs or Gods. He's the only God to be worshipped. Calls himself Aten these days. This is new. Must have been triggered by the collapse. He always was an opportunist, always figuring new angles, the bastard. You'll probably fall in love when you meet him. He's practically a Smiter himself." So saying, he switched his attention back to the priests.

Is he calling me a narcissist?

"It's the first good news since we arrived. You and Horemheb may be compatible."

Myriad reappeared in the doorway. "Rudwulf! Come here!"

I complied. I figured I might as well, since I had nothing else to do.

The next courtyard was identical to the previous one except for one thing, an open-air Roman-style latrine.

"Thank you," I said. "Will come in handy later, I'm sure."

"No, look," she insisted, pointing at a group of baldies clustered at the near end of the latrine where water poured from a lion's-mouth spout set high in a mudbrick wall. They appeared to be lashing planks together to form a wooden trough. I was immediately curious.

A query in the local language drifted past my ears. It came from Titus, who had followed me while munching on a locust. One of the baldies who accompanied him answered back in testy tones, annoyed at being interrupted. What are they speaking?

"Sounds like a bit of a pidgin mix to me, some Egyptian, some Coptic, Arabic, maybe some Aramaic. Figures Titus is fluent. But what's important is what they're saying."

Which is?

"Ask Titus."

I looked to Titus. He gulped down the last of the insect, then said, "The locals are frustrated. Gigantic though this temple complex is, that spout is the only source of water. They want to divert part of the flow into a plaster basin they have yet to construct. But first they want to see if their runoff gizmo will work. I don't think they know what they're doing."

I noticed a standard leaning against the wall near the spout. An image of an ostrich-feather fan sprang naturally to mind. However, the spray of feathers was represented by three sponge-on-a-sticks sprouting from a crossbeam. I pointed. "What's with that?"

Titus grimaced. "Some kind of fetish. Further proof they're ignorant."

"I think they're honouring the water source," Myriad said. "They're being respectful."

"There are several fan standards visible in the temple reliefs they haven't covered up yet," added Tlaloc. "I think this is meant to imitate them. See? Art can be influential. Important, even."

"You understand what this means?"

That the techgrid's plan is consistent? A Roman latrine everywhere the mushrooms sprout?

"No, it means you are right. The techgrid screwed up. This reborn temple isn't user friendly. It's poorly designed, or at least, incompletely designed. The master plan cut short, as you said. Our future may not be as utopian as the tech intended."

So? Just means we improvise, like these baldies.

"Don't you understand? The techgrid planned for us to survive its demise. This flaw indicates their plan isn't fully in place. Maybe we're doomed. All of us. The entire human race."

For a moment I contemplated the abyss. Then…

Screw it. Let's get drunk.

CHAPTER EIGHTEEN

Exploring further proved the baldies had set themselves up quite nicely. Other mudbrick courtyards teemed with servants who, unlike the priests, had hair, albeit close-cropped. They were bustling about, stockpiling goods brought by endless lines of porters, who not only had hair but wore loincloths instead of kilts—all clothes made from good Egyptian cotton. I was unable to locate the entrance gates because I couldn't resist settling down where fresh-baked bread and pitchers of beer were plentiful.

"Shouldn't you be drinking water?"

My hangover this morning isn't extreme, but I do have the strange conviction that if I pull all my teeth out with a pair of pliers, I'll feel better.

"Serves you right."

Shouldn't you be capable of absorbing my pain on my behalf?

"You've mentioned this absurd theory of yours many times. Fortunately, my mind is completely separate from your body abuse. My mind is clear as a bell."

Empty, you mean.

"You're the void king, not me."

I was sitting with my legs splayed out in the dirt of the courtyard, my back pressed against the outside of a cell wall. I could hear Seneferu snoring inside. A nameless servant had been dutiful enough to place three pitchers of weak beer within easy reach. That was good. The others had awakened before I did and gone off to explore. That was bad. Weren't we supposed to stick together?

Yet another batch of baldies filed past. Six of them. I had to draw up my legs to avoid being stepped on.
They have the full width of the courtyard to wander in. What motivates them to detour in order to trample me?
"I don't think they even noticed you. They're intent on carrying on the purification of the temple."
Is that what you call the whitewashing?
"So Seneferu claims."
I stared after the priests as they trotted into the next courtyard. *What's with the mops and metal buckets? That's old tech.*
"Yes, and I've noticed they use metal safety pins to keep their kilts closed. Almost as if they're not reconciled to entering the new stone-age."
No sooner had the priests left than Myriad appeared in the same doorway, bearing a large ceramic mug. She knelt beside me and offered it to me. "Be careful, it's hot."
I took the mug in hand. Warm, but not hot, and cooling rapidly. "What is it?"
She smiled. "Coffee, I think. Tastes like it anyway."
I gazed at the black liquid. Sniffed it. Sure enough, it smelled like coffee. *Where'd the Egyptians get coffee?*
"Ethiopia is only a month or two distant by camel."
But the ancients never drank coffee.
"True, but their modern descendants started at some point."
When?
"I don't know. Does it matter? Maybe this is leftover ersatz from the sustenance vats. More proof the current crowd is clinging to the past."
What happens when they run out?
"Well, then, they'll have to round up some camels to start trading with Ethiopia. If they can find any. I have a vague memory they went extinct."

235

Myriad chuckled. Her eyes sparkled. She appeared to be in fine fettle for someone who had drunk twice as much beer as I did. "Why do you always take so long to make up your mind? Drink! It's good coffee. It'll snap your thoughts into sharp focus."

"Terrific. All the better to enjoy my headache." Nevertheless, I started sipping. Didn't know whether it was going to wake me up, but it was definitely strong enough to aid my digestion.

I'm grateful for small, mundane triumphs at this point. With increased consciousness my ambitions will return.

"Typical addict. Focused on micro-details. Obsessive."

I'll focus on the world's problems once I can think straight.

I became aware of Tlaloc looming over me. He had something cupped in his hands. "Look what I made," he said. He knelt and placed the object on the ground in front of us. It was a bust of Myriad four inches in height. The likeness was remarkable, considering it was made of wet mud and straw that hindered fine detail.

Myriad's eyes shone with delight. "Beautiful! I love it."

"Yeah, it's pretty good," I admitted. What else could I say? Left to my own talent all I'd be capable of doing is drawing a lively stick figure of her.

"Best not to. She wouldn't be impressed."

"I found where they were making mud bricks to add to the complex," Tlaloc said. "I grabbed a fresh one when they laid it out to dry. They didn't seem to mind. Well, maybe the scribe keeping count did mind a little, but he didn't try to stop me. Once they saw what I was doing, they all seemed impressed."

"Of course," Myriad said. "Everyone loves what you do."

I glanced up at the cloud cover. It seemed as dense as any I'd ever seen. But was it brighter here, and warmer? How long does it take mud bricks to dry?

"*Longer than it did thousands of years ago. So what? Not your problem.*"

Seneferu came bumbling out of the cell, half-awake, and looking half-dead. "Is that coffee I smell?" He spotted the mug in my hands. "Give that to me. I need it."

I raised the mug high, but Seneferu stumbled forward to grab it and trod the bust into the dirt without noticing. Behind him, Tlaloc shot to his feet, visibly enraged. Myriad gestured at her lover to sit back down. "It was only a test study," she murmured. "You'll do better once Horemheb lets you have a block of marble."

The anger faded from Tlaloc's eyes. He looked thoughtful, contemplative. "Yes… Luna marble. You'd look good in Luna marble… as Isis. As the Goddess Isis…. Seated on your divine throne. I'd do you as a full figure. Statuesque. Dignified. Overpowering."

Myriad clapped her hands in glee. "Sounds wonderful. What kind of get-up does she wear?"

"As little as possible," I suggested.

"White tunic and blue robe," Seneferu said. "Or the other way around. Damn, that coffee was good. Makes me feel almost alert enough to outwit my father."

"You may get your chance." Titus had joined us, along with Beedlewood and Mark and Olaf. They appeared preternaturally alert too. Excited, even.

"This isn't good. Something's got them worked up."

"We just came down from the roof of the temple," Mark said.

Beedlewood swept his arms wide. "Fantastic view. Overlooking the Nile. What a magnificent river! The Thames is nothing in comparison."

"You'll like it, Tlaloc," Olaf added. "There are ships everywhere along the bank. A forest of masts. Dozens of ships."

"More to the point," said Titus, "there's a procession coming up from the ships. Hundreds of men. Dozens of standards and banners. I think it's your father." He smiled sweetly. Diplomats love bearing bad news. Always.

Seneferu scratched the tip of his pudgy nose. "Is there any more coffee? I need more coffee."

Drums. Already I could hear drums, and peculiar horn blasts that made me think of bubbles of sound bursting against piles of wet meat in asynchronous rhythm. It was the mother of all marching music, all beat, no melody, and it was getting louder. I hated it.

The chief baldie appeared. Imperiously, he snapped his fingers, then sauntered away.

"That's how you can tell that his Lord and Master is coming. Trickle-down power on display."

Seneferu dropped his coffee mug and trailed after the priest in his usual ponderous fashion. "Might as well get this over with. We all have to die sometime."

Speak for yourself.

"No, an opportunity to get rid of Wolfgang, I hope."

Glumly, we followed Seneferu through courtyard after courtyard. At last, we reached the temple forecourt and joined the priest who had led us there. I found it odd there were no other baldies present. Too scared, perhaps?

The musical atrocities halted. Now we were conscious only of the sound of marching feet. Sure enough, a military band, instruments now silent, came through the main entrance and halted just inside, to right of centre. I figured the drums must be standard issue, though the massed tubas were a surprise. But what really got my attention was the fact all the band members were wearing lederhosen. Cotton lederhosen.

Then entered a parade of beautiful young women wearing diaphanous gowns of sheer cotton. They carried ceramic beer steins, one in each hand, but disappointingly bereft of beer. The girls wound up standing to the left of the gateway.

You call me obsessed with detail? Methinks Hermann Horemheb is a good deal more obsessed than I am.

"Yes, with his ancestry. *I am beginning to question his sanity.*"

A phalanx of priests—bald, shirtless, wearing lederhosen instead of kilts—now came through the gate. They advanced with the solemnity of coffin-bearers, except their burden was a large, ornate desk, probably stolen from some museum. They set the furniture piece down in front of us, then moved away.

Behind them, a pair of especially solemn priests brought forth a traditional office chair, complete with fake leather cover (depressingly black and wrinkled), and equipped with uncomfortable arm rests. Definitely a museum piece.

Then it got worse. A squad of grim-faced men wearing modern khaki uniforms, including sturdy boots and even sturdier helmets, trotted forward and formed a line immediately in front of the desk. They didn't come to attention but rather stood at ease, keeping their weapons pointed straight at us.

"Ooooh," Mark moaned. "Wonderful. Ak-47s. I've only seen pictures. I want one."

"Me, too," Olaf said. "Best resumé possible."

"I don't think I'll risk killing the old boy," Myriad whispered in my ear. Tlaloc shushed her. Sensible fellow.

More soldiers entered and took up positions behind the desk, filling the space from wall to wall but leaving a wide corridor in the centre. Instead of AK-47s, each bore an axe resting on the right shoulder. Axes with metal blades.

Those are steel blades! Where'd Horemheb get those?

"This guy hates the new stone age."

The Pharoah came in alone, striding confidently down the aisle to plop himself nonchalantly into his cruddy chair like a minor executive. I was disappointed. Instead of a gold-encrusted kilt and a fan of lapis lazuli covering his chest, not to mention the traditional, majestic double crown of Upper and Lower Egypt, he sported a charcoal-grey business suit, shiny white shirt, blood-red tie, black leather shoes, and gold cufflinks. He looked like a cliché figure from the past, a pre-war icon. A man with no imagination.

"At least he's not wearing lederhosen."

The pharoah leaned forward and rapped his fingers sharply on the desk. "Let's call this meeting to order. I demand a quarterly report!"

"Majesty!" Titus shouted. "I am the leader of our expedition. Allow me to—"

"Shut up, worm! I know who you are. I'm not interested in talking to you. I never talk with my enemies." His gaze turned upon his son. "Wolfgang, why isn't Titus dead? Why did you disobey my orders?"

What? What-what?

"*Listen. Concentrate and listen.*"

Seneferu slowly settled into a crosslegged sitting position. He looked curiously comfortable, as if he had truly come home. His fear had entirely left him.

"Revered Father," he began, "I launched the missile, and its aim was true, but unfortunately Titus survived. The Grand Smiter, in his infinite wisdom, chose to save him, undoubtedly in order to serve our purpose."

"So, you were never the target?"

Quiet. Don't distract me. Our lives depend on this madman and his whims.

Horemheb glanced at each of us in turn. "Which one is the Smiter? The hairy one?"

I raised my hand.

"You don't look like much."

"I like to blend in," I said. "Easier to kill that way."

"Hmmm." The Pharaoh studied me for several long moments, his expression unreadable. Then he smiled and put his feet on the desk, and we could relax.

"You have a fantastic reputation," he said. "Near mythological. A regular Hercules. Slaughtered more people than anyone I know."

Beedlewood uttered a heartfelt gasp but made no comment.

"I am efficient, and will serve you well," I replied, keeping my voice firm and rock-hard.

"Of course you will, and I will shower you with gold as your reward. Just be aware that if you betray me the shower will consist of molten gold."

I bowed low. "I never betray my clients."

"So I have heard. You are an amusing fellow. I like an honest murderer."

"May I ask a question?"

The Pharaoh frowned. "Don't worry. It will be pure gold, not adulterated."

"No, not that. I want to ask, since you sent Seneferu halfway around the world to hire me, why attempt to kill me? Seems contradictory, a waste of effort."

Horemheb smiled, showing a brief twitch of menace at the corners of his lips. "The contract was utterly sincere. But when Titus boarded your aircraft, and my son informed me of this, the opportunity to strike a blow against the machinations of the Triple Alliance was too useful to ignore. In comparison to that, you were expendable."

I purposely did not react. Said nothing and remained as inert as a statue.

The Pharaoh's smile became genuine. "But there's no need to speak of this. Your incredible skill saved you to further my aims. As the living God, I praise myself for ordaining my good luck."

Seneferu spoke up. "Don't forget me, Father. It was I who signed Smiter. I who safely brought him here."

Titus could contain himself no longer. "Traitor!" he shouted. "You serve Ashurbanipal and Mussolini! Have you forgotten your Pharaoh father condemned you to death?"

"Pay him no mind, Divine Dad," Seneferu said quietly. "Titus suffers from the proverbial professor's vice. All abstract rationalizations and no deeds. He thinks too much."

"Yes, we took advantage of him," Horemheb commented. "A ploy to plunge his mind into the unreal. I relish fooling creatures who depend on flowcharts and algorithms. They never know when to strike. They're too busy figuring out how to react."

He swung his legs off the desk and leaned forward, his eyes intent and glittering. "You see, although I am a magnificent CEO who appreciates a proper pie chart as much as any state-sanctioned philosopher, what I really am is a predator, a lion of the desert. I do so enjoy stalking."

Open-mouthed in shock, Titus abandoned his anger. He slowly raised his jaw and cast down his eyes. No doubt he regretted his indiscretion.

"Stupid fool. Always was too impulsive."

I can do better.

"Majesty, I am eager to get to work," I stated. "I require a comfortable base of operations, a few dozen servants, free transportation, easy access to everything, the total cooperation of your bureaucracy, police and military, absolute immunity to law and taxes, an expense account—gold will do if you have no monetary system—and, oh, a dozen AK-47s with plenty of ammo."

The Pharaoh blinked. "*This* is how you mingle unseen with my loyal subjects?"

"The power you grant me will enable me to survey your kingdom with utmost efficiency and tact. Only then I can start reducing the excess population to your satisfaction."

"Wolfgang, was any of this in the contract?"

Seneferu appeared to search his memory. "I believe the appropriate clause was, 'All measures appropriate to the Smiter's function will be granted, including freedom of action, etc., etc.' My intention was not to amend the contract till he actually showed up, subject to your approval."

The Pharaoh produced another mirthless smile. "That's unimportant now. Rudwulf, I note that your contract is to destroy the Assyrian army, yet your demands imply that you think I want you to cull my people."

"Oh, damn. Another job prospect shot all to your Norse version of Hell."

Patience. I'm sure he wants me to kill somebody. Otherwise, we'd already be dead.

Horemheb leaned back, hands clasped behind his head. We were in for a lecture. "I ran the kingdom smoothly when the techgrid was up. Accomplished wonders. But for some stupid reason both the soil and the people were mostly infertile. No matter how cleverly I employed technology to exploit our resources, there was never enough. Our resources shrank faster than our population decreased. Cross purposes, you might say. Of course, I could have ordered a massacre or two, but the people were already on the verge of revolt, what with starving and all. You see my plight. I could solve their problem by killing them, but they wouldn't like that. I could lose my throne."

"It's every ruler's dilemma," I replied. "That's where I come in. I am the solution."

"You were, yes, till the techgrid crashed and everything stopped working. I nearly went insane."

"Cross out the word 'nearly.'"

"Fortunately, I recovered quickly. I remembered how Eve had plucked the Ur-AK-47 from the tree of knowledge and given it to Adam, thus emboldening him to lead Eve out of the boring Garden of Eden and enter the exciting wild lands where they transformed into the Gods Shu and Tefnut, the progenitors of humankind."

"Right, and I'm the queen of Sheba."

Quiet!

"Divinely inspired by my divine self, I made use of all salvageable technical relics, including the arsenal I had had techgrid assemble for me—blessed be my divine insight—to instill order. Then the miracle occurred, undoubtedly according to my will. People began to fuck like crazy, and as a result the soil regenerated. The land is fertile again. Aren't I great?"

I bowed low. "It goes without saying, Majesty."

"So, you see, I can afford my people now. I have no reason to exterminate any of them."

"And yet, surely, there are enemies. There are always enemies."

"Not among my people, no," replied the Pharoah, pleasure and delight momentarily visible on his face. "My people love me now. They are so sweet. But beyond my frontiers..." His face clouded over. "Filthy scum and jealous perverts, drenched in greed and avarice. And that's just their ordinary followers. Ashurbanipal and Mussolini are beyond vile. Pesky demons. How dare they! I want them killed. And their minions. All of them! Every last one! I want no native problems for my settlers. That's why I contracted you to defeat Ashurbanipal. Understood?" Pharaoh had risen to his feet, his face flushed dark red.

It was difficult not to laugh, but I managed. "Rest assured; measures are in place. I have planned carefully. I will not fail you."

"Good. Good. Keep it up. Then we can plot our escape."

For once, it seemed, Titus and Beedlewood had achieved unity of thought. They both appeared terrified. Myriad, on the other hand, remained calm and serene. She had seen it all before. Seneferu, too, was placid and relaxed. But I had the distinct impression that Mark, Olaf, and above all, Tlaloc, were puzzled and deeply concerned. Good. Could this be the beginning of a rift between him and Myriad?

"You're distracting yourself with stray, useless thoughts. Focus. Focus!"

Horemheb was drifting toward calm. "You see how wise I am? Thanks to me, you don't have to waste time getting to know my people. You can concentrate on the idiot inhabitants of Assyria and Italy. And as you say, 'measures are in place,' so you are already primed and ready. You have but to give the command and they are destroyed. When will you do this? Now? Tonight? Perhaps tomorrow? Don't keep me waiting too long. I've been dreaming about this for years. Many long, long years."

"Majesty, it is a bit more complicated than that," I said, bowing low once more. A good habit to indulge in, I thought. Certainly, Horemheb seemed to like it. "Genocide comes easy to me. It is my profession, and no one is better at it than I."

"But you have some kind of excuse to delay?" muttered the Pharaoh, eyebrows rising, forehead furrowing. Mustn't let him complete his suspicions.

"It's not enough simply to kill them. You must witness their downfall firsthand. Be able to splash in their blood. Delight at their dying screams. Revel in their anguish."

"True, true. It must be personal. You can arrange this? I would be grateful beyond your imagination, especially if you have Ashurbanipal and Mussolini stuffed so I can cart their bodies around for display wherever I travel. I want to amuse and impress my people. They need to know their living God has a sense of humour. A touch of the human, you might say."

"It must be done right. Choreographed to perfection. The greatest ritual ever conceived. There are certain… ah, secret activities I must direct in order to finish my preparations. A month should suffice. Five weeks at most. Guaranteed."

Horemheb smiled. He was pleased.

All at once, a flash of blinding blue light erased the daylight.

"Not again!"

CHAPTER NINETEEN

The light faded, or withdrew, dissipated or disappeared. Main thing was, it went away. I didn't care how. I needed to rub the blue from my eyes. Needed to make them stop hurting.

"Was that flash sky-blue?" Horemheb demanded. "I've never seen the sky. Was that colour authentic? Anybody know? Am I about to have a revelation? Was that me? An expression of the divine? What's going on?" He was beginning to sound frantic.

"He's looking for an omen."

I'll make something up. Give me a moment.

Drums sounded. They boomed within the hypostyle hall of the temple, as deep and thunderous as the great drums of Pochtlan. Had Tizoc sent a follow-up embassy?

"Or perhaps an invading army?"

Impossible. That's impossible. Isn't it?

A shrill trumpet wailed and shrieked. Truly annoying.

Except for Titus. He was jumping with glee, wearing an ecstatic expression on his face. "The sacred horn of Tiglath-pileser! It's the Great King Ashurbanipal!" He turned to face Horemheb, actually shaking his fist at him, saying, "Now you're going to get yours." Among the drumbeats and trumpet blasts, I heard a raft of human activity. The measured tread of soldiers. Shouted commands. The full panoply of jangling accoutrements. Many things noisy and powerful.

The Pharaoh blanched. He waved his soldiers forward. "The enemy is in the temple. Kill them!"

"Sorry! Sorry! Sorry! Sorry! Sorry!—"

Buddy-bod was screaming in my mind. His thoughts drove me to my knees. Out of the corner of my eye I could see Myriad writhing on the ground.

"Sorry! Sorry! Sorry! Sorry!—"

Seneferu too. The Pharoah. Titus. Beedlewood. Everyone with a Mate.

"Sorry! Sorry! Sorry!—"

Tlaloc knelt over Myriad, trying and failing to gather her into a calming embrace.

"Sorry! Sorry!—"

Mark and Olaf were standing back-to-back, sword and axes at the ready.

"Sorry!—"

Meanwhile, the chief baldie was rocking back and forth with laughter. He was having a great time.

I was in agony.

Flash! Another blue flash. Then another. Another. A strobing effect. Continuous flashing. Continuous waves of blue light washing everything from sight. A torrent of light crushing my soul. A relentless tide of light. An ocean of light. And it was all so damned blue.

It wasn't fair. Blue was my favourite colour, but not when it was this painful.

Make it stop. Make it stop. Make it stop!

Everything quit—the light, the martial racket—leaving nothing but sharp, residual pain. Slowly, my eyes adjusted to the daylight filling the courtyard. I lay sprawled on the pavement, panting hard, out of breath. I found myself staring at Horemheb's legs. They were sticking out from behind his desk. He'd been knocked flat, too. His left shoe twitched. Still alive then.

Buddy-bod, why did you do that?

"I didn't. I was overridden. Hurt me as much as it hurt you."

I struggled shakily to my feet. *Overridden by whom?*

"The techgrid, I guess. No other suspects spring to mind."

I shook my head, desperately trying to clear my thoughts. Plus, I was hoping to put an end to the chills running up and down my spine.

It spoke through all the Mates simultaneously? Has that ever happened before?

"Not that I can remember."

Why would it apologise?

"Because it knew it was about to screw up?"

So, it is still alive?

"Felt more like it was dying."

The others had regained their footing and were staring silently at something behind me. I turned to see what they were looking at.

My gaze alit first on the AK-47 guys. They'd been blown off their feet and now lay where they'd fallen, some on their backs, some on their bellies, but all pointing their guns at—

It took me a good several seconds to comprehend what it was they were aiming at. The temple doors had been torn off their hinges and flung to the pavement. In their place was an extrusion similar to freshly squeezed toothpaste spilling out of its tube, now frozen into an immobile blob of flesh and cloth and metal resembling a 3-D collage of texture and material constructed by a butcher. There was remarkably little blood, or any other bodily fluids, for that matter. Liquid couldn't flow when bodies were so tightly compressed. Merely a little seepage visible. But what caught my attention was something unique. Something important.

"Did I do that?" came the wavering voice of Horemheb. He sounded riddled with doubt.

"No. I did." I stated loudly. I sauntered casually toward the blob, exuding all the confidence and triumph I could muster. Years of experience were coming to my rescue. This would be my supreme moment. Or maybe it wouldn't.

"Yes. Don't blow it."

I reached up and knocked loose the helmet I'd spotted projecting from the blob, catching it as it fell. Of course I'd recognized it. Had seen it often enough in the tabloid vids. Myriad always thought it quite fetching. Made of gold—though more likely it was a gold alloy—it sported two horns, each a foot high, with a radiant sun disc suspended between them. The horns were bent and the disc slightly crumpled, but it remained a beautiful piece of megalomania, nonetheless.

"Behold the crown of Ashurbanipal!" I shouted. "It is as dead as he is."

Paranoid or not, Horemheb abandoned his habitual caution to rush forward and grab the helmet from my hands. He turned it over and peered inside. "Look! Look! Still a bit of flesh inside. Isn't it delightful? Isn't it wonderful?"

Slowly, solemnly, he placed the helmet on his own head. He shivered in triumph. "I adopt the crown of the vanquished. Hail me!" Never mind that it clashed with his business suit. Somehow the blood trickling down his forehead tied the whole ensemble together.

Again, I bowed low. Now would be a good time to ask the Pharaoh for favours. For some reason, however, my mind was a blank. I couldn't think of anything to request.

"Don't push our luck."

Horemheb folded his arms and regarded me thoughtfully. "How did you accomplish my triumph? How could you possibly arrange this?"

"I must have my trade secrets," I replied. "Don't want to give my enemies any pointers. Surely all that counts is the final result? The rest is mere detail."

"Fair enough. Only losers question success. But tell me this much: do you have something in mind for Mussolini? Something equally entertaining?"

"Absolutely. Guaranteed."

The Pharaoh's eyes focused on the carnage behind me. "Pity there's nothing left to stuff. Nothing that can be separated out, anyway. People will be so disappointed."

"I'll make sure Mussolini falls into your hands. You can have him stuffed while he is still alive."

"Capital idea. I like the way you think."

A whiff of bodily fluids caught the attention of my nostrils. Worse, the condensed mass of Assyrians would soon begin to break down. "Majesty, this sacred temple is about to be profaned by bodily decomposition on a scale not seen for centuries. Most unsanitary," I pointed out. "Might it not be wise to have your men fill this courtyard with sand? And lime?"

For a moment Horemheb appeared thoughtful, as if seriously considering my proposal. He looked up to contemplate the clouds. Then he laughed.

"I rather like the odour of death," he said. "It's good for morale. Besides, the vultures are gathering."

"Never any danger of them going extinct."

I glanced upward. Yes, there were large black birds circling in the thermals. They seemed to be gathering from all directions. Sharp-eyed bastards.

"That's fine," I said. "They'll take care of Ashurbanipal and his escorts. But have you forgotten the thousands of dead jammed inside the temple like a large haggis in a small can? They don't even have room enough to rot."

"And have you forgotten vultures like to burrow through corpses to get at the good stuff?" the Pharaoh responded gleefully. "They'll be tunnelling like moles. Reduce that army to bones in no time."

"You'll wind up with thousands of vultures flopping about so stuffed with human flesh they'll be unable to fly."

"Great idea!" said Horemheb, gripped by a gust of enthusiasm. His eyes gleamed. "They'll be easy to catch. I'll have my men stuff them and mount them high on the walls gazing down at the bones with beady glass eyes. The effect will be dramatic. The temple will become a place of pilgrimage for young school children. They'll grow up impressed with my power."

"I bet they will."

"By the way, what's a haggis?"

I hesitated. I'd remembered the proverb but wasn't clear on the details. "Something the clans of Scotland used to eat to terrify their enemies."

"Really? Usually, my name alone does that. But it's worth looking into. Would haggis grow in this climate?"

"No idea."

"Hmmm…" Shifting his gaze to the baldie, Horemheb issued a series of short, precise commands. The priest nodded his head and took off at the double. Then the Pharoah turned his attention back to me.

"I've given instructions that you and your party are to be well served. I even grant you Titus as a war trophy, or souvenir, however you interpret my gift. Interrogate him. Annoy the piss out of him. But be ready by nightfall to attend a banquet on my floating palace. And bring your friends. And Titus. He'll be good for a laugh."

I risked bowing low once more. "As your Majesty wills."

"Naturally." Horemheb snapped his fingers. "Wolfgang! Come here."

Seneferu approached his father-God. He was probably attempting to stride manfully. Truth to tell, however, his gait more closely imitated the rolling strut of a corpulent goose. "I am here, Holy Dad."

The Pharaoh put his arm around Seneferu's shoulders. "You are back in my good graces. Come back with me to my barge. We have much to talk about. Your sunstone, for instance. And the fate of your son."

Seneferu uttered a pained-sounding sigh. "Do I have to? I've walked so much already today, and the Nile is like a thousand miles away."

Horemheb gave his son a quick hug. "You could lie on your back and I'll have my men drag you by the heels. Your belly will be a comfortable place for me to sit as we talk."

"I'll walk. I'll walk." Seneferu declared quickly. Then, apparently desperate to change the subject, he blurted out "So, how's mom these days?"

"The Queen, my sister and the mother of your child?" Horemheb asked, frowning slightly. "I'm not sure. We don't seem to have much to talk about lately. But I imagine seeing her son-lover again will perk her up. Keep in mind that I'll kill you if you ever touch her again."

"Wouldn't think of it. Just want to say hello."

As Horemheb began leading his son away, a detail of guards quickly formed up around them. The last fading words I heard were the Pharaoh saying to Wolfgang, "Did I ever tell you about the time I had your older brother flayed alive?"

"I'm looking forward to the party he's throwing for us."

Don't be sarcastic. I'm sure it'll be fun.

"You *are* a monster!" Beedlewood rushed over to me, an expression of horror etched on his face. That and confusion.

"Really?" I replied. "Compared to Horemheb? You think he's a saint?"

"I'd decided you were too easygoing and stupid to be a mass murderer."

I gestured at the Assyrian blob. It was definitely starting to reek. "Yet this happened. You have to admit this will enhance my reputation. Be good for business."

"How can you be so callous? That was thousands of innocent men!"

"These guys? Assyrian soldiers? Cogs in a killing machine? Innocent?"

"Don't ignore his anger. Tell him the truth. Otherwise, he might interfere to the point of getting us killed. The wrong word to Horemheb and we're dead."

Oh, all right. I hate the way you prioritize options. Takes away my sense of free will.

"Beedlewood, think about it. How did I trick Ashurbanipal into pushing an army through the portal? How did I arrange for the portal to go berserk and malfunction at precisely the right moment? How did I murder all these men?"

"I don't know." Beedlewood's voice was suddenly soft and weary. I was getting through to him. Or maybe his mind was going.

"Point is, I didn't. I had nothing to do with it. It just happened. That's all. Nothing to do with me. I simply took advantage of the event, the happening, the miracle, call it what you will."

There was no expression in Beedlewood's eyes. The mind staring through them had evidently gone blank. Not surprising. It was hard to argue against the existence of something that didn't exist.

"The world is in a mess," I explained. "Not enough resources. Too many people. I hire myself out to cull populations, but I don't actually have to do anything. Something always happens. A famine. A failed revolution. A botched coup. A natural disaster. All sorts of inevitable catastrophes. All I do is take credit for them. And get paid.

Handsomely. Because the disasters keep getting worse, and my reputation more formidable, so my price keeps rising. Best job I ever had. Even when the rest of the Smiter's Guild was still alive, I was always the top earner."

That did it. Beetlewood's lips were quivering. His expression appeared to alternate between fear and despair. Made me certain I'd broken his brain, and that he was now teetering on the verge of a mental collapse. Not a happy man.

"Rudwulf is a fucking con artist," Myriad added. "Never harmed a dung beetle. I, on the other hand, have killed more than a dozen fools who tried to cross him. Make sure I don't have to add you to my list."

Beedlewood dropped to his knees, clinging to his staff as if it were the only thing keeping him upright. "I don't believe it. I can't believe it."

"Too stupid for words? Reality can't be that dumb?" I smiled. "That's why I get away with it. My service is my best camouflage, my best protection. Nobody wants to believe that I could be that lucky. Therefore, I *must* be a miracle worker."

"The average person has one or two Lucks dwelling within them," Myriad explained. "Rudwulf has an army of Lucks. He's the luckiest man I know."

"*Indeed. Look at the others. Look how they are reacting.*"

I took a quick survey. Tlaloc was beaming at Myriad. His respect for her had obviously increased. Olaf and Mark were gazing on me as if admiring me. So, I had gone up in their estimation. Titus, on the other hand…

Titus was sitting cross-legged, absently tracing patterns on the pavement with his fingers. The obsequious schemer was apparently gone. Instead, he had a distant, defeated air about him.

"So," he said with a sigh, "how are you going to deliver up Mussolini to Horemheb? What diabolical fate will be his?"

I shrugged. "I don't know. I never know. But one thing is certain: the unexpected always happens. I can take that for granted. And take credit. No matter what goes wrong, I always wind up celebrated and rewarded. Every time. Without fail. Makes for a stress-free life."

"Liar. You'd worry yourself to death if it weren't for me."

"Musso has many Lucks but not as many as yours," Titus stated in a calm voice.. "He can't win. Sooner or later, you are going to defeat him."

"Which is why Horemheb is going to give me a shitload of gold."

"And why I am switching my allegiance to you. Can't go against the Fates."

"True," I said. "The Norns are implacable."

Olaf clapped his hands. "I've got it!" he cried. "Every time you kill a fool, his Lucks abandon his carcass and take up residence in yours! No wonder your success grows exponentially with every hit."

I couldn't help noticing Mark was gazing at Olaf the same way Tlaloc looked at Myriad. Smitten with admiration. Truly bonded. Well, good for Mark and Olaf, but thinking of Myriad and Tlaloc in those terms was not good for me.

I shook my head to refocus my attention on the discussion at hand. "Ah, but I didn't kill the Great King. The Norns did. For which even you have fallen into the trip of giving me credit. You see how it works?"

"And I thought I was a successful fraud," Beedlewood muttered.

"What are you saying?" I demanded. "That you're something like me?"

"No, no, never mind. I remain true to my faith… er, well, true to me at any rate."

"That must mean I have your support."

Beedlewood was silent for several long moments. "I can't work with Horemheb. The joy of his citizens is the last thing on his mind. I need to keep a low profile. Therefore, I'll be your humble footstool, nothing more."

"Good."

"Congratulations, you've managed to tame both Beetlewood and Titus."

Oh, they'll betray me soon enough. A temporary reprieve, that's all I've got.

Baldies entered the courtyard. Several carried bowls of scented water. They dabbed clean cloths in the water and gently wiped our faces and hands. It was annoying but also refreshing. Almost made up for the stench of the dead Assyrians. One of the baldies spoke calmly and made a sweeping gesture with his hand, apparently waving us towards the servants' quarters.

"Titus? Can you translate?" I asked.

"They've prepared a meal for us, and comfortable couches to recline on."

A dozen hungry vultures thumped down on the pavement and headed in ungainly hops toward the blob. More birds were swooping in to join them. This was not going to be a pretty sight.

"Let us leave their feast and go to ours," I said, fancying that I spoke with a lordly air. "But don't eat too much. Leave room for the delicacies Horemheb will serve us."

"Probably Seneferu, boiled and stuffed with ostrich."

Fine, you eat him and I'll eat the ostrich.

"Methinks you are enjoying your temporary streak of luck too much. It's not as if it's going to last. Especially with Horemheb around."

A chill clung briefly to my spine. You want to be serious? Okay, how about this. What happened when the techgrid made you shout? Was it a two-way connection? Were you in communication? Could you access the memory banks? Was it like old times? Bosom buddies again?

"No. Nothing like that. I just had an uncontrollable urge to shout."

In unison with Fuzz Bucket, Fucky Loo, and the other Mates? Because that's what happened. Did you see into their minds? Were you one with them?

"I couldn't see into anyone's mind, not even yours. My own mind was a blank. All I could think, all I wanted to do, was apologise."

And why in Frigg's name would the techgrid want you to do that? It did what I needed it to do. Kill a bunch of Assyrians.

"I think... I suspect... it apologised for being out of control, for breaking down. If Ashurbanipal's army had successfully exited the temple, Horemheb would be dead, Seneferu would be Pharaoh, and both he and Ashurbanipal, not to mention Titus, would be praising you to the skies for their success. Because, of course, you would have taken credit. And, as always, the idiots in charge would have believed you."

Would they though? Seems a bit farfetched.

"Weirder than normal, you mean. But you set the stage. Back in Pochtlan you abandoned your role as Smiter and pledged allegiance, by implication at least, to Beedlewood and his lust-ridden dreams. So, naturally, it follows you would have arranged to defeat Horemheb."

Uhmmm... right... sure.

"And if you had failed to take credit, I would have prompted you. Not that I would have needed to. You took responsibility for the destruction of the Assyrians right away. I'm sure you would have done the same for Horemheb's demise had the Assyrians triumphed."

Well, yes. I would have responded appropriately no matter who won. Such is my nature.

"Let's face it. When push comes to shove, your survival instincts are as ruthless and relentless as these hideous vultures. You possess a singular lack of conscience. Remember that. You're the biggest bastard on the planet, not Horemheb. Otherwise, you're quite a decent chap, of course. No reason why you can't be both."

You've restored my high spirits. Only… one thing still bugs me. Used to be I could count on the techgrid to help me out. Breaking down to the point of ending civilization is one thing. But breaking down to the point of abandoning me is going too far. That's something I cannot forgive!

CHAPTER TWENTY

The noise level was surprisingly low. Turned out Horemheb's idea of a party was a subdued gathering of Horemheb worshippers. To be sure, the low tables scattered about the deck of the pleasure barge were crammed with food and drink, mostly sausages and beer, but hardly anyone was indulging. They didn't dare risk getting drunk and saying or doing something the Pharaoh might find insulting.

As a result, he was the only one having a good time, the only one wearing a party hat—if Ashurbanipal's helmet can be called that. And he was the only one besotting himself. A miasma of fear drifted about the assembled partygoers. What state would the God-king drink himself into? Temporary oblivion for him? Or permanent oblivion for others?

"You don't have to worry. He likes you."

I hope he's not the kind who turns mean when drunk. Considering his state of mind when sober, the result would be... unsettling.

"Wonder if he's had the helmet cleaned."

I doubt it. I get the impression he's the type that revels in flesh... the scattered flesh of his enemies, that is, not the usual sort of flesh-fetish.

"What about the naked boy chained to his table? That indicates his personal taste, don't you think?"

I squinted at the raised dais where Horemheb's table was located, on the stern of the barge. Details were a bit hard to make out, because the electric lamps on the wheelhouse railing shone directly into everyone's eyes. (Presumably, the lights imparted a divine glow to the Pharaoh's presence.) Nevertheless, I could see the boy. He was squatting on his haunches, with his arms tightly wrapped around his legs and his head resting on his knees. He looked thoroughly miserable. Every now and then Horemheb pelted him with a fistful of sausages, then laughed uproariously.

I observed this while leaning against the gunwale of the ship. Seneferu sat beside me, staring morosely into the stein of beer he held between his outspread legs. He hadn't touched a drop.

"Wolfgang," I inquired. "Is that your father's bumboy?"

Seneferu shot me an angry glance. "No! He's my son. His name is Fritz Psamtek. Today is his ninth birthday. His Granddad mistreats him but would never hurt him. Lucky bastard. Wish I could say the same."

"Bit of a dysfunctional family, if you ask me."

"I don't understand," I said, adopting a soft, soothing tone. "Why is Fritz chained like that? Why is he on such horrible display?"

Seneferu took to staring at his beer again. "Pharaoh had a dream about six months ago. Seems he saw into the future, saw Fritz succeeding him and tearing down his monuments to erase his memory and exile his Ka for all time. Pissed him off."

Hmm, Horemheb is pretty handy with AK-47s. Wonder why he didn't kill the kid?

"Because you can't kill your successor, not when the Gods guarantee his succession."

So, deep beneath his self-worship, Horemheb is superstitious? That's good to know.

"And *I'm* pissed off," Seneferu added.

"Why?"

"Because it means I never get to be Pharaoh. The double crown will pass directly from Horemheb to Psamtek. My father took great pleasure in telling me that."

"Better not tell him it probably means the Pharaoh is looking forward to executing his son whenever he gets the urge."

Wolfgang probably knows. Considering how much beer Horemheb is slamming back, it could happen tonight. No wonder he's glum.

"And this is a crummy barge anyway," Seneferu growled. "When Cleopatra sailed up the Tiber to have sex with Nero, her ship was festooned with purple sails, silver oars, and gold foil hammered onto every surface. Not to mention a barge-load of naked Nereids prancing about. No wonder Nero had no problem getting it up. But this barge is a public cemetery, with everyone waiting to be tumbled into their open graves. Standards have declined; I tell you!"

"I don't think Nero ever met Cleopatra."

That's right! Wasn't he famous for having a hard-on for Victoria, Queen of the Britons?

Shouting erupted, coming from the dark of the desert. I twisted around to see what I could see.

Silhouetted in the glare cast by the lamps in the stern, figures were abandoning rows of stationary bicycles and staggering wearily into the night as newcomers took their place. Moments later, multiple pairs of legs were pumping once more, generating electricity for the massive battery that powered the lamps, along with whatever other machinery was hidden inside the barge.

"Wolfgang, why does your father cling to the past? I mean, the near past, rather than the distant past?"

"Oh, well, we're German. It's traditional for Germans to love machines." He paused, his features contracting as if contemplating unpleasant memories. "Besides, it's always rankled him that the Romans were building five-hundred-story palaces back when our ancestors were lying around in dismal huts getting drunk."

"Is that true? Did they?"

"According to a surviving letter by Barbarossa's mistress. Anyway, point is, when the techgrid informed all the world leaders it didn't know how much longer it could hold on, what with resources dwindling, it insisted that nations begin converting to a stone age economy to ensure their survival. It became all the rage to revive ancient polities, but Horemheb absolutely refused to go along."

I was astounded. "What? The techgrid did what? When did that happen?"

Buddy-bod! Why didn't you tell me?

"First I've heard of it."

Seneferu sighed. The subject clearly bored him. "Of course, back in the day, technology was not subject to human control. My dad pleaded with the techgrid to fashion sophisticated tools and machines that we could direct and manipulate. It allowed him a few things. But then the techgrid disappeared, and my father's grand scheme collapsed, almost before it had begun. I think that's what drove him insane… Not that he was all that jolly to begin with. Always had a morbid streak."

"I doubt the Egyptians can manufacture spare parts. All of these gizmos will cease functioning someday. And then Horemheb will be forced to knap flints whether he wants to or not."

Or he might just go berserk and kill as many people as possible.

"More work for you."

No, I want to be long gone by then.

Seneferu was muttering at his beer. Not *into* it, strictly speaking, since he still hadn't taken a single sip, but the head had disappeared. He was looking awfully drowsy now. The entire steinful would probably evaporate before he moved another muscle.

"Hermann can be very stupid," he mumbled. "Hasn't even touched the caches yet. He knows they're there, but he won't open them. Can't believe his sperm grew into me. Some sort of mistake... stupid mistake..."

I don't know whom I should feel most sorry for—Fritz or Wolfgang.

"At least Fritz has a guaranteed future. As will the Egyptians once they empty out the caches. But the sooner they get off this tech kick the better."

Seneferu's head fell forward. He had fallen asleep from exhaustion. At least he wouldn't wake up with a hangover. Provided his father let him live that long.

All due respect, Buddy-bod, but I'm getting bored talking to you.

"Fine by me."

Got enough of an overview of the party. Time for company.

I stood up and stretched. Then I wove my way through the tables to the one near the bow, where Myriad sat along with Titus and Beedlewood. No idea where the others were.

"Plotting our next move?" I inquired as I made myself comfortable beside Myriad. Both Titus and Beedlewood glared at me.

"Still hiding from Horemheb, if that's what you mean," Myriad replied. "These two haven't said a word. They're feeling too sorry for themselves to think straight."

"Of course we're depressed," Beedlewood said. "We both know our lives depend on what you do next. And we're equally aware you haven't got a clue what that is. In short, we know we're screwed."

I studied the nearby tables. As best I could tell, they were occupied by Egyptian officials, apparently in a catatonic state. Frozen in terror, most likely. Only the ship's stewards were in motion. They wandered about, staring soberly at the untouched plates of food and the steins not yet emptied of stale beer. Understandable, really. They were ready to refresh and renew but were stymied by the total lack of consumption. Prevented from doing their jobs. What would happen to them if Horemheb noticed their plight?

"Probably force feed them to his guests."

Quiet. I just noticed something curious.

"Where are the baldie priests from the temple?" I asked my companions. "I don't see any of them here. Anybody know?"

"Oh, they've been touched by Horemheb's sense of humour, or irony, or whatever," replied Titus.

"What do you mean?"

"He assigned them the task of catching as many vultures as possible to hand over to his taxidermists. No matter how long it takes to mount the dead vultures on the temple walls, the baldies have already begun worshipping them. A vulture-cultist guard of honour for a mound of Assyrian bones. Hilarious." But Titus wasn't laughing. In fact, he seemed downright resentful.

"The baldies are just being self-serving," he continued. "They know Horemheb despises them because they resist accepting him as Aten. So, they've been trying to worship high tech, like the sponge sticks, to put themselves back in his good graces. Unfortunately, their attempt to divert the water feeding the latrine into an efficient and reliable water catchment has proven a failure, and Horemheb is not impressed."

"And that's the whole problem right there," Beedlewood stated. "The Egyptians can't get anything to work."

I pointed at the cloud-reflected beams of the searchlights on the riverbank. "They're the only ones I know still using high tech."

"Low high-tech, you mean, and only as long as it lasts. I know this is true because I had a long talk with Seneferu yesterday while you slept with your mouth open."

"What business is it of yours if I choose to catch flies in my sleep?"

"Listen to me!" Beedlewood pounded his staff on the deck planks. "Seneferu is terribly frustrated. His father still refuses to dig up the sacred caches with their treasure store of resources and knowledge. Still refuses to adapt to the new reality. People are dying because of this."

"Interesting. Normally I'd take credit for that, but Horemheb would probably interpret that as a criticism or personal insult." I pretended to give the matter some thought, then smiled. "Safest to stick with slaughtering foreigners."

Beedlewood looked grim, as if channeling the prophets of old again. "Take beer, for instance. You think the Egyptians brewed this crap?"

"Didn't they? I though beer and wine represented the height of early Egyptian ingenuity. What they invented before pottery and the wheel."

"That was a long time ago. All this beer going to waste is the last of the brew from the nutrient vats. Since the loss of the memory banks, today's Egyptians are clueless. No written sources. No oral tradition. Nothing."

I searched my memory, a process that felt akin to examining scores of empty bubbles floating on the water at the base of a waterfall. "Don't you just mash stuff up and ferment it? Leave it alone in a sealed jar until it bubbles and reeks?"

Beedlewood shook his head. "No, no, you still don't get it. Of course, the Egyptians are experimenting, but so far, they're getting nowhere. When the last of the vat beer is gone, they won't have any booze at all."

"Well, then…" I cast about for a solution, beginning to feel as frustrated as Seneferu had appeared. "I'll suggest to Horemheb that if he ever gets a Gogetter or two up and running, he should start importing pulque from Pochtlan. That should make everyone happy."

Beedlewood snapped his mouth shut and worked his jaw muscles so hard that I half expected his teeth to shatter and spew from his lips.

"You have a talent for upsetting people needlessly."

Nothing wrong with finding out what's really bugging them.

"My Druid-Mayan Reform Movement is a return to nature and its simple pleasures and resources," insisted Beedlewood. "It's fully in line with what the techgrid was planning for and insisting we prepare to accept."

"Or so Wolfgang claims," I replied. "He probably just made up the story."

Ignoring the bait, Beetlewood continued stiffly, "However, Horemheb refused to take advantage of the limited amount of time available before the techgrid crashed."

"And your point is?"

"That the Egyptian Empire is the least prepared and most vulnerable of nations. When Horemheb's idiotic dependence on the pathetic remnants of old tech blows up in his face, he'll be looking for scapegoats. That's us. That's me. We're doomed."

I snatched up the stein on the table in front of me and took a sip of the brew. Possibly I was the first person at the banquet to do so, other than the Pharaoh. The beer was a bit flat, but it tasted pretty good. I swallowed several more mouthfuls of it.

"There you go again," I chided him while enjoying the sensation in my stomach. "You're being all gloomy and negative. Hell of a worrywart. You should stop it." I wondered if I should try one of the sausages. If they were vat products, they'd be quite safe to eat. I pointed upward at the beautifully glowing clouds. "Why don't you just relax and enjoy the light show? Probably won't be another one for a zillion years."

Beedlewood spared a glance overhead, then turned back to me, wearing a sour expression on his face. "Horemheb said he's never seen the day sky."

"So? Worship the clouds instead. Make them the new definition of eternity."

"That was my epiphany, you see, the realization that both the Druids and the Maya studied the stars. Night after night, standing in forests of mistletoe, climbing atop pyramids and henges to get a better look, reading the night sky the way we used to consult the techgrid. It was a religion full of profound beauty, an ethos devoted to the contemplation of stars that twinkled in the darkness. I know. Twice, in my childhood, the stars were visible from England. They were lovely. I miss seeing them."

"Didn't other ancient cultures follow the stars? I thought they all did."

"Nope. Just the Druids and the Maya. They must have been one and the same."

"So that's his angle."

I pondered the possibilities. Yes, a good gimmick. Nice and simple, appeals to equally simple minds.

"Advocating unlimited sex is even simpler. Appeals to everyone."

Beedlewood rested his head in his hands. Overdoing the woebegone bit, if you asked me. "Now everything is buggered up," he went on. "I can get killed for preaching what I preach."

"Only in Egypt. I'm sure you'll find millions of willing perverts elsewhere."

"You really think so?" He sounded hopeful, as if grasping at straws.

"There you are," thundered Tlaloc, crashing down between Myriad and myself. They clung to each other for a moment, kissing passionately. Then Tlaloc turned to the table and grabbed a stein of beer. He gulped down half the contents. "Uggh. Tastes the way the Death God smells, but good enough."

"Where have you been?" I asked, purposely ignoring the adoring gaze Myriad had fixed on Tlaloc. *Will she abandon him if I sneak up to him in the night and shave off his chest hair?*

"Unlikely. He'd wake up and kill you. Then she would be devoted to him one hundred percent and they'd both live happily ever after."

"I've been checking out the ships," Tlaloc replied. "They're weird as hell. Symptoms of Horemheb's delirium."

"They let you do that?"

"No one tried to stop me. The Pharaoh seems to have given us special status, or immunity, freedom of the whatever. Anyway, seems I can go wherever I want and poke about. So, I took full advantage."

"And discovered what, exactly?"

Tlaloc emptied the stein, then scratched his forehead with its bottom edge. "This barge, for instance. It's flat-bottomed."

"Aren't most barges?"

"Traditionally, yes, in order to carry as much cargo as possible. But the bottom of this one is insane, composed of small blocks of wood tenoned together in a pattern like that of a mudbrick wall."

I failed to see any worthwhile significance in this. "Advantage of flexibility?"

"The pieces could work themselves loose in a dead calm, never mind in a storm. The strakes are done up the same way. There's no ribs. No keel. This thing wasn't built by shipwrights. It was put together by cabinet makers working with scraps."

"We should think about getting off."

I scanned the deck with new, worried eyes. "Is the deck secure? Is it safe?"

Tlaloc laughed. Not a comforting sound. "Yeah, sure, reinforced by thick cables anchored on the outside of the hull, but since they're exposed to passing waves, they've already begun to rot. This thing isn't a ship, it's a giant basket woven by children just starting to learn their craft. And that's not even the worst part."

"Which is?"

"What they're using for ballast, namely dead machines, all kinds, though mostly engines, I think. As if Horemheb thinks they'll spring to life and drive this bilge bucket forward."

"What about the other vessels?"

"Much better designed, judging by the two I checked. They've got rounded hulls, ribs, and keels, but everything is built from teeny, tiny scraps. I'd be surprised if the whole fleet isn't on the bottom by morning. And you know what's most brilliant about their construction?"

"I assume you're going to tell me."

"The masts," Tlaloc said, grinning as if he were delivering a punch line. "They're goddamned repurposed streetlight poles, with no give at all, and poorly braced at that."

"Egypt always was famous for its lack of suitable trees."

"Hmm. Well, it's interesting, but no concern of mine. Tell me, were Mark and Olaf with you while you explored these wonders?"

"Them?" Tlaloc thought for a moment. "Last I saw of them they were volunteering to help man the bicycles. Said they needed the exercise. They're probably still pumping away. Pissed out of their minds by now, most likely, but still pumping… which reminds me…" He slid a stein toward Myriad. "Let's get drunk before we drown."

"Watch it!" Titus hissed urgently. "Here comes Horemheb!"

The Pharaoh swept towards us, his eyes gleaming as if they were lamps lighting his way. Something had gotten him extremely excited. He was pumping one fist in the air, clutching a dagger in his other hand, and grinning maniacally. The sight of him roused some guests to action. They were not only moving out of his way but also leaping overboard.

"Rudwulf, my beautiful man, my miracle worker, where are you?" Horemheb demanded.

I rose reluctantly to my feet and bowed low. For once, Buddy-bod kept silent. Out of the corner of my eye I noticed Myriad nudging Tlaloc. She had seen the very thing that was painfully obvious to me. Horemheb was carrying an impressive bulge beneath the front of his kilt. Evidently, he

271

was *very* excited. I would have to choose my words carefully.

"Rudwulf, why didn't you tell me that you had planned your surprise for this night?"

"Because I wanted it to be a surprise?"

Without warning Horemheb pulled me into a hug. It was an awkward moment all around. I noticed his bodyguards passing uneasy looks back and forth. At last, the Pharaoh released me and stepped back.

"You wonderful man," he said. "I just got word. An Italian invasion fleet has entered the Nile. Mussolini will be here by noon."

"As I planned. You can hold another banquet tomorrow night, only this time Musso will be the centrepiece."

"Glorious! Glorious!" Horemheb gushed, before dialing down his joy a trifle. "But now I must go. Got to make preparations. First the menu for the victory celebration, then my plan for the battle." He shot me one last smile, then strode off to exit the barge.

Titus spoke up, sounding plaintive and worried. "I'm not certain I picked a good time to switch my allegiance."

CHAPTER TWENTY-ONE

"Remember the Emperor Norton's proverb, 'The Gods help those who help themselves'? Well, I'm a God, and I'm helping myself."

No one dared to dispute the Pharaoh. That included me. *"Low-profile time. Let's see how this plays out."*

Horemheb brought his glee-ridden face within inches of my own. A low profile was clearly out of the question. "So, miracle man, you witness my preparations. But you are the man who will tip the balance. How do you plan to do this?"

"I arranged victory so long ago I've forgotten how it will unfold."

"Modest to the last, eh?" he replied with a smirk. "I like a man who takes his reward for granted. That's all arranged too. I think of everything."

Pharaoh went back to pacing the width of the bow. Meanwhile, my group occupied a couple of benches nearby. We literally had front row seats to watch the battle. The pleasure barge remained with its port side tied to the left bank of the Nile and a merchant vessel lashed to its starboard side. These two formed one end of a string of Horemheb's flimsy ships, all joined side by side in a curving blockade that reached the far shore of the river, three miles away. Fortunately, the seaward-bound current was sluggish, and the small craft loaded with boulders and deliberately sunk upriver provided firm anchors to hold the fleet in place. For now. Only the Gods knew what would happen if Musso's fleet were to ram into us.

"The Egyptians proved magnificently industrious. Spreading ropes like a spider web across the river to weave every ship into place. They're good at some things."

I'd never bitten my nails before but was contemplating developing the habit. The Italian ships in the distance were a solid black mass of menacing hulls, their towering masts bearing furled sails. Musso's fleet also spanned the width of the river, as if in response to Horemheb's strategy. The enemy was in motion, creeping closer, ever closer. Packed together with just enough space between the ships for the oars to play. Their decks and rigging appeared crowded with troops.

Armed with what weapons?

"I hope we don't find out."

There were but four soldiers on the deck of this pleasure barge, and a fifth lying prone atop the curved swan neck that passed for a figure head. They were armed with AK-47s, and innumerable boxes full of ammo, but still... It was hardly an awe-inspiring display of military strength. The rest of the fleet was even worse off. Only a single Ak-47 gunner per ship. Didn't strike me as the stuff of victory.

"You're forgetting the steel-axe men."

I studied the army positioned on shore. Yes, a line of axemen. Two or three hundred of them. And crowded behind them seethed an undisciplined mob equipped with a motley selection of "modern" weapons like crowbars, sledgehammers, lengths of rebar and Gods knew what, scavenged from derelict warehouses.

My stomach felt unusually empty, as if host to an expanding vacuum. I hoped it didn't mean my Lucks had abandoned me, but rather that they were out scouting the enemy and preparing to annihilate him... somehow.

"Don't give up. They've never failed you yet."

Seneferu, claiming to be too fat to sit on the bench, sat on the deck to my immediate left. Myriad stood behind me, her hands resting on my shoulders, and Tlaloc beside her. He had borrowed one of Mark's stone axes. Beedlewood sat to my right, clutching his staff as if preparing to wield it like a hammer against the foe. To his right sat Mark, holding a stone axe comfortably across his lap while, beyond him, Olaf toyed idly with his obsidian-bladed Aztec sword. Anyone looking at us would think we were eager for battle and confident of success.

Poor Titus was crouching below the gunwale just behind the swan neck. Something about the Pharaoh wanting him to translate when Mussolini chose to surrender. Titus occasionally cast longing looks at us, as if wishing he could sit with us where it was safer. Safer? We couldn't be any more exposed even if we were shot at the enemy from catapults. Alas, no such weapons were available. In fact, the Egyptians had never heard of them. AK-47s and steel axes were the best Horemheb could provide, and not many of those.

Seneferu was playing with something in his hand. I leaned forward and saw that it was his sunstone. As good a luck charm as any, I supposed.

"What the Beloved of Ptah are they doing?" Horemheb cried.

To my surprise, the Italian fleet had suddenly veered to our left, every ship attempting to ram its bow ashore. At this distance, I couldn't tell precisely what was happening, but it appeared the ships were crowding one another, wedging themselves together to create a solid platform. And spilling masses of men out onto the desert sand.

"The bastards!" Horemheb shouted. "They're converting my naval victory into a land battle. I was going to spare most of them, but I'll show no mercy now. How dare they insult me. I'll kill them all." He turned to face us.

"You lot. You're with me. Stick close." Then he disembarked, issuing instructions to his underlings as he went, with us tagging along behind him as commanded.

After considerable confusion, and much to our disgust, we found ourselves well in advance of the rest of the army, with just a single line of AK-47 gunners lying prone in the sand in front of us.

"Majesty, is this wise?" I inquired as Horemheb paced past me.

"Of course, you want the best view of the enemy crumbling before the Smiter, don't you? How often do you get to enjoy the fruits of your machinations up close and in your face? I do this as a favour to you."

I bowed low. I wished I could bow lower and burrow into the sand forever. "Delightful, Majesty. I am honoured."

"Here come the legions. Stupid outfits, but at least they know how to keep formation."

Indeed. Line after line of men were approaching, all wearing black shirts above their waist and skirts of Roman armour below, the latter to protect their groins. Curiously, that was the extent of their battle dress. Apparently Musso hadn't issued his men boots, grieves, or helmets. Just floppy hats with drooping black feathers. And rectangular Roman shields that looked authentic yet strangely insubstantial. They seemed to wobble in the breeze. The way the soldiers held them was unmilitary, projecting in front of them at arm's length, as if hoping to ward off the battle entirely.

Closer and closer they came.

"This is exciting," Horemheb said, smiling fondly at me. "I can't wait to see what you're going to do."

"I'm feeling pretty much the same. By the way, do you see any weapons? I don't."

That's odd. Neither do I.

All at once the Italians dropped their shields and charged, their formation instantly dissolving into a formless mob. They were shouting what I assumed were battle cries and slogans.

"Aiutami!" They cried. "Salvaci! Cazzo Mussolini!"

Horemheb raised his arm and commanded in techgrid, "Get ready to fire!"

Titus raced to confront the Pharoah, flailing his hands to get his attention. "Don't shoot! They're surrendering!"

The Italians dropped to their knees, then prostrated themselves. "Abbiamo bisogno di Acqua! Dacci da mangiare! Lascia che ti serviamo!"

Horemheb looked at Titus. "What are they saying?"

"They're starving. And dying of thirst. They beg you to help them. They're willing to serve you, to fight for you, but they need your protection, your generosity."

"Why? And where's Mussolini?"

Titus hastened to find out. He moved into the crowd of desperate Italians to converse with them.

Horemheb turned to gaze into my eyes. I expected to see triumph in his, but instead was met with a cold, calculating stare. I felt naked and exposed. I had been revealed.

"He's afraid of you. Seeing your power for the first time."

But I don't have any power.

"Too late to tell him that now. He won't believe you."

"Even I dare not underestimate you," Horemheb said in a low voice. "Good thing I've prepared your reward well in advance."

Titus came scrambling back. "It was the chickens!"

"What?" The Pharoah's cold expression slipped into one of anger.

Titus dropped to his knees in front of Horemheb. "When the fleet reached the latitude of old Alexandria, Musso was astonished to find nothing there, just water. He forgot about the rising of the oceans. So, he consulted the sacred chickens."

"How?"

"He let them out of their cage. Pile of food on the left, another pile to the right. Depending on which they pecked, the fleet would either go back or press on."

"And?"

"Stupid things refused to eat. So Musso had them thrown overboard. They drowned."

"I fail to see how this led the Italians to surrender."

Titus must have realized the Pharaoh was growing impatient. He began speaking twice as fast. "Everybody got disgruntled when Musso insisted the voyage continue south. Yelling something about Caesar burning his boats, he ordered all the food and water rations flung overboard. Claimed they had no need of them. That they'd be at New Alexandria within twelve hours."

"Impossible!"

"Exactly. Especially when the wind died down and they had to resort to oars. Four days later, when they drew abreast of the great pyramid, they flung Musso into the Nile and hastened to beg your forgiveness. He's dead. They're alive, and they'll do anything to stay that way."

"Rudwulf, you planned this?" Horemheb asked. Not that he was doubtful, but I sensed he was perplexed and genuinely in search of an explanation. I blurted out the first thing that came to mind. It was stupid, and therefore plausible.

"I put a hex on the chickens," I said.

"That's it? That's all?"

"Look at the result. It was enough."

A loud, crunching sound assailed my ears, and I turned to find its source. An odd-looking catamaran, its twin hulls composed of narrow lifeboats, had come ashore. The platform connecting them looked flimsy in comparison to their metal hulls. The rowers appeared a surly lot, the guards with the AK-47s even more hostile. They beckoned to us with short, jerky movements.

Smiling smugly, Horemheb placed his hands on his hips. "Off you go, all of you. One last mission. Then you'll get your reward. Seneferu will explain."

I would have protested if the Pharaoh's bodyguards hadn't raised their AK-47s and pointed them at us. We trooped down to the shore and clambered aboard the platform. In seconds, our boat was shoved fully into the Nile. The rowers were powerful men and soon had the catamaran racing along with the current. They didn't look pleased, though. Kept throwing scowling glances our way.

Seneferu sat in the centre of the platform. The rest of us squatted around him.

"Wolfgang? What's going on?" I asked.

"Don't worry. We're going to a happy place. Back to Pochtlan."

"That's a surprise all right. A nasty one. What if we get mushed, like the Assyrians?"

"Via another Gogetter? One that works properly?"

"So I'm told. We don't have a choice. But I'd rather party with Tizoc than with my father."

"Me, too," Beedlewood declared. "I love Tizoc! He's a saint compared to Horemheb."

"I say, let's rush the gunners," Tlaloc said. "We can take them if we move fast enough."

"No!" This was Myriad, her voice sharp and clear. "Too risky."

"Oh, all right," Tlaloc muttered. We were passing the jumbled collection of Italian vessels. "Look at those things. Impressive from a distance, but just as gimcrack a mess as the Egyptian boats when seen closeup. Even if the planks *are* longer."

"Who cares?" Olaf said. "Have any of you noticed there's no food or drink aboard this craft?"

"Doesn't matter. We've not far to go," Seneferu stated.

Indeed, after an hour of staring at the banks of the Nile, I realized the river was widening. Soon, we lost sight of the far bank. Not long after, the left bank curved away and we appeared to be on an open sea.

"Wolfgang!" I snapped, alarmed. "Where are we? Where are we going?"

"Still far south of where the delta used to be. Look ahead."

Sure enough, there was something sticking out of the water. The closer we got to it, the more clearly I could see that it was a truncated pyramid with a flat top, rising maybe thirty feet above the surface of the water. Its sloping sides consisted of yellowish stones, carelessly placed and roughly three feet in height. Climbable, I thought, should we be marooned there.

And reachable. No waves beat at its base. In fact, the sea was extraordinarily calm around it, making it appear quite otherworldly.

"Which one is this? Anything famous?" I asked.

"You could say that. Khufu's tomb. The Great Pyramid. The biggest of them all."

"That little thing?"

I was flabbergasted. "The ocean rose that much?"

"And the land sank. Something to do with an earthquake. Anyway, it's a Gogetter. A passing fisherman observed a double flash of blue light a week ago. Somebody popped in and out. As we will."

Seneferu fished his sunstone out and held it to his right eye. "I can see a blue flickering. It's definitely active and, judging by the radiance, fully charged."

When the catamaran banged up against the pyramid, we all leaped onto the stones at the water's edge to avoid being pushed or prodded there by oars. Then, smiling cheerfully, the rowers bent to the task of returning home. As the gunners waved goodbye to us, I had no doubt they were imaging our slow and unpleasant death atop the pyramid.

Seneferu studied the slope. "Too steep. I'm too fat. I can't make it. Won't be able to activate the Gogetter."

"Close your eyes," Tlaloc said, grabbing him under the right arm, as Mark grabbed his left. "We'll hoist you up." Unsurprisingly, their progress was swift. I was pleased Myriad clutched at me to assist my climb. It fit in with an old fantasy of mine.

"Don't get excited. She's just doing her job."

In no time at all we were atop the pyramid. The platform was uneven, a strange conglomeration of stones varying from one foot to four feet in length. Fortunately, one section was a remnant of the missing next level and provided a sturdy bench to sit on. I couldn't help but notice that the stonework wasn't particularly close-fitting, and that the interstices were filled with bright orange nanotech plastic. More proof that the Gogetters were of techgrid origin.

Seneferu sank onto the stone ledge with a sigh of relief. Evidently, he considered it firm enough to support his "vast" weight. It had to make for a pleasant change.

Titus plopped down beside him, looking rather disconsolate. "I hate this place. Let's get out of here."

Seneferu was slowly twirling the sunstone in his hands. "Don't rush me. The words in my incantation have to be correctly chosen if we're to reach our destination."

I hunkered down in front of him. "Wolfgang, why has your father betrayed us? The Italians had barely begun to grovel and then, all of a sudden, we're being kicked out of the Kingdom."

"Isn't it obvious?" Seneferu replied, with a smile that was more like a grimace. "He may be mad, but he's not crazy. He doesn't want to share credit for the twin victories, is all. Apart from the mob of people around him, none of the population at large will ever learn of your existence. He alone will be the saviour of the country. He is the one the fellaheen will bow down and worship. You are nothing. Be grateful he is sparing our lives."

"I hate politics," Titus muttered.

"We can recover in Pochtlan. Get back in Tizoc's favour."

How? We bring him nothing. We'd be no better than refugees.

"Describing the glorious victories will amuse him. Explaining Horemheb's regime in detail will confirm his opinions. We will show him proof that it is wise to remain aloof from old world affairs. No, don't worry, he will be glad to see us return. We bring good news."

There wasn't much to see at the apex of a drowned, broken pyramid. Nevertheless, Tlaloc was nosing about as if in search of treasure. Pausing at the far edge of the platform, he looked down and let out a shout. "There's a man here! Help me help him up!"

Tlaloc leaped over the edge, followed by Myriad, moving fast. I stood up and crossed to the spot as well, being careful not to trip on the uneven surface of the platform. No need to rush. I knew the two of them would have matters under control.

A man was clinging to the face of the blocks at the surface of the water. He was half-submerged, with most of his body resting on the level underneath him. Motionless, he appeared to be dead. Some might have left him there. But Tlaloc plucked him out of the water as though harvesting a lotus bloom and carried him swiftly up to the platform. Myriad raced alongside, offering cries of encouragement, but whether they were directed at Tlaloc or at the waterlogged man I couldn't tell.

"Leave it to you to concentrate on which one she is paying attention to. Jealous, are we? I should think this drowned rat is more important right now."

By now, the rat was lying flat on his back, with Myriad checking his vital signs and Tlaloc kneeling beside her. I stepped over for a closer look.

He was dressed all in black—shirts, pants and socks—and his face seemed oddly black as well, as if decay had set in. Nonetheless, his chest was visibly rising and falling in steady rhythm, a strong indication that he was indeed alive, and his eyelids were twitching, as though he was in REM sleep.

Something about his face was familiar. It was fleshy, and somewhat jowly, putting his age at around forty. His features were a trifle ugly, even brutal. And somehow, I felt I ought to recognize him.

"Musso!" Titus roared, dropping down to straddle the body and slap its cheeks. "Wake up! Wake up! Don't leave me."

I was dumbfounded. This was Mussolini? The self-proclaimed world leader? He looked a lot different from the last time I saw him. Had let himself go. Still, though drenched, he was alive.

"The Italians did claim they dumped him overboard in the vicinity. Makes sense he'd swim to the pyramid."

If they wanted to kill him, shouldn't they have bound him and tied on weights to drag him down?

"Who says they wanted to kill him? Seems like they were just trying to get rid of him."

Reacting to the slaps, Mussolini's eyes shot open. He cast a most baleful glare on all of us, full of hate and anger. "Merda," he declared. "Che mucchi di brutti bruti. Deve essere all'inferno."

"Oh, Musso! You recognise me! Thank God!" Titus shouted. Eagerly he embraced the Duce, who grunted and slipped back into unconsciousness.

Now I noticed an unexpected resemblance, a most unwanted fact. "Titus, are you and Musso related?"

"He's my younger brother, my dear, wonderful younger brother."

Oh, great. Can't leave him behind then.

"Won't leave him behind in any case. The Gogetter will take everyone within reach."

Right. Damn. We're stuck with him... wait... we can offer him to Tizoc! A trophy!

"Or potential ally, or advisor. Whatever. I'm sure Tizoc will be pleased."

"But he's cold... so very cold... he may be dying," Titus moaned. "Seneferu. Activate the Gogetter! Now!"

"Hang on, hang on... got to be sure," Seneferu said quietly. "Let me concentrate."

Titus got to his feet, his fists clenched. Was he going to assault the one man who knew how to activate the Gogetter? If so, what a fool.

Myriad and Tlaloc rose beside him. They'd restrain him in time. No doubt of that.

"Take us now! This instant!" Titus insisted, not being as intimidating as he evidently thought he was. In fact, he appeared rather comical.

"Titus!" I shouted. "Calm down!"

He whirled to face me, his face suffused with rage. "Why should I? Musso needs help!"

"And once he's been helped and is back to his usual jolly self, what do you think he'll make of your traitorous switch of allegiance to me? You want me to tell him?"

"You idiot! That's no threat," Titus said, his voice dripping with contempt. "He understands diplomacy very well... necessity... opportunity... politics... all that good stuff. But nothing counts more than family. And I'm family, damn it."

"I'd back off if I were you. In the presence of Mussolini, Titus has a backbone."

Yeah. Right. Fine. He's not important anyway. Musso is the one to suck up to, to manipulate and control. We can forget Titus.

"Sounds like an interesting new hobby. But don't underestimate either of them."

Seneferu slid forward and dropped to his knees, staring intently into the sunstone. "Jade to the left of us, jade to the right of us, jade all around, jade above and below, to Pochtlan, city of jade, embrace us!"

Again, the world was made blue, nothing but blue. The universe was blue. Time itself was blue. Disorienting, but pretty. A brief flash of pleasure. I was getting used to it.

Then the blue faded. I struggled to adapt my eyes. Wherever we were, it was nighttime.

"So beautiful," Beedlewood whispered, gazing upward. "It's a sunny night tonight. No clouds. Look at all the stars. Are we in England?"

"No such luck," I commented disgustedly. "Two moons in the sky. We're on Mars."

To be continued…

Made in Canada by LoginPOD
Powered by Publishers' Graphics
loginpod.ca